OXFORD'S HAUNTED

A COLLECTION OF GHOST STORIES INSPIRED BY OXFORD

Edited by
Henry Cockburn, 'Doc' David, Jude Jones,
Peter Meinertzhagen, Sarah Milne Das & Tiffany Williams

OXFORD'S HAUNTED
A collection of ghost stories inspired by Oxford

First published by Oxford Writing Circle Press in 2017

Text copyright © Individual contributors
Cover design: Alexander Walker < www.alexander-walker.co.uk >
Book layout: 'Doc' David

The moral rights of the authors have been asserted.

A CIP catalogue record for this book is available from the British Library

ISBN paperback **978-1-9998832-0-1**
ISBN ebook **978-1-9998832-1-8**

CONTENTS

Dear readers of *Oxford's Haunted*,

It is with great pleasure that I can introduce the second anthology from the Oxford Writing Circle in the space of a year.

If our first book *Debut* introduced the Oxford Writing Circle and its members to a wider audience, marking the first time in print for some of its contributors, then *Oxford's Haunted* cements our community of writers as one rich with talent.

The brief for *Oxford's Haunted* was a simple one: to write a ghost story connected, if only loosely, with Oxford. From one common beginning we have 19 very different stories, each bearing the imprint of a city whose architecture and history carries ghosts of all kinds.

This book would not have been possible without the immense effort of its editors: Sarah Milne Das, Jude Jones, Henry Cockburn, Tiffany Williams, and 'Doc' David (who also laid out and produced this anthology). From leading the events where many of these stories were first aired to reading and editing the final submissions, their own mark is shown in the quality of the final product.

I would also like to give thanks to those establishments kind enough to house us over the past year, most notably the Albion Beatnik; Dennis, you've been a support in more ways than wine.

And with that I invite you to find somewhere comfortable, lock the door, and keep those curtains closed: for *Oxford's Haunted*.

Peter Meinertzhagen
Founder, Oxford Writing Circle

OXFORD'S HAUNTED

A COLLECTION OF GHOST STORIES INSPIRED BY OXFORD

THREE WEEKS OF RAIN

Megan Davis

My mom died when I was ten years old. Lung cancer, though she swore she had only ever smoked one cigarette in her thirty-two years, but since when has life ever been fair? We lived close to the graveyard, and we buried her there. I could see her headstone through my window. I visited every Thursday. Thursdays had been her favourite day of the week, and I took her a single gardenia whenever I visited. They grew in our back garden, and she cultivated them carefully until the beds were filled with this beautiful flowering shrub. I screamed when we left them; when we left her.

In our old home, the sun shined hot and bright, and when it didn't shine, it poured in a downfall that left you drenched within moments, but it was warm and welcome in the almost stifling heat. In Britain, the rain was the most dreadfully dull affair. Sometimes it poured for three hours straight and caused floods and destruction and chaos to the country, but most of the time it was this awful, pathetic drizzle that persisted for the entire day, making you uncertain whether you could carry out any plans you may have made. It hovered in the air as a mist — the sky this boring grey, so pale it hurt to look at; the clouds so thick they appeared as one large, bleak blanket covering the world. You thought, *Perhaps the sky was never blue at all. Perhaps it had always been this dreary, pallid monotony.* The droplets were so tiny, so fine, they left you wondering whether it was raining at all, or if it was just your imagination — at least, until the puddles began to form slowly (oh so slowly), and you could see thin ripples in them as sorry proof.

My father and I moved to Oxford two years after my mother's passing, and that damnable rain was one of the first things I ever truly hated in my whole life.

I detested the quiet of the new city. In my old home, I had been used to busy, bustling streets filled with people, regardless of the time of year. In Oxford it was quiet (less so during tourist season), and so green. There were trees everywhere. Trees belonged in the country, not lining the streets and avenues, no matter the size or population. In most places, yes, there may be one or two large parks, but in Oxford, it was as if the people had tried to interweave their city with the countryside surrounding it. There were so many spaces filled with grass and rivers and even, though it took me two or three visits to believe it, entire meadows cultivated within the city limits.

Where were the tall, overshadowing skyscrapers? Where were the blocks of apartments and offices, with windows on every floor? I missed the gleam and shine of the sun when it reflected on the buildings, half-blinding and yet somehow comforting. Everything in Oxford was a dusty, golden colour; everything was topped with a tower or a spire; and everyone was an academic.

I missed the yells of angry cab drivers as they braked sharply to avoid people who stepped, without looking, into the road. Bicycles were the mode of transport in Oxford, never mind the cobbled pavements that lined many of the streets, never mind that the people who rode them cared not if they ran you down. Every way was their right of way.

The only place in the city where I could escape was the cemetery in old Headington, down the road from our house. There I did not mind deafening silence, different as it was from the lonely quiet of the city; the world so green it was as though you had put on special lenses.

Nobody bothered you in a cemetery. Stand there long enough, gazing at one grave, and everyone assumed you were mourning, and that was respected, and you could be left alone. Every time I felt overwhelmed by my new home, and sometimes when I felt underwhelmed, I would walk to the graveyard and visit a different headstone. Sometimes I brought flowers. My mother had always encouraged this — she believed they appeased any unruly spirits upset by the presence of the living in their place of rest.

In a graveyard, the world became peaceful. When you're dead, I imagined things no longer mattered, and that calmed me.

On a cold and dismal Thursday in November, almost a year after we first moved to that inauspicious country, when the rain was falling oh so feebly, I took myself along to the graveyard.

Time had done nothing to leaven my hatred for that foreign place. I still detested the city and the country and our life. My school was filled with clones — with neatly cut hair; designer trainers; their school uniforms — who laughed at my accent and my name and my hair. Kids don't care if they hurt your feelings. Kids don't care if you're homesick. Kids are cruel. They didn't want to be my friend, and I didn't want to be theirs.

My father, desperate, tried to force friendship upon me by turning up at the school gates and asking the people I walked out of class next to (never with) if they wanted to come over for snacks and games. They laughed in his face and called him a creep, and I, embarrassed and angry, ran home with my head in my arms. On his second attempt, I punched a boy. My father did not come back after that. He watched me come in through the back door after my detention and dump my school bag on a chair, and he sighed and he was sad, but he did not try again.

I knew he wanted the best for me, but I knew the best for me was at my old home, where all my old friends were, where my old life had been. I knew he worried that I spent all my time in the cemetery, but that was where I felt closest to Mom, and if I couldn't be at home with her, then this would have to do.

On this particular Thursday, I went and sat on the bench opposite the grave of someone named Mabel Dawkins. The inscription read: *1897–1978; Beloved wife to Robert Dawkins 1894–1963, Mother to James Dawkins 1923–1997, loving Grandmother and Great-grandmother; Gone but not forgotten.* I wondered what Mabel Dawkins' grandchildren and great-grandchildren were doing now. I wondered if they visited her grave. There were no flowers laid there. Perhaps she had been forgotten after all. I hadn't brought anything with me today, and I felt strangely guilty.

The rain drizzled gently onto my face as I sat and stared at Mabel Dawkins' headstone. One or two of the delicate droplets fell like tears into the corners of my eyes, and I thought perhaps they *were* tears and I was crying for this woman that I had not known.

I pondered how she had died. Had it been painful? Was she at peace now? I always hoped those who had suffered could finally find somewhere... better. Or maybe during her life, she had been a terrible person, and therefore she now deserved to be in someplace awful, made to repent for all the dreadful deeds she had committed.

A voice interrupted my thoughts.

"She wasn't."

Irritated at having the peace and quiet I sought so rudely

disturbed, I turned to the intruder to tell them off, and flinched.

A boy, my age or perhaps a little older, stood next to me. He was silvery and transparent, and I knew at once that he was a ghost. He could hardly be anything else. He looked slightly distorted as though I was seeing him through glasses that had been prescribed incorrectly. His hair might have been blond when he was alive, for it was only a slightly darker shade than his skin. It stuck up all over the place as though he was perpetually trapped in a strong wind. His expression was unconcerned and a little aloof. He did not mind he had caught me unawares or that I wanted to be left alone.

I discovered I was curious, rather than afraid. Maybe I had spent too much of my youth in and around graveyards to be scared of the beings that might haunt them. My mother had believed in all things supernatural, and she had impressed upon me that bad things will only befall those who are cruel or disrespectful. Still, this was my first time meeting a ghost, and I was prepared to be wary.

I realised I had let my mouth fall open upon seeing him and shut it quickly. He gave a small smirk. I glared at him.

"What do you mean, 'she wasn't'?" I asked.

"*She* wasn't a terrible person." He flicked his gaze to Mabel Dawkins' grave and back to me again.

"How do you—?" I began to ask and then stopped. It occurred to me that I hadn't said what I'd been thinking aloud. How had he—?

"Ghosts feed on thoughts."

Another ghost had joined us. A small girl, her unwashed dress tatty, stood next to the boy. I blinked in astonishment, trying to gather my thoughts into some logical formation.

"You feed on thoughts?"

"There ain't a lot else a ghost *can* feed on," the girl said, insolent.

I thought about this. Both ghosts stared at me, their gazes never wavering. It was unnerving.

"I suppose that makes sense..."

The boy smirked again.

"We're ghosts. Nothing about us makes sense. But you're not scared of us..."

There was something confused, a little vulnerable, in his voice. I supposed they sent most people running, terror gripping them to their very bones. This was clearly a new experience for us all.

I shrugged.

"It defies a lot of things I learn in school, yes, but I always hoped ghosts would be real." I was talking about my mom.

The boy smiled. The girl continued to watch me, a strange glint in her eye. She moved a step closer. A low growl issued suddenly from the boy, and she jumped. His expression was menacing.

"Stop it, Greta."

The girl turned a paler shade of silver, which I took to be a blush, bowing her head. Without glancing at either of us again, she faded into nothingness. I stared into the space she left.

"What was that about?"

This time, the boy shrugged.

"Nothing much. Sometimes the living get uncomfortable if we are too close."

I frowned. He grinned. He was fond of smiling.

"What are you called, anyway?" he asked.

When I told him, he cocked his head to one side like he was intrigued.

"That is unusual. I like it." He nodded decisively as if I had asked his opinion in the first place. "I'm Teddy. Stokes." He made a movement, as if to offer his hand, before remembering we couldn't shake. Instead, he nodded his head at a grave a few steps to my right.

"That's me there."

I walked over to the grave. It was old and worn, covered in multicoloured moss. The image of a sleeping dog had been carved into the stone above the epitaph, faded and almost illegible. I squinted. It read, *Memory of Edward Stokes. Son of Lord Michael and Lady Georgiana Stokes of this Parish who died July 1835 Aged 13 years and 8 months.*

"You're older than me," I observed. "Why the dog?"

He gave a noncommittal jerk of his head.

"Family pet. I think I was partial to it. It was a long time ago."

I looked around. The rain had ceased, and a sliver of blue was attempting to push through the grey curtain hiding it. Small silver droplets coated the leaves on the trees and the stalks of grass, spinning the world topsy-turvy in their reflections. A man bearing a red umbrella, accompanied by a small white dog, was making his way through the cemetery towards the gate, whistling tunelessly.

"Can he see you?" I asked, anticipating the answer.

"No," said Teddy. "Only you can see me. Not everyone can see a ghost. You would not believe the number of people I've tried and failed to engage in conversation."

So he was lonely. I was lonely too, though I only admitted that to myself when the world was silent and I lay curled up in bed, sleep having evaded me.

"Tell me about yourself," I said.

"Will it make me more sympathetic, if you know my backstory?"

I shrugged, nodded.

We wandered through the graveyard for hours, though it felt but minutes. Teddy pointed to the graves of those he'd known before his tragically early demise, telling me stories and anecdotes about the life they'd shared. He had been privileged, though I guessed from his gravestone that his parents were members of the aristocracy. He had spent much of his time running wild with the offspring of his parent's servants — the youngest of seven children, he was not the son destined to inherit his father's fortune, nor was he the cleverest or the most handsome, and had thus been allowed to do as he willed with his free time. When I asked whether any of them had become ghosts also, a frown furrowed his brow and he shook his head vehemently.

"They all moved on," he said.

I was not allowed to consider this however as, with a cry of delight, he spotted a familiar grave and swiftly ensnared me in thrilling tales of a young girl he'd known, with whom he had experienced many great adventures.

We stopped when dusk fell and it became difficult to read the epitaphs. My father would be expecting me back for dinner, if he wasn't already worried about where I was. Teddy gazed after me as I headed towards the cemetery entrance.

"Will you come back?" he asked, tremulously, like a much younger child. I found myself nodding automatically. I had enjoyed our conversation and his company.

The joy that split his face buoyed me all the way back to my house, and when my father commented upon it, I was able to truly say I had made a friend.

Over the next two weeks, I spent almost all my time in the graveyard. During school I daydreamed, thinking of everything Teddy had told me the previous evening and doodling in my textbooks. At the end of day, I grabbed my bag and was out the door with the bell. At the weekends, I slipped out of the house when the sun rose, leaving brief notes to my father, and returned when the gates closed. We talked about everything, me and Teddy, from favourite toys to childhood memories to wildest dreams. Many of Teddy's stories were outdated and I had to explain as much of the technological world as I could to him. He was particularly fascinated by telephones and how they connected so many different people. He had never travelled outside of England, and I thoroughly enjoyed describing my old home to him.

The question I had been most desperate to ask only arose towards the end of the second week. I had not dared to bring it up, and if Teddy had read it in my thoughts, he had refused to acknowledge it.

We were discussing my mom, and my favourite memory of her — the last day we'd ever gone to the beach, just a week before she found out about the cancer (something else Teddy had never heard of; a heart-achingly difficult topic to explain). We ate ice cream and pretended we were mermaids or sharks, swimming as far out as we dared and grabbing the other's legs under the water.

For a moment I lost myself in nostalgia and there was a lull in the conversation. I sat on the bench, my hands tucked beneath my thighs, gazing at my toes. Teddy leaned against his own headstone, holding his knees against his chest. He had told me it was considered impolite to touch another ghost's grave.

"Teddy?" I asked, hesitantly. He met my eyes. "How did you... become a ghost? You don't have to answer if you don't want," I hastened to add.

He frowned, contemplative rather than angry.

"I think," he began slowly. "I think I was so angry that my life had been cut short, that my spirit, or whatever it is that makes one a ghost, refused to accept death and sort of... floated out of my body. And here I am." He laughed humourlessly. I took a breath.

"I meant—"

"I understood. You want to know how I died."

I blushed.

"But you really don't have to tell me! Just say, and I'll never ask again, I promise! I just wondered… you're so young."

"No," he said, solemnly. "I'll tell you. I'm not upset by my death, not anymore." He stood and turned to his grave, running his fingers over the letters on the headstone. "It is not a very exciting tale: it was the morning of my eldest sister's wedding. We weren't the closest of siblings, and I did not want to go to the ceremony. My parents were furious — well, Mother was. I do not think Father spent much thought on me. Mother told me I was coming whether I liked it or not, and I said some fairly unpleasant things to her in return, before running out of the house and off towards the woods. I used to go to the woods often when I was angry with my family. Anyway, the dog — the dog here, in fact" — he gestured to the carving — "chased after me. She was the favourite of my sister, and Mother had instructed one of the maids to put a special ribbon around her neck. I told her to go back because I knew Mother and my sister would be furious, but she did not. I even threw stones. In the end, I had to chase her. We were some five minutes away when a carriage appeared, heading to my sister's wedding. It was going at speed and the driver did not see the dog. I knew they would crash, so I did the only thing I could think, and ran out in front, pushing her aside."

He paused for a moment, skimming his hands over the grass, not looking at me.

"I think I was so bitter I had died saving a dog for my sister that I returned instantly. It was peculiar, looking down on my crushed and broken body and listening to everyone talking about me." His voice became softer. "The whole world turned grey, that was the first thing I remember noticing. All the colour had disappeared. And they put the dog on my headstone. Punishment even after death." He was silent for a while, lost in memory.

I shifted slightly, and the movement seemed to jog him back to the present. He shook himself and laughed a little shakily.

"I have thought not about that for a long time. Being dead, yes, of course that is always on my mind. But my death? Not for years."

"Sorry," I said. "I didn't mean to bring back bad memories."

"No, no, I don't mind." He grinned. "Now, less of the morbidity? Let's do something fun!" He came over to me. "May I visit your home?"

We walked slowly. Teddy kept trying to go faster but I purposefully made the walk as slow as possible. I never liked being at the house, and I was reluctant to share it with Teddy. My father would not be back for a few hours, and whilst it would be a good idea to make sure Teddy left by then, there was no immediate rush. I got the impression that Teddy had not spent a lot of time outside the cemetery, though it was clearly no problem for him to leave. There did not seem to be a specific distance tying him to his grave, but he was delighted by the streets and the houses that had not been there when he was growing up. When we reached the house, I showed Teddy my room and my books and my belongings, though they were few. What possessions I owned were those only from my old home. I was not interested in collecting things here. I had had a lot of things in my old life and I had left them behind. All the money I possessed was spent on the flowers I bequeathed to the lonely and unknown in graveyards.

Fascinated by everything, Teddy ran his hands along the bookshelves and the walls, his hands moving through the trinkets atop the chest of drawers and the bedside table, as though he could actually feel them. He gazed at the photos of my mother and my father. He was particularly interested in my mother.

There was a photo of us visiting an ancient war memorial a few miles from our old home. We stared solemnly up at the marble plinth on top of which reared a man on a horse, sword pointed at the sky. My mother held my hand. Her head was covered by a blue scarf, hiding her scalp, bald from the chemotherapy that didn't work. It was the last photo of us together. I think my mother knew she was going to die soon. I think that is why she held my hand so tight. She needed to draw courage from me, and from the brave General riding into battle.

Teddy peered at the pair of us; his nose, if it could, would have smudged the glass. He closed his eyes and breathed in deeply. A shiver ran through his silvery form, the colour deepening for a second. He pulled back and noticed me watching him.

"Sorry," he said, not looking particularly so. "This photo has strong emotions surrounding it. This is your mother?"

I nodded, curtly. I was protective of her.

"I can see you were close. You miss her terribly," he said, simply.

A frown creased my forehead, and I blinked away the tears attempting to form. I hadn't wept for my mother since we had left — at least, not with anyone watching.

"It is okay to cry," Teddy said, his voice soft.

I glared at him.

"Don't you know it's creepy when you respond to my thoughts?" I demanded.

He raised his eyebrows.

"We've been through this. I am a ghost. Everything I do is 'creepy'. Anyway, I care not. I have always enjoyed being a bit... sinister." He lowered his voice on the last word, a faux dark shadow crossing his face. I rolled my eyes.

"I don't need to cry. My mom and me were best friends. It sucks all the time, but I'm *not* about to cry in front of you." I fixed him with a glare. "Come on, I'll show you the garden. It's the only part of this place that I don't mind."

"Your enthusiasm has me intrigued."

I strode out of the room, pausing at the door to check Teddy was following. He had his hand over the picture of my mother and me, and his eyes were closed again. I wanted to tell him to leave the photo of us alone, but an odd feeling in my stomach told me I was intruding on something private. I turned away quickly and hurried down the stairs.

Teddy re-materialised in the tiny garden behind our house. It was overgrown with weeds and the grass desperately needed cutting. During the summer, the garden was filled with a wide display of colours and flowers. A small pond at the end of a well-concealed path sheltered a family of frogs during the warmer seasons, but it was currently filled only with slimy, dark green algae. If the water got cold enough as winter progressed, it froze over, and I, in one of my more daring or perhaps masochistic moods, might attempt to stand on the ice and hope I didn't fall in. Or hope I did, depending on my temperament. On a bad day, I might gaze down at the black pool and dream of jumping in and there being no bottom and sinking deeper and deeper until I could no longer glimpse the sky above.

The flowers were all dead now too and, reflecting the mood of the clouds, the garden was dismal and unappealing. I made my way over to the dilapidated bench that rested beneath an awning coated with holly and ivy. The little red holly berries were the only bright spot amongst the greenery. Sometimes I plucked them and flicked them around the garden in an attempt to spread their brilliance.

Teddy joined me as I sat and stared back towards the house. I was still thinking of my mother. She would not have let the garden get to this state. She had loved to keep things looking beautiful. She would have left a corner to be wild, though, so that the mice and the birds had a place to hide.

We remained in silence for a while. He ended the quiet.

"I was thinking—" He broke off, looking awkward, giving me a sideways glance. "I was thinking about your mother."

"What about her?"

"Well..." he hesitated. The next words came in a rush. "Would you want to see her again?"

I sat still. He fidgeted nervously with the cuffs of his sleeves. I could feel my heart racing in my chest. See my mother again? Of course I wanted to, but how... how could I? She was dead, buried far from here — even her ghost could not travel this distance. Why would he ask such a thing, when he knew how much I missed her, how I longed to hear her voice, to be enveloped in her warmth? It was all right for him, he was dead. Everyone he had cared about died long ago, and he must have got over them by now, but my mother's passing was still fresh and raw. I would give anything to see her again, but it was impossible. It was unfair that he should ask such a thing of me!

I grew angrier and angrier as I thought about his tactlessness, his insensitivity. He did not appear to be listening to my thoughts this time, for he continued. He should have shut up.

"There is a special network, for ghosts," he said.

I cut him off.

"I think you should go." My voice was ice. He peered at me. I did not meet his gaze. I was actually shaking now, not just because the air was cool. Tears once again pooled in my eyes, betraying me this time and leaking down my cheeks. Tentatively, Teddy put out a hand, but I shied back.

"Go away!" I shouted. I jumped to my feet and rushed back to the house, slamming the door behind me. In my room, I collapsed onto my bed, the tears coming steadily, my face a blotchy red mess.

I lay there for hours, hating Teddy, missing my mom. My father came home and cooked dinner but I was not hungry and he let me be.

I was determined not to give a single thought to the proposal Teddy had offered, but my mind failed me, straying instead to it often. At first, I remained furious at him for even suggesting I might be interested in something so heinously impossible, but slowly, gradually, the notion settled. I knew of the spirit world only from what Teddy had told me, but he, as a ghost, must surely have much better knowledge. He had been dead for so long that he would be intimately familiar with all its aspects. As the night drew in, the idea possessed me with a fervour I had not before experienced. There was nothing in the world I desired more than to see my mother just one more time.

I made up my mind in the early hours of the morning.

When dawn broke, I ran to the cemetery. There was a fine mist swirling through the streets, parting like a tide as I sped through. The chill air clung to my skin, turning my nose red and biting at my ears. Tiny sparrows sat fluffed up on the telephone wires overhead, chirping loudly at each other. Early morning workers passed in their cars, their eyes puffy from sleeplessness. At the graveyard, the groundskeeper was just opening the gate, his face comically surprised as I dashed through. I heard him call as I wended my way up the hill towards the place Teddy was buried, but I did not stop.

I was still upset with him for having sprung this upon me so unexpectedly, and I did not want to seem too eager to see him. I was not ready for forgiveness just yet.

Teddy appeared when I had reached Mabel Dawkins' grave.

"You came back!" he said in a hushed tone, almost disbelieving. His face was a mixture of relief and contriteness, unable to completely hide his smile.

I refused to smile in return, and his slowly faded. He chewed his lower lip.

"Yes, I came back," I said, curtly. "But I'm still mad at you. I'm here for my mom, not for you."

He nodded.

"I understand. I am sorry for making you upset, that was not my intention. I wanted to let you know there was a way to speak to your mother again, but I told you at the wrong moment, in the wrong way, and I apologise."

I glanced at the ground. It was impossible to know whether he was telling me what I wanted to hear because he could read my thoughts, or if he genuinely meant what he was saying. I didn't think I wanted to know the answer. I was too desperate to see my mom again.

Cautiously, I asked, "How would this work?"

We arranged it for the next Thursday. I was eager to see Mom as soon as possible, but Teddy advised circumspection.

"You might want to think about it," he said. "Remember that you have not seen your mother in two years. Time is not a generous friend to memory."

I was certain that nothing could ever change my mom so much that seeing her just one more time would damage the way I thought of her.

"I want to tell her I love her."

I was surprised; I had felt sure that the sun would shine on such a momentous occasion, but the day was grey and cold, the wind strong and blustery. School dragged longer than usual, painfully stretching so that my nerves almost reached breaking point. On my way to the graveyard, I stopped by a florist to purchase a bouquet of lilies. I would have preferred gardenias, but they were not in season, and I needed something beautiful for my mother.

Teddy was waiting by his headstone. He beckoned me when I appeared, and I laid my flowers gently on his grave. Together we sat on the ground, the grass damp beneath my legs.

He held my gaze.

"Are you sure you're ready to do this?"

I hesitated, only briefly. I was about to see *my mother* again.

"Yes," I said, firmly. His face relaxed into a beautiful smile. I knew it was the first true smile I had seen upon it.

"Close your eyes," he instructed, and I did so. I felt his hands press gently against the sides of my head, his forefingers at my temple, his thumbs resting on my forehead. The pressure began to intensify; not his physical touch, but deep within my mind, running through my body like hot liquid, towards my heart. The red behind my eyelids darkened, deepened, went pitch black.

And the world exploded.

I was screaming, although my mouth remained tightly shut. The blackness of my surroundings turned white. Terrified I was blind, I opened my eyes.

Something was different.

I could see, that was certain. I was still in the graveyard. The sky above me was as grey and bleak as ever. But so was everything else. It was as if someone had dropped me into an old monochrome movie. Gone were the greens of the trees and the grass. Gone were the pale flowers laid at the base of Teddy's grave. The petals were no longer those of the brilliant white and yellow lilies. In fact… the flowers laid there were not lilies at all, but roses. I had not brought roses.

Suddenly I realised Teddy was not in front of me. I looked wildly around for him. He crouched a few yards away, hunkered down by the grave of Mabel Dawkins, where we had first met. He stared at me… *was it nervously?*

I remembered why we were here. Where was my mother? I could not see her anywhere. I turned back to Teddy. My voice was hoarse, as if long unused.

"Where... my mother?"

A flash across his eyes. He could not meet my gaze. His face was ashamed.

"Didn't it work? I demanded. "Why can't I see her? What happened to my eyes?"

A cackle erupted to my left. Greta was laughing at me. A Greta suddenly sounding much older than the little girl I had met before, though her face was still that of a five-year-old's.

"Of course you can't see her, you foolish child! Don't you realise what you've done?"

A noise from the entrance to the cemetery interrupted us.

A procession was making its way up the path. It moved slowly, everyone in it dressed in black. Four pallbearers carried a small coffin. Behind them trailed the mourners, though they were few. Amongst them... my father. Tears poured down his cheeks. He looked as though he had not slept for days. His normally tidy hair was unkempt. Unbidden, my own face flashed into my mind momentarily. I turned again to Teddy. A hard resolve had stiffened his expression and he gazeed steadily at me now.

"I had to. It was the only way. One day, you will understand."

The funeral procession passed between us.

"What have you done?!" I cried.

Greta giggled again, horribly.

"No, you silly girl," she crowed, though the people walking nearby did not hear. "What have *you* done?"

On the other side of the path, Teddy turned his head in the direction of something I could not see. A peaceful, gentle glow lit his face as he began to smile. His body seemed to brighten from within, the light growing and growing until it consumed him, and he raised his arms to whatever it was that he could see and I could not. Slowly, he faded into nothingness. I cried out and ran towards him, but he was gone.

In desperation, I turned to Greta. She no longer looked amused.

"You're stuck now, like me, and how Teddy was. 'Til you can get some fool…" she left her sentence unfinished. "He got you good, he did. You even let him suck your soul right out your head, way only ghosts can."

She pulled a disgusted face.

"Did he trick you with his sob story about dying saving his sister's dog? He didn't save no dog. He's always been a sneaky, conniving boy, sweet-talking everyone, stealing all he could, borrowin' off people he shouldn't of been borrowin' off. He got caught one time, and that was that, BAM! Dead Teddy. Living world was better off without him. Surprised it took him this long to catch someone else to take his place. He's much cleverer than me. I wanted you but he stuck his claws in quick." She laughed, sourly, her expression pitiless as she stared at me.

But I was not ready for this. I was not ready to be dead.

I hated Teddy.

I hurled myself at his grave, screaming obscenities and kicking out. My intangible feet passed straight through the granite and I fell, landing face first on the grass I could not feel.

It was all my fault. I had invited Teddy into my life and my home. I shared with him all of my memories and he used them against me. As soon as he knew I wanted to see my mom, he had me caught. It must have been so easy.

A sob stuck in my throat.

Greta watched me.

"You'll get used to this. Being a ghost ain't so bad, and now you know you got to be trickier. Gotta get them like he did."

One silvery, ghostly tear ran down my cheek, falling from

my chin.

Around us, the wind howled through the trees, stronger and stronger. Leaves whipped about in the air, passing right through my ghostly grey form, and the hateful English rain began to fall.

LOST

Jude Jones

The whole hideous ordeal is due to end on Wednesday. Finally.

It began with a phone call, gargled half-sentences that stirred my stomach into a queasy panic that never quite dissolved. Every morning there are a few bleary seconds when I forget — and she is still alive — and then the jumpy, vomity, fever sets in again, and boom: "I am so sorry for your loss".

For the first few days I was hurt and comatose. I wandered with the search party, I swept my torch around the parks and rolled my heart between the trees, hoping for her to step forward and repair it. But as the weeks wore on, her light was growing fainter. Her features morphed into an alien death mask. I demolished a display of melons in a supermarket because I could no longer remember the exact slope of her nose.

I don't know if it was lack of morale or lack of probability that brought the searches to an end. The first signs of wear were in the fringes of our group. When I called for volunteers my friends' appointments, once easily rescheduled, were suddenly unmovable. There was no one to look after Lily's kids, no one to feed Malik's dog, no one to cover Jonathan's shift. Our search party diminished into an intimate family gathering.

Soon after, the apathy spread even to the inner circles. The last time I checked in with her mother, Joanne, to ask if she needed more posters she just shrugged at me.

"What's the point?"

I asked myself that question a thousand times that day, and scribbled a thousand answers onto cafe napkins, the corners of waiting room magazines, and the backs of bus tickets — an oddment library proving 'the point' of her. The next day I received an email from Joanne informing me that the search was over. I rang, and I knocked, I texted, stalked, shouted through her letterbox. But my persistence went ignored. I tried to print more posters at work the next day, but received a gentle memo from IT about using the printers for personal use.

I resisted the rot the longest. But I too became a casualty of diminished probability. The police gave me their reasons for stopping the search — there were statistics I could use to try and programme some detachment into my mind, but the real final severing of hope for me was performed by an email from my landlady.

"Are you going to be paying the full rent for the flat now? Or will you be looking to sublet her room?"

I asked for time to consider my options, and spent that time violently erasing every painful reminder from our flat. I tore down pictures, I emptied out her drawers, and I smashed half of all the crockery I could find until the house was a mausoleum filled with the broken bones of a life ripped in two. I gave the landlady my notice the following morning.

I spend a lot of time at work now. I take extra shifts at the library to avoid returning to the shell I live in, but the emptiness follows me. I try to lose myself in repetitive tasks, emptying shelves down to their thin metal skeletons and refilling them again, and again, until the ringing of a bell tells me that I can't stay there anymore. An empty, sterile tunnel links my part of the library to an older section, and I retreat there when the quiet slip of pages turning becomes too loud to bear. Each hour drifts by and I along with it. Floating, flotsam, forgotten and plagued by memories of —

A clatter and shuddering air. I am ripped from my stupor by the sound of books cascading from the edge of a table. A hand is resting where the tip of the pile was a moment before. My eyes meet the eyes of the offender, and my body spasms in frantic, horrified joy.

"Y-you're...!" is all that I can manage. She runs, kicking the puddle of books to one side. I dash after her on buckling legs, following glimpses of long black hair through the stacks and around computer desks. She is making for the tunnel — the heavy door slams shut for a second before my fingers reach the handle, and I wrench it open again.

"Dana, wait!"

The corridor stretches ahead in front of me, white and harshly lit and deserted. The fluorescent lights hum, the lino smells new, and there is no one there but me. There are thick black lines running down either side of the tunnel, and the end looks like it might be diminishing in height and width, smaller and smaller, and empty.

I suddenly feel ill. I stumble forward, hands clapping loudly against the plastic walls to either side, the sting and sound convincing me that I am awake, but I can't understand. The tunnel brings me to a staircase, and I keep running and climbing with half-breaths until I reach the old library on the other side. It is a maze of creaking wooden shelves and frayed binding and shelf-mark labels, and I grab the shoulder of every woman who might be her until I am guided to the exit by a colleague.

"What the hell's the matter with you? Go get some rest and we can talk about this in the morning."

I can't wait until morning. I sit on the steps of the library, trying to still the tremors in my chest and contact the police. Eventually I am put through to the detective who had been co-ordinating the search for Dana.

"Hello?"

"Yes — hello — I've seen her!"

"Woah, calm down. You've seen Dana Mitchell?"

"Yes! Today — just ten minutes ago, in the —"

"That's not possible."

"I'm sure! I saw her! She's alive!"

There is a pause. I hear a heaviness in her breath, a weight being prepared for me. "You can't have seen her. We've found her. We've found the body."

She says this as if she is anticipating the effect it will have on me. But there is no way that the detective could understand how my brain slows to glacial numbness at her words. The evening commuters around me disappear, and everything is reduced to a drag of black of white.

"I'm sorry," I say. I can hear my voice is weak. "What do you mean?"

"I mean that unfortunately we have found Dana's body in the river, near the boathouses. Her mother has verified her identity. Perhaps —"

"No, I saw her, here. Ten minutes ago!"

"Perhaps you should come —"

"N-no, no, no!"

I throw the phone away from me and it somersaults across the cobbled square. Blurry people stop to stare, but I am beyond them. I tear down the steps and through the library entrance gates with little sense of where I am going. All I can see is Dana dancing ahead of me, cutting through the crowd and swinging out of sight again. It isn't real this time, I know. My mind is tricking me. My conviction in having seen Dana doubles as I fight these new hallucinations.

I reach Joanne's house with barely a thought, and slam my fists against her door. Every organ in my body feels like it is tangling itself against the prison of my skeleton, yearning for Joanne to come and untwist them with an explanation. Better yet, for a moment I allow myself to entertain the thought that Dana is in there, having tea at the kitchen table or lost in a soap opera with two bites of toast left on her plate. A million lost domestic scenes assault me, all the sharper for their dullness.

Joanne finally answers the door. Her face is pink and swollen with tears, a grotesque confirmation of the detective's story before I even ask.

"You heard then?" she says. It is barely a question. She nods to herself as if I answered. "Suicide, like they thought. Threw herself in the Thames." Her puffy eyelids squeeze together over a crumpled paper bag mouth. She is full of water and sadness, empty of thought, soaked in loss. She continues blathering as if I am answering, requiring no input in return. My mouth moves to try and tell her what I saw, but as she lays her thoughts before me I begin to pick out a pattern in her words: relief. Relief, and release, selfish and ashamed of itself, but unmistakable.

"At least that's it all over now," Joanna finishes, watery eyes peeking past the lids again. "We know now. It's the not knowing that was killing me."

And just like that, my moment is lost. I can't tell her. I want to — the words are trapped but waiting, just behind my teeth, on the tip of my tongue and aching to burst forward. But it doesn't. Instead, we share a pot of English Breakfast, and we talk about her in the past tense.

I take the next few days off work on compassionate leave and try to live in my sadness and loss for a while. She is gone, so I grieve — I cry and I am comforted by relatives, and I don't get dressed for days, and I stop caring because that is what you do when someone is gone. I perform for Joanne, for myself, and for her. I perform at the funeral, hand resting on her closed casket, spinning out my tears in exchange for sympathetic pats and shaking heads. We all wear black, because that is what you do. We all sob during the sermon, we all throw a handful of dirt in the grave, we all talk about what a wonderful service that was while we all ignore the fact that she hated the Church and that the Reverend doesn't believe suicides get to Heaven.

We all act the way sad people act. But all through the day I hear the same glimmering life jacket being thrown from person to person through the ocean of grief.

"It's over now, at least."

"We know what happened now, at least."

"Her poor mother can start to move on now, at least."

The more I hear it, the less it seems to mean. Closure, acceptance, relief — it was the least, they were right about that. I could wrap myself in the warm embrace of "it's over" like them, but I hadn't felt my heartbeat since that day I thought I saw Dana in the library. Even though the ground had swallowed her, I felt —

A clatter, and shuddering dirt. A few loose stones tumble down the small mound that covers her grave. My skin crawls cold, and I glance at the other lingering mourners to see if anyone else felt the tremor but they are leaving. The gravedigger lays his shovel down, work complete. It happens again — I swear I saw the tombstone shake.

"Are you ready to go?" Joanne's hand on my shoulder makes me leap a foot into the air. She steps back. "Are you alright, darling? It's over, it's time to go."

I stand between Joanne and Dana — the grave, I meant. Or was it still her?

"Are you ok?" Joanne repeats.

She extends a hand — comforting, beckoning me to forget what I felt and what I saw. Perhaps she saw it too. Perhaps they all did, and they made a choice to ignore it, and close their eyes on the past. The light of the future was blinding, and that wasn't a bad thing. But still, I knew I felt the earth move beneath me. I knew I saw her amongst the stacks in the library.

"I'm not ready," I say. The colour drains from Joanne's cheeks as I pick up the gravedigger's shovel. "And you never let me see the body."

ARIADNE'S AFTERDARK AFTERLIFE AMBLE IN OXFORD

Richard Edwards

I'll try to make this as quick as possible. Let's skip over the first hour of the tour, the uncomfortably bad impersonations our guide peppered throughout the whole evening, and jump right into it.

"And that's when the devil himself appeared!" A flash of flame shot from the lady's hands. It left purple afterimages dancing across my vision.

I licked my finger and stuck it in the air. Nothing. Not a single spark of infernal power. The big man himself tends to leave a fairly noticeable tang that hangs around like a bad smell. He leaves a bad smell as well, sulphur, but that doesn't persist quite so dutifully.

Still, the tour guide was doing her best. The flame elicited a few 'oohs' and 'ahhs' from the crowd. I smiled and clapped along. Anything to keep my cover as an interested tourist. For me, this was a job. A job I didn't want to be doing. A job my agency had sent me on without telling me anything about it.

"Roger Eckford could hear the cries of the damned and, as he looked across this very graveyard, he could see the souls of the dead rising from their eternal slumber! His murdered wife was out for revenge!"

Have you ever tried to wake the dead? It takes more than an alarm clock and a spot of vengeance. Bringing back one spirit takes a lot of effort. Bringing back an entire graveyard at once would take nothing short of the apocalypse. Mr. Eckford's wife might have had suitable motivation — a lot of people who get murdered end up with a spectacular grudge — but that would not extend to everyone buried in St. John's cemetery. Why would they care enough to come back?

Simply put, those corpses, long ago rotted to skeletons, didn't have any skin in the game.

I nudged the man next to me, intending to share this thought, when I remembered no one knew who I was. He turned to me, expecting me to say something.

"Sorry," I whispered.

He scowled and turned his attention back to Ariadne of Ariadne's Afterdark Afterlife Amble. She'd put as much effort into her costume as she had her business name and stood before us all, a vision in white with ghastly facepaint, jangling bells and multicoloured ribbons. Miss Havisham takes fashion advice from a fortune teller.

"Roger Eckford turned from this scene, from this unholy commander and his satanic army, and fled for his life! He tore across the graveyard to his townhouse, the one that sits across from this gate. When he arrived home he found someone in his sitting room. A woman with a thick earthy smell and black, unkempt hair, waited in his favourite chair. The one that overlooked the graveyard. With a trembling hand he touched her shoulder...

"The next morning Roger's cleaner found his body, strangled, beneath the corpse of his wife."

Her voice tailed away to a whisper, leaving us in a stunned silence. We all looked down at the grave Ariadne had led us to.

Roger Eckford — 1865–1901

"Now, follow me as we tread in Roger's footsteps across the graveyard!" Ariadne was suddenly all smiles again, dispelling the spooky atmosphere she'd worked so hard to create. "And, although we'll be going at a more sedate pace, I must warn you… if you feel a hand reach out and grab your ankle, the rest of us will abandon you to your fate!"

Laughs, and we set off. I lingered at the back just long enough to perform a quick headcount. I didn't get the result I expected, so I made a quick note, jotting the number and time down on the back of my ticket.

We hadn't lost anyone.

The city had its fair share of churches. With only two spires, most agree St. John's was one of the less impressive ones. Poor builders. They work their whole lives to create a legacy to stand the test of time and then, 100 years later, someone decides to build another church right next door. Of course the later one is going to be bigger and better.

In the unlikely event I ever build a giant, gothic building, I'd be grateful if you would all appreciate it for its own merits.

Anyway, as we filed out of St. John's graveyard onto Broad Street, Ariadne grabbed our attention again.

"Now, as we come to the heart of the city, we enter the heart of darkness. Steel your nerves and take courage, for we draw closer to… the Black Bag Society."

She hissed the last bit. Like a snake. Some of the tourists, the ones who had a tenuous grasp of English, had their friends translate.

"This collection of nefarious ne'er-do-wells reigned over the city in a storm of terror. Over the span of nine years, starting in 1892, they kidnapped more than 60 people, committed

24 brutal murders, and blackmailed almost every member of the town's elite. Some say they were psychopaths, others claim that they worked with organised criminal gangs coming in from the continent...

"Still others hold that they were in league with powers beyond our comprehension. But the truth of it is..." Ariadne paused for effect beneath a lamppost, drawing her shawl about her. The tourists leaned in to hear what came next. "*They were the undead!*"

Leading with the twist. Brave. As surreptitiously as possible, I took a small black book from my inside pocket and flipped to an orange bookmark. My notes confirmed that, for once, Ariadne told the truth. Black Bag Society; led by Lord and Lady Winderton, a pair of renowned, confirmed occultists. I closed the book and replaced it in my coat.

I listened with rapt attention, keen to know what Ariadne would have to say about this one. She led us down Broad Street and turned onto a beautiful example of a narrow English alleyway sandwiched between two University buildings. About halfway down the street, a tree overhung the path.

"This is Oak Alley, so called because of the tree. The tree with a grisly history. It was the original meeting spot of the Black Bag Society."

The first time she'd said the name, there had been a frisson. Now we'd heard it once, the only thing we did was look upset. She sensed our impatience and hastened to explain.

"Of course, now we know the society was made up of students from all over the country. Once here they would receive an invitation to a private supper if, of course, they caught the eye of Lord Jeremiah and Lady Cybil Winderton. It would arrive in a black envelope, addressed with scarlet ink, and yet bear no stamp. No servant, no postman, no commoner ever saw such a letter. They appeared as if by magic, and..." Ariadne faltered, holding a hand up for silence, as if she heard something from another world and needed to concentrate to pick up the details.

This could be it. I took my hands from my pockets and held them by my side, widening my stance, tensing my muscles. I strained my ears, listening for the faintest bit of magic.

"What's that?" Ariadne swooped down to one of the children in the front row. She grabbed him by the shoulders, staring deeply into his eyes, her mouth agape with horror. "Are you a smart child?"

The child, terrified into inaction, looked to his parents for confirmation. They laughed and said he was. I could hear their pride a mile away. Ariadne drew back at once, retreating to the shade beneath the tree.

I scanned the tree. Nothing. So what was —

"I fear that Lord and Lady Winderton have taken notice of us this evening," Ariadne said, pointing a trembling finger at the child. "Check your coat pocket, child."

I frowned.

The kid had drawn a black envelope, addressed in scarlet ink, from his pocket. It was difficult to read in the dark light of the alleyway but, by straining and standing on tiptoe, I could make out the first few lines of the curling script.

The Smart Child, Front Row, Ariadne's Afterdark
Afterlife Amble

Ariadne motioned for him to open it. He pulled out a single black page.

"What... what does it say?"

The kid read it aloud in a high waver. "We're watching you."

The crowd broke into laughter and I finally relaxed. This had to be one of Ariadne's conjuring tricks. Admittedly, I hadn't seen her put the letter into the coat pocket, but then she started running these tours years ago. She would have practiced this trick for days on end until she could pull it off under the closest scrutiny. Or at least until she could fool a willing audience in the dark.

"What?" she asked in a flat tone.

"We're watching you," the kid said again. Had I been the eyebrow-raising type, I would have done just that.

"It doesn't say... It doesn't invite you to a supper in the garden of Mary's College?"

"Nope." The kid turned the envelope around for her to see. "It says 'We're watching you.'"

"But..." Ariadne took the letter from him and read it twice. Then, stumbling over her lines a little, she said, "It seems the spirits have their eyes on you, child. Perhaps we should attend this supper."

"Which supper?"

"It's well known", Ariadne had almost fully recovered, "that the Windertons held their private suppers in plain sight, in front of Mary's College. If they're watching you then...we should go. Follow me everyone! It's this way!"

One by one we passed underneath the oak tree as Ariadne strode off, letter crumpled in her hand, in the direction of Mary's College.

I counted them as they went, noting the total on my ticket.

The college grounds were open to the public. I felt a shiver of something unearthly as we crossed the threshold and entered University property. The majority of the gardens were shrouded in total darkness, presided over by the dark shape of the building itself. A few windows were lit, doubtless students desperately racing against their deadlines. Jack-o-lanterns stared down at us.

"Do you notice anything strange?"

The question came from a man with a backpack. In all my years, I've never once had cause to trust a man who thinks a backpack is suitable attire for anything less than an overnight stay.

He was exactly the type of person I avoid on the street: 40 years of privileged life captured in an overweight bag of meat topped with greasy hair, wearing a gothic style outfit with a pentagram tattoo. The whole package was propelled into absurdity by the camera hanging around his neck and the spiral bound notebook clutched in a deathgrip. He had tucked a pen behind each ear. Guys like him make me leave the room at conventions.

"A few things," I replied.

"I thought as much," said the man. He thrust out his hand for me to shake. I took it and noticed his handshake was firm despite his flesh yielding so easily against mine. Not a single callous on his sweaty skin. "Gideon."

"Ryan."

"Good fun, this, isn't it? Under the circumstances."

"What circumstances would those be?" If I didn't ask he would tell me anyway, and somehow that would make me feel worse.

"Well, she's a hack, isn't she? Still, a free ticket is a free ticket whatever the price." Before I could tell him I didn't think that was the case, Gideon went on, speaking with an air of smugness that only comes from a lifetime of practice. "You have to keep up with the competition, don't you?"

"I don't know."

"That reminds me," said Gideon, waving his hand in front of my face. I frowned at it, wondering if I should intervene at all, when he snapped his fingers and conjured a business card out of thin air.

I boggled. Actual magic. There was a telltale *fizz* in the air, the residue of a simple arcane manipulation. I took the card and read it twice.

Gideon Crow: Master of the Dark Arts, Wizard of the Ninth Seal, Grand Sorcerer of the Mystical Lodge (Oxford). Tour Guide.

Then a LinkedIn profile.

"Wizard of the Ninth Seal?"

"There are ten," said Gideon dismissively, "but we forbid anyone from breaking the final seal."

"Really?" I asked. "What would happen?"

"We never say." Gideon tapped his nose mysteriously.

Do you want to know what happens? I could have told him what happens when you break the Forbidden Tenth Seal. You find out there's an Eleventh. Break that, guess what? Number Twelve appears. And so on. For a while it was a hobby of mine. I made it all the way to Seal Fifty-Eight before I got bored.

The only problem is, as soon as you break seal number Four, things start trying to kill you on a regular basis. The puzzles lose a lot of lustre when that happens.

"Grand Sorcerer of the Mystical Lodge?" I asked. "I've never heard of you guys."

"We're a secret organisation."

"With business cards."

Gideon shrugged. He motioned toward Ariadne. "So what strangeness did you see?"

"There's extra guests. We've picked up six new people since the tour began."

"What?" Gideon performed a quick headcount. "27... How many of us were there when we set off?"

"21."

"Are you sure?"

"Yes." I showed him the back of the ticket where I had crossed out the number 21.

"Did you include Ariadne?"

"Yes. But even if I'd forgotten to count her, that still leaves us with five more than we're meant to have."

"Should we report it to the police?"

"What?" I couldn't hide the surprise in my voice. "You would call 999 for that?"

"You're right. Perhaps a quiet word with Ariadne might —"

"That wouldn't be wise."

"Why not?"

"Look at her."

Gideon did.

Our tourguide now wore a petrified expression to go with her costume. At first glance, she appeared to be floating several feet off the ground, which went some way toward explaining her fresh terror. I blinked a few times, noticing new details in the snatches of light between the darkness.

The ghost of a woman held her by the neck. A black bag covered the spirit's head, but a large, crinoline dress revealed her gender. Ariadne kicked her legs madly, swatting at her captor's arm. Together they drifted higher into the air.

Gideon looked back to me. It seemed Ariadne's expression was contagious because there it was again, written across the features of my new friend.

"See what I mean?" I asked. He nodded. "Now take a closer look."

I put my hand on the top of his head and twisted gently against the grease until he faced the crowd. The tourists were still there but now they all wore black bags over their heads. I expected six of them to be undead — not all of them.

For a second time, Gideon looked back to me.

"What's going on?"

"You're the Grand Sorcerer," I said, searching for my mobile phone, "How about you tell me?"

"Are they ghosts?"

"Yes." I swiped through my phone and speed-dialled number one.

My boss answered straight away with her standard friendly greeting: "What do you want?"

"Hi," I started. "That job you sent me on. The ghost tour. Who reported the first sightings?"

"A woman who identified herself only as 'A'."

"Thank you." I hung up and turned to Gideon. I punched him gently in the upper arm, just to make sure he wasn't undead. "See, these are ghosts and I am a necromancer. My employer runs an agency that deals with weird shit like this."

"Did you ever see Ghostbusters?" Of course Gideon would ask that question.

"It's nothing like that. We use magic, not lasers. Sometimes the magic *is* lasers, I grant you, but..." I patted my coat pocket, trying to remember if I had a weapon or not. The comforting bulk of something there put my mind at ease. "You should know this, if you're a grand wizard."

"Grand Sorceror." Gideon bristled. "Anyway, we don't go looking for trouble."

"What if it comes looking for you?"

"I do know one defensive spell... It takes some time to cast, though. If I start focussing my centre now..."

"How long?"

"Ten minutes?"

The black bag and crinoline ghost had tired of our conversation. She dropped Ariadne on the cobblestones. Our guide landed with a thump and cried out in pain. To his credit, Gideon was by her side in a heartbeat, helping her up.

"So what do I call you?" I shouted up at the floating ghost. The black bag covering its head revolved until, I assume, it could see me.

"I am Lady Winderton of the Winderton Estate, Founder of the Black Bag Society, First Grand Sorcerer of the Mystical Lodge."

"Huh." I pointed at Gideon. "So you two work together?"

"No," said Lady Winderton.

"No," said Gideon, a fraction of a second too late to matter.

"The Lodge has become a laughing stock in recent years, full of vain windbags who defile both its glorious purpose and feared reputation."

"Hey. We do our best." Gideon's voice cracked as he spoke. He and Ariadne, clutching each other for support, limped toward me.

"That explains why he's here. You guys want revenge. What about Ariadne?"

"Her tours are terrible. They disrespect our legacy."

"But that's your legacy," I said, pointing at Gideon.

"Our legacy is our reputation. We were feared once, and now we're nothing but a sideshow."

"Well, you have a point," I said, trying to remain jovial. "So let me get this straight. You all decided to host a long overdue reunion to issue her with a cease and desist order and, I assume, give Gideon some pointers on how to run a secret society?"

"We intended to kill them both."

"Ah." I placed myself between Lady Winderton and her targets. Gideon and Ariadne broke apart and stood defiant.

"I provide a valuable service!" Ariadne snapped, her voice full of fury. "People need to know the history of the city!"

"Why?" I asked.

"Because otherwise we'll forget it!"

"I think that's what Cybil Winderton wants."

The black bag on Lady Winderton's head nodded.

"Is there any chance these negotiations are going to come to a peaceful end?" I asked.

This time the black bag shook slowly, left and right. I sighed and drew the weapon from my coat pocket.

"Bit of advice for you, Gideon. Never take a knife to a gunfight —"

"You think that's new advice? Everyone knows that." Gideon looked at me across his shoulder. "That advice is common knowledge."

"You didn't let me finish. There's an 'unless.' Do you want to hear the 'unless'?"

"Sure."

"Unless you don't have a gun. Then you may as well bring a sharp bit of metal."

"You're telling me you have a knife?"

I held up my penknife for his inspection. This is what you get for packing in a hurry.

"Bit small, isn't it?"

"It also has a corkscrew. Look." I flipped the tool down and held it between my ring and middle fingers. "Question is, do the Black Bag Society have guns?"

We both turned to Lady Winderton.

"I think he's asking you," Gideon said.

"No," Lady Winderton shook her head. Then she gestured to her team of ghosts. They dropped all pretense of being happy tourists and, as one, they drew their weapons: a diverse collection of swords, cudgels, and knuckledusters. "We have these."

"It's a good thing my best friend Gideon has a gun."

"I don't have a gun."

I groaned. "That was a bluff."

"You should have said something."

"Like what? *'Excuse me, Gideon, but I'm about to tell a barefaced lie and I sure would appreciate it if you backed me up.'*"

"Maybe not in so many words —"

"Stop it," Ariadne cut in. "What's the plan?"

"Take this," I said, handing Gideon a flat stone. He turned it over in his hands, noting the sigil carved into one side.

"Why have you carved a rune of —"

"Shut up," I interrupted. "Shut up, shut up, shut up."

Gideon shut up. Just as well — I didn't need the ghosts knowing I'd enchanted the stone to let me sense its location. So long as I was within ten miles of it, I could close my eyes and walk straight to it. Dodging traffic usually proved the hardest part of the ritual.

"I'll hold them off as long as I can. Just get away from here!"

They ran. Well, Gideon waddled quickly and Ariadne limped faster than she had before, which wasn't going to win any medals, but it was better than nothing.

The ghosts charged and I stood my ground. Our battle lines — theirs significantly the larger — closed in.

No matter how many times it happens, I will never, ever get used to the pain of a broken nose. Unfortunately for me, the swing of a cane caught me square in the head and I felt a significant portion of my face twist out of shape.

I thrust my penknife at the man with the cane. It traced a silvery line through his stomach.

The Smart Child, the one I remembered from the front row, kicked my shin. I hopped back, cursing as I lost balance and pitched over backwards. The whole tour, ghosts. All of them arrayed against me.

I'm not a gambling man. I would have put good odds on me dying but, when you're a necromancer, death doesn't hold the same fear. It becomes more inconvenient than anything else.

"Come on then! Do your worst!" I screamed, hoping the ghosts would fall on a hopeless target and give the others the time they needed to escape.

They didn't. They floated right by me, in hot pursuit of the two people I was supposed to be protecting.

I stole a car.

Now that you know what I did, you're an accessory to a crime. I think that's how the law works.

If you decide to turn me in, good luck to you. Especially when it comes to convincing the judge neither of us are insane.

In hindsight, there might have been a better, more reasonable course of action available to me. Didn't know it then, don't know it now. Isn't life better when you don't dwell on your mistakes? Besides, as they say, needs must when the Devil drives.

The ghosts were easy enough to follow — their mob wasn't subtle at all. I followed them in a circle around a church, their ethereal forms glowing softly in the darkness. Somewhere ahead of them would be Gideon and Ariadne, fleeing blindly in terror. That they chose a circle irritated but didn't surprise me. If the two of them had been able to tell me their route in advance, I could have cut ahead and picked them up.

As it was, I didn't want to drive through the quicksilver river of spectres. If they were capable of breaking my nose, then they were capable of a lot worse. Besides, when you're consigned to an eternity of endless wandering the idea of rushing anything becomes comparable to insanity. I had time to follow at a safe distance and wait for my chance to strike.

More spirits emerged, dazed, from the buildings on our sides. A few broke out of the ground surrounding the church and shambled after, moaning and shaking chains. A headless highwayman rode behind, maybe thinking this strange metal beast part of the procession.

Say what you will about Oxford's undead: they're traditionalists.

A flash of inspiration struck me and I retrieved Gideon's business card. If I could phone him... But no. The man had a

LinkedIn profile and nothing else. Angry, I dug through my pocket for my phone and loaded up the app store. With one hand on the wheel and my eyes constantly flicking between highwayman, mob, road, and screen, I typed.

The procession turned a corner onto Cornmarket street — a pedestrianised zone — and I broke another law. (Together, you and I descend further into criminality.)

At night, the road was silent. There were no buskers, no high-street fashion addicts, no students looking to kill the time between lecture and pub.

I looked at the screen and found autocorrect suggested I download Ink Run instead, a cheerful looking game with terrible reviews. I scowled, corrected my mistake and installed the app.

One tap later and LinkedIn was asking me to create an account. I swore, noting that the horde of undead were taking a sharp right. They funneled into an indoor shopping centre. Together we were about to break a third law.

I braked, slowing to a crawl, and swung to follow. It looked like Gideon had blasted a door open using some magic or other. The ghosts drifted through after them without leaving a trace. I had no such luxury. I braced for impact and smashed into the darkened building.

It was still too narrow to overtake the ghosts safely but, fortunately, we were now moving at a snail's pace. Ordinarily it should have taken around ten seconds to career through this place in a rush of squealing rubbers and breaking glass. I took this opportunity to quickly tap in an email address, a username — GhostGuyRyan2 because my first choice was taken — and get to the password entry screen.

No time for that, though.

I broke through the far doors into a narrow road and turned hard right. This road was particularly long and I could make out Ariadne up ahead. It looked as though they were barely staying one step ahead. That settled it. The ghosts were making sport of them, moving just quickly enough to scare them.

I chose the password qwerty12. A popup told me I'd receive a confirmation email.

The highwayman overtook me as I tapped the activation link and searched for Gideon. The spiritual horse whinnied at me, as if it knew I might be dangerous.

There was Gideon, hiding behind the picture of a younger, happier man. I sent him a request to connect and waited. Feathering the accelerator I crept after the parade as it took a right turn and made its way back toward the centre of town.

My phone pinged. Gideon, it seemed, wanted to become business associates. I fired him a message with my phone number and — seconds later — he called me.

"Ryan?" he asked.

"I'm following in a car. Are you and Ariadne okay?"

"Winded." I could hear asthma fighting to silence him. There was a brief fumble and Ariadne's voice took over.

"Your friend isn't doing so well."

"He's not my friend."

"He has your number."

"We're associates. Look, I'm about to drive a car through all these ghosts. I don't expect my plan to go well but, if it does, I want you both to be ready to jump in."

"Will do."

I grit my teeth — and floored the accelerator.

The car jumped forward, and I raced toward the silver wall of ghosts. I passed through the first few, feeling the familiar chill of the grave wash over me. The ones who touched me collapsed instantly; the living complain that ghosts make them cold, but think about the searing heat they experience. It scars the unprepared, leaving them a trembling wreck.

It was the highwayman who first saw the car with enough time to react. Don't ask me how he did that without his head, all I know is he fired a black powder pistol at one of the car wheels. It scored a direct hit and the vehicle lurched.

Another ghost punched the driver-side window, shattering it. Supernatural physics is a strange thing I don't pretend to understand, but quick moving glass is something I know all too well. I felt lines of pain trace their way across my cheek. Small rivers of blood wet my face.

I spun the wheel in a vain effort to correct the car's route. It was too little, too late. When you're in a car crash the world moves in strange ways — sliding by uncomfortably, somehow appearing all the faster for the sudden change in direction.

One of the tires hit a raised cobblestone, or the curb, or a bench. Something — I don't know. What I do know is that suddenly the world was upside down and my seatbelt was being put to the test.

This was the fault of the car, the engineers who thought it a good idea to make this model so top heavy, the tire manufacturers who didn't make their product bulletproof and, just a little bit, mine.

More shards of glass. Rushing, cold air. Man and vehicle rolled once, twice, then almost went over a third time before the car rocked back onto its tires. I fumbled for the door handle and fell onto the street.

Gideon looked down at me.

"Should we jump in?" he wheezed.

"Probably not..." I coughed, horribly aware of a coppery taste in my mouth. "Do you know what a broken rib feels like?"

"Like two smaller ribs and a lot of pain."

"Har," I coughed again, "har."

All around us the parade of ghosts had slowed, forming a circle. I pulled myself up the side of the car until I stood, wobbling, alongside the others. "I have some bad news."

"Is it the ghosts?" asked Gideon. "I think it might be the ghosts."

"If this is your definition of bad I'd hate to be with you on a terrible day," I muttered.

Apparently he heard me because he replied. "I'm an optimist."

"What does your worst day look like? A minor apocalypse?"

"What's your bad news?" Ariadne cut in. I turned my attention to her.

"I lost the penknife."

"We'll need better weapons anyway," said Gideon, picking up a shard of glass. We watched him use it to draw a thin, scarlet ribbon across his arm. I winced; blood magic can be very, very dangerous, especially if you're behind on your tetanus shots.

A single drop of Gideon's blood splashed against the road where it sizzled, burning a small divot in the concrete. The world's tiniest pothole. I shook my head, realising what Gideon was planning. Flames already licked at the corners of his mouth.

I tore part of my sleeve away to wrap around my own shard of windscreen. A quick incantation gave it a blue sparkle. Regular glass would be useless but, with a few short words, I was ready to shank a ghost.

Ariadne reached into her inside pocket and levelled a revolver at our enemies. I gasped with envy.

"Family heirloom," she said, "passed down from my grandfather. I've changed the bullets since then, mind."

"Can I just...?" I shuffled closer and put a forefinger on the barrel of the gun, giving the weapon its own blue sparkle.

Behind her, Gideon exploded into fire, growing taller, his eyes replaced with rolling magma. Two enormous wings broke out of his back, sending flecks of burning flesh in all directions. I shook my head in disbelief.

"Well, there goes your soul," I said.

Gideon either didn't hear me or didn't care to admit what he'd done. It's not like we were ever going to meet up in some magical social club where I would out him as communing with dark forces beyond understanding.

I looked him up and down one more time, envious. "Can't believe you know how to do that."

Gideon didn't turn to look at me. He answered in a deep, rolling voice, conjured from the pits of hell itself. "It is the coolest spell."

I couldn't disagree.

Never take a knife to a gunfight, unless a knife is all you have.

On that note, sometimes bringing an enchanted shard of broken glass to a war is the best you can do. But when that war can be described as an all out melee between spirits, a demonic mage and a tour guide with a magical gun, a four inch prison shiv is a terrible weapon.

In order to hurt me, the ghosts had to become solid. That gave me a great opportunity to slash at them or, when I was desperate, punch them in the face. Of course, nothing would kill them without the right enchantments on it. Once I tried to charm my hands and gave myself some nasty burns which were a nightmare to explain at the hospital.

I dispatched one stick thin ghost, just in time to see the highwayman charging toward me. I sighed, seeing the pistol raised against me, and prepared to get shot.

There was a flash of orange light and Gideon landed in front of me. He bellowed in anger, the concrete beneath his feet melting in the heat. I watched as he swiped at the highwayman and sent him — horse and all — spiraling into the air.

Ghosts are not heavy. Gideon was strong. His attack threw the spirit clean over the rooftops of Oxford.

Something exploded. I remember hearing it, then I remember hearing nothing but a high pitched whine. I spun to confront Ariadne, who offered me an apologetic smile before firing again. A second ghost collapsed, withering away to nothing more than a puddle of ectoplasm.

Behind her, Cybil Winderton was raising a sword.

Instinct took over. I dashed forward, ducking beneath Ariadne's line of fire, and plunged my shiv into Lady Winderton's stomach. Her eyes opened with surprise — this would be the first time she felt pain since her death. Pushing my advantage, I followed up with a few quick, horizontal slashes. Each one sent a trail of silvery residue out into the air where it lingered, beautifully caught by the moonlight.

It's strange what you notice when you're in shock.

Something hit the back of my leg. I felt my knee buckle and went down, turning as I fell, raising my glass knife as if to ward off my attacker.

I didn't need to bother. Gideon tore him in half.

"You okay?"

"I think so. We need to kill Winderton."

"On it."

Gideon jumped into the air and flapped his wings once. He didn't quite fly; he climbed rapidly and then fell back to earth, ready to jump again. Cybil fled before him. A trail of fire followed.

It really is the coolest spell.

Cybil was finished. She couldn't outrun Gideon forever and, through some fluke I didn't quite understand, he was extremely powerful. Not as strong as yours truly, but reckless enough to use the wrong sorts of power. The dangerous kind that costs the unthinkable. I didn't want to imagine what might happen when they finally met, and nor should you.

Stop imagining it. Let's move on.

With their leader fleeing, the ghosts of Oxford were hesitant to continue the fight. Together, we watched both Grand Sorcerers of the Mystical Lodge — first and last — continue their chase into the heart of the city.

"Don't kill her!" Ariadne ran after them. "She's the best bit of the tour!"

I caught her by the arm. "She's dangerous. She has to be stopped."

"But all the things she could teach us!"

"Should never be taught." I could feel her pulling away, trying to follow. "Look, you called me here, didn't you?"

That gave her pause. She looked me square in the eye. "When I thought my audiences were in danger."

"They were, but not tonight. Let Gideon do what has to be done. Save your own life and let this tourguide business go because the Black Bag Society want to kill you and they have no reason to stop trying."

Ariadne went limp, no longer trying to chase them. I let go, glad she finally understood.

That's when she shot herself.

"Fuck," I said. I looked at her corpse, at the slowly expanding pool of blood, at the ruined face. There were no other words that summed up exactly how I felt. What other word could encapsulate so many feelings? First, there was the shock. Ariadne had obviously loved her job and, presumably, her life. Then came the realisation that I had failed, that when I got back to the office I would have a mountain of paperwork and several awkward meetings with my boss.

The bits of brain on my shirt were enough to warrant their own curse.

As I watched, Ariadne — the real one, not the body — rose

up. She gave me an apologetic shrug. "You said they wouldn't stop until I was dead."

"I didn't mean you should help them."

"But this is perfect. Now my tours will be the most authentic in town. Look at all the people I can interview to get the stories right!" She waved at the crowd of ghosts, most of whom were just as stunned as me.

"Right." I said, coming to a decision. "I'm going to go home. Is anyone going to stop me?"

None of them did.

Now that you know what happened, I can leave my rating.

One star out of five. Would only recommend to my worst enemy. The only reason I'm giving it one star is because Ariadne is very, very dedicated to her job.

Or, because every good review needs a pun, I suppose I should say 'dead-icated.'

Ariadne's Afterdark Afterlife Amble TripAdvisor Review by GhostGuyRyan2

URBAN EXHUMING

Anna Lewis

The bombing of Morland Hall should not have happened. Oxford was never a target in the way that so many other cities were. All it had taken was one rogue pilot to knock it out of history at the tail end of the Second World War, twenty years too early to ever become a fully recognised college like the other women's societies. The buildings were utterly destroyed and in their place grew a mess of shops and fast food restaurants.

The first time Rose went there, it was with Benny. She was dancing with the thrill of being the one to show him a new place. She'd made her first tentative forays with the university society and now here was a ghost all of her own.

He barely bothered with the society but did impromptu trips late at night. He went alone but liked to shoot videos, which he would edit and put up online to a considerable following. When he came to see her afterwards, smelling of paint and rubber from the old manufacturing plants, he brought into bed the cold.

He watched her with reserved pride, wary of patronising but full of affection for her newfound skills. When they found the passage to dead Oxford, she took to it with practiced ease and looked back to see if he was following.

They walked in straight through the Lodge, the gate swinging easily open for them. This was a new thrill. Normally they would have to find some way to sneak in, carrying their anachronistic selves apologetically into the past, but Morland welcomed the two students as natives.

"It's so actualised," she said in fascination as they stepped onto the quad. In the past it was a cloudy day, damp but warm. She could feel the drizzle on her face. The grass smelled strongly of growth.

They walked around the lawn, and through steel-framed windows Benny saw studies fade into view with piles of paper and books all over the place. "This level of detail is unusual, yeah. You've found a well-preserved one."

He stopped to study a noticeboard outside the common room and she stopped too, smiling at the compliment. Most of the text wouldn't quite resolve but the outlines of words were clear. He pulled out his phone and carefully framed a photo, then chose a filter that sharpened MORLAND HALL in gold lettering across the top. "Do you know when we are?"

"I think around the 20s. The forums say that's the most common time."

"Look at you, reading the forums." He put his arm around her waist and they explored the two quads, marvelling at the solidity of the stone. Some of it they recognised from their present, but most was new territory for them, structures that had collapsed under the onslaught and been built over following the war.

Rose let out a little squeak of excitement when she saw the library and tugged on Benny's arm. "Can we?"

"You go ahead." He laughed and pushed her towards it. "I don't think it'll let me get that far. My roguish charm might disrupt the ladies' learning."

"You'll wait for me outside?"

He was already looking through the lens of his camera to set up some more serious shots. "I'll keep myself busy."

Inside the library were long, well-lit wooden tables piled with books. It was quiet, not silent like the quad outside; the peace of a working library. The college showed off, essays sprawled across tables as if undergraduates might return to work on them at any moment. Rose walked between the shelves mouthing the Dewey Decimal to keep track, marvelling.

She glanced over the desks, but the handwriting was too blurred to satisfy her curiosity. The shelves were the same, full of books with indistinct titles, but their orderly nature allowed a pattern to be discerned in splotches of colour and texture where generations of women had focused their attention. Some (set texts, she assumed) had clear, precise lettering. Rose could muster little interest in the science and so on, but she found English Literature eventually at the foot of a staircase and ran her fingers over the spines.

She pulled one out at random. The book felt heavier when she held it, as if it had gained permanence on the journey from the shelf to her hands. The pages were a mess of grey lines. Words, but not if you looked hard enough.

When she closed it again, she saw that the cover had mustered up its title. *To The Lighthouse*. She held it a moment longer then, on a whim, slipped it into her bag.

Outside, Benny was sat on the steps. He scrambled to his feet the moment she came out. "Satisfied?"

"Very much. You're done already?"

They set off at a brisk pace. "I can't go into any of the residential buildings, so there's not much I can explore. I got some good film, though. It comes through well on camera."

"It's absolutely beautiful. The library... as if it had just been left. I wish I knew what the students were like."

He pulled her closer as they walked out of the lodge, under one of his gangly arms. "It's dangerous to get too invested."

"No, I know."

She watched the college collapse behind her as they stepped back into life. This only made his frown deepen, her interest in the precise moment of transition.

In living Oxford it was warm, or perhaps just clammy, in that way that caused sweat to build up. The book was in her bag. She put her hand in to rest on the spine, so she could feel it growing less substantial with every step she took.

She went back to explore the parts she hadn't seen yet, that Benny would never see. She took pictures to show him, but he wasn't so interested in seeing it through somebody else's eyes. She learnt the college's secrets. Its nooks and crannies became real for her as she built up a map in her head, one she validated late at night pulling up old blueprints from the 20s on archive computers.

She tested the limits of the college and found where it could not be recreated. There were entire rooms that were fuzzy and indistinct. When she stepped into them she felt herself slipping away. In these rooms, the real world felt closer to her skin than any other time, and she worried that if she focused on the feeling it would pull her back to living Oxford.

She avoided these rooms.

Other areas surprised her with their crispness. The kitchens, for example. Even in her own college she was always on only one side of the servery, but here she could slip in through the back door. She found herself almost overwhelmed by the clanging of pans, the indistinct chatter of voices that were always just out of sight and knives ringing as they sliced. She only wandered through, never stayed too long to listen to the cooks. Though their voices were the loudest in college, she had the strange sense that it died down somewhat as she entered. She would never have come here when Morland was alive.

She came back to the library most of all. Technology in ghost buildings was a complex job, but she could carry in books and paper and while away time writing in the presence-filled quiet which was so different to a silence.

Then, a few weeks in, it began to visit her.

At drinks she was in a group of people scrolling Benny's photos and making curious eyes at him across the room. His disdain for this easy kind of fame was the main reason he rarely attended society events, but they had plans for dinner with some of the committee afterwards so there he was. She kept stealing glances his way too, trying to place a niggling unease that had for some reason percolated in her mind.

She had been looking for a way to excuse herself, but was distracted. Too slow. "He took you with him?"

She brought her attention to the man who said this, his scrubby hair and perfectly round eyes. "Yes," she said. "Actually, I found the way in."

"I suppose he needed you with him. Women's college and all that." The man lingered over a picture of the library on his phone. It took a moment for Rose to see herself, halfway through the door with her back turned to the camera. "It's a pity the term card's all filled up. We could go as a group."

Rose was barely paying attention to him, because now she saw it. They were in one of the modern college bars, the kind that looked like the architect had been on a budget and had some concrete going spare, but over on the wall behind Benny all she could see was clean-cut stone. Now she'd noticed it came in and out of focus. It swapped with the concrete to look normal for a moment, then re-appeared in the corner of her eye.

"I could take you," she said. They lit up, though a few of them at least tried to disguise it. She had to clarify. "Just us five. I like the college a lot."

They did the maths of the group and realised this did not include Benny. Interest waned. Rose saw her chance to leave, in the gust of discontent, and went to join her boyfriend at the bar. By this time the ghost had gone. The wall was just a wall.

She was in a tutorial when it came down fully. There had been more flickers here and there for the last few days, so it wasn't entirely unfamiliar, but that didn't make immersion any less unsettling.

It was her, a partner, and their tutor, sat in uncomfortable chairs scribbling notes on Chaucer. Then it wasn't, and she was alone. She sat on one side of a vast oak desk, scattered with papers, and on the other side an abandoned pen dripped ink onto a professor's open book. A fire crackled in the grate.

She looked around, completely still, her eyes wide. It was as if the study had just now been left in the middle of a meeting.

"Rose?"

She was back in the tutorial. Her partner and the tutor were looking at her with concern. She wondered for a moment if they'd seen, but realised she must have just spaced out, her head somewhere else. "Sorry," she said. "Tired, I guess."

As she was walking home from the tute, Bea leaned out of a first floor window and waved at Rose to stop, then clattered down the stairs to speak. They had met on a few expeditions with the society. Bea had a tendency to wander off on her own and find her way back to the clubhouse hours after everybody else. She was suspected to be going for Treasurer or something similar.

"I'll come, if you go again," Bea said. "I heard you were talking about it from Sophie — she's equipment manager, so we can sign out anything we need. We could get a group. Probably just girls, so we can see it properly."

Rose had forgotten the invitation, had in fact forgotten that anybody knew about Morland College but her. She hesitated before agreeing. "You know Ben won't come with us?" She was certain of this.

"Oh, of course. He's already photographed everything, right?" She rolled her eyes a little then caught herself. "That's fine. It's not why I'm asking, if that's what you think."

So they agreed a day and time to meet, and Bea said she would invite some others.

Rose asked him to come later that week as he edited, nose close to the screen, but he didn't want to. "I feel like I'm locked out. I couldn't go in any of the buildings. It's the whole opposite of the reason I do this."

"I can't go to some of your favourite spots without getting catcalled," Rose pointed out. It was never aimed *at* her, just part of the groundswell of background noise in deserted rooms, but she heard those echoes and Benny didn't. It made her feel uncomfortable, and at worst unwelcome, which she had overcome by intellectualising to the extent that she could use it to pinpoint what era they were in. Men of their time.

"But you *can* go." He sipped the coffee she'd made him. "Mm, this is good, thank you. It's not great for my viewers, either. They have to feel like I'm giving them something exclusive."

"We can't go because it won't get you ad revenue?" She was ready to leave at this point, sick of half-focusing on her essay to have the conversation. She yearned for solitude and focus. The smell of old paper and varnished wood came to her. A yearning or a haunting. Either way, she wanted more.

Benny spun in his chair and caught her hand. He kissed it, carrying off the archaic gesture with a seriousness that touched her. "The channel pays for my cameras. It pays for all my detectors, and for chrono-proof GPS, and for access to journals..."

"I know. I know." She closed her eyes. The blue light from their computer screens filtered through. "You don't have to come with me."

"It's not just that. I don't understand why you keep going back at all. You were so frightened the other night." She had turned up on his doorstep, late, because her room in college was too similar to start with and kept slipping into Morland. It had kept her up.

She shook her head, but he pressed. "I know how you look when you're scared."

"I was disconcerted. There's a difference."

He sighed. "You don't have to let this take you over. It's dangerous to spend too much time. They start clinging onto you. You don't even *do* anything while you're there."

"I wrote my essay in the library yesterday. I read my book. I just like being there."

"You went *back*?" He sat down again, this time next to her, so he could put his arm around her. "This is what bothers me. Most people, something like this, they'd be frightened."

"You go to the old car factory all the time. There can't be anything left for you to photograph there."

"I don't make it my house." But now that he was this close to her, she could smell oil and something more acrid, too, the smell of mechanical things. She thought about how, when she'd arrived for brunch with him that morning after a long week of work, he had already seemed wide awake and switched on. The images he was editing tonight were filled with early dawn light, all pink and fresh.

"It feels so hollow," she tried to explain. "I want to occupy it. To fill it up."

"They're all hollow. That's their nature. You can't occupy them, you can only ever move through them. Do you understand? You're transient. It's not a transient emptiness."

"It feels so real," Sophie breathed, nervously smoothing her skirt. She was a member of the small group that dressed up for expeditions. Rose hadn't yet managed to discern whether this was simply to satisfy her own make-believe or whether she genuinely thought it affected the experience, as if the ghost buildings would welcome her more warmly because of it.

Bea had already assembled all her favourite instruments and was eagerly leaning over them to see the first readings. "Off the charts," she agreed.

They explored together. Rose was happy to walk with them and see new things in their company. The others were right. The college was opening up with even more to show her than before.

In the kitchen, a mess, halfway through preparations for formal. A table stood laden with hors d'oeuvres. Rose popped one into her mouth, slyly. There was very little taste before it dissolved in her mouth — just a brush of umami and smoke. She caught Bea watching warily from behind one of her contraptions and held the other woman's gaze.

"Be careful," Bea said.

Rose smiled conspiratorially and offered her a hors d'oeuvre. Bea grimaced but took it and chomped down in one big bite.

The accommodation was something you'd find anywhere in Oxford, cold stone counteracted by big fireplaces that burst into momentary flame as they walked past. A lot of it was hazy as usual, but they delighted in small instances where the college remembered itself: a diary sitting open on a student's desk, or the echoes of viola practice teasing through the corridors.

A couple of them gave up on doors and started to walk straight through walls, calling out their discoveries from the other side while the rest hunted for the way in. "It doesn't like it when you do that," someone mumbled. The two soon returned, complaining that the rooms had grown monotonous and dull.

Soon after this, the group split. Sophie and Bea, following the data, wanted to test how far the college's grounds went.

The rest preferred to explore the minutiae of the common room, studies, the bar. Rose made a show of joining in but was inexplicably irritated by these others who she — after all — had invited here. She lingered in the common room and rifled absently through the student publications on display until the others had moved beyond her range of hearing.

The room grew into vibrancy as she examined each section in turn, looking for nothing in particular but enjoying the way that details swelled towards her. Rose took her phone out and thought about adding this deserted common room to her camera roll, but the emptiness of it had started to bother her. She was too keenly aware of the bodies that failed to fill this space. It looked cavernous on screen.

As she replaced the phone in her bag she saw *To The Lighthouse* buried at the bottom, its black and white cover catching her eye. She stared for a moment then pulled it out and examined the swirling design on the cover, clearer now than ever before. So real, she wanted to pinch herself.

Rose looked around again at the miserably empty common room. She sank into a sofa, kicked her shoes off and curled her feet underneath her on the leather. With every page she turned she expected the book to disintegrate, for the trick to be over, but each was perfectly legible. The room was warm and comfortable.

She woke up in the dark. It was cold.

For a moment she was nowhere, could not have named even herself. Then a car rolled past with a flash of headlights and she felt the rain pattering down. She had been bone dry, but was quickly getting soaked.

She got to her feet, stumbled, leant against a wall until the dizziness subsided. Then she managed to drag herself into the blank light of a McDonald's down the road and order something hot and salty. As she ate she sunk her fingers into the plastic of her chair, hard enough that she punctured through to the foam beneath.

Her phone, when she thought to check, was blinking urgently. Bea, Sophie, Benny. She sent them all reassurances and apologies. To Benny she added, *coming over*. It was late but she saw ellipses jump up immediately as he typed a response. She didn't wait to read it.

On her way to his, she walked fast but took a long route, avoiding cobblestones and libraries. Instead she let neon and concrete guide her home.

RUIN

Alexander Walker

We all know about the noises at night. Echoes, in the dark. Those creaks you never seemed to notice before but now, well, now you're alone those creaks could be just about anything working their way to your door.

How I long for someone, hell, something, anything, to be climbing those stairs, crossing the landing, rattling the handle. I think anything would be better than this, this absence. Because even when I can't stand the creaks, when I creep to the door but bolt it open, there are no wraiths shackled in chains, no shuffling corpses, nor lost lovers. Only the void stares back, and we all know how that story goes.

The bedroom was gutted first, it was sparse, tidy, undeniably mine. The rest of the house, though, had a while to go yet. These old Oxford houses are all the same, you used to say. With the bay windows and the draughts under doors, the spits of grass out back and those fucking pigeons too. We'd made the room our own, for a time, at least. I would later live to see it empty and what do we say, if only the walls could talk? Could I bear to hear what they would have to say? Would I wish them mute all over again?

I remember ruin, that awful time after you had left and I had yet to. That strange limbo, living in a space once shared, a space for two, a room with a view. All for one, and none for all.

Your things still gathered dust on desks, your bags still cluttered halls, your toothbrush remained an idle sentry on the shelf. All the remnants of a person, of a life once lived, just without the humanity that bound them together. It hurt to be reminded, from every smiling face in frame, to first sips from every gifted comedy mug. Living in the wake as life passed by. Trapped in a museum, no, mausoleum of a time now long lost, but not forgotten. And yes, over time it hurt a little less. In fact, a little less every day. And now? While the mugs have lost their memory, their scrawls now faded from the wash; while your bags lie piled in storage, now deflated from trips to goodwill; it is the photos that haunt me most. Those smiling faces that while I recognise, I don't strictly remember. I don't remember feeling as happy as I look in those frames. You too, for that matter. They paint a largely fictional narrative of a happy life once shared. They belie no captured frame of fights behind closed doors. No snapshot of tear tracks down cheeks or of throats hoarse from shouts. No photo could capture the silence that grew between us, such a deafening sound of silence, even as we lay next to one another. How every sigh was the shortest of fuse. Every comment a jab or riposte. Pores that swelled with poison. Tongues that spat with venom. And while our fists remained firmly at our sides, it was the door jambs that suffered most, now lying dulled and splintered from the slams.

Now those photos remain firmly packed away, yet I know they are still there like some old spirit that lies contained, a genie in a lamp, a witch in a bottle. Wraiths live amongst those pages and to peek but once would be to release all the old phantoms of the past. Yet, I cannot bear to part with them. I am them, after all, and whatever form they may take in my future, they are a part of my past for good. My history. And maybe now or never again they serve a grim reminder, of the time I loved a ghost.

BRASS LION

C B Blakey

The ghost of a narrowboat drifted through Jericho, but none who live saw it pass. I had wandered along the canal-side in the morning's early hours, my head thick with the afterglow of my birthday celebrations. My carefully chosen clothes were dishevelled, robbed of any remaining dignity by the storm that had struck without warning. My rain-soaked shirt now hung on the back of a chair, replaced by a threadbare towel my host had draped over my shoulders as I sat clutching a mug of sweet tea, the steam caressing my face which still felt rubbery and slack from the rum I'd consumed earlier that evening. The boatman watched me closely, his face deeply lined beneath close-cropped grey hair. It was a solemn face, with heavy jowls like a bloodhound.

"You've seen better days lad," he observed, his voice grating as he spoke. I nodded, trying to keep my grip on the mug as I shivered, my elbows constantly slipping off my knees. "So where do I take you?"

"Take me?" I asked, peering up from the mug. The man nodded slowly.

"Got to take you somewhere lad, whole point of a boat."

"I can walk from here," I answered; my voice came out higher than usual and I coughed before continuing. "I can walk home when the rain stops. It's not far."

"No sense walking if there's no need." His voice was reasonable, if a little insistent. I was silent for a moment as I tried to peer through the fog in my mind, struggling to find the words to dissuade this man's unnecessary generosity. I was about to offer some half-coherent desire to use the walk to clear my head, when something caught my eye. On the wall by the door was a set of brass coat-hooks crowned with the image of a lion. The old man followed my gaze, then looked back at me. "Something the matter?"

"Long story," I muttered. "It's nothing really."

"I've got time, only thing I'm not short of. Besides, I reckon that tea you're holding's worth a story." I stared at the man for a moment, but he seemed to be waiting patiently for me to begin. With a growing discomfort, I began to realise that I must be this man's first visitor in some time, or at least that visitors were neither planned for nor expected. There was solitude ingrained in the scattered books, the table set for one. There was no television, no radio, no newspapers. The outside world did not intrude here, and there was no one who brought it by invitation. I pulled the towel tighter around my shoulders.

"It was a dream," I said at last.

"A dream?"

"More like a scene within my dreams. Same thing every night for about a month." I must have been around five years old, and my nights had been the usual mix of nonsensical imagery and distorted memories; a stairway that rippled like water, a merry-go-round hidden behind a rack of coats in a department store, a soft toy that wept until I unzipped its mouth only for the tines of the zip to stretch into needles framing a tongue red as grenadine. I shuddered, more from the cold than anything else. "It was a man," I muttered. "I never quite saw his face. I knew him though, I recognised the voice, or at least I did during the dream." I could remember the indistinct features, bristled lips parting to utter stern words.

"He spoke to you then?" The boatman's face remained impassive, but his eyes held a spark of interest. I nodded, my thumbs leaving streaks in the condensation on the rim of the mug.

"Better hurry up, he'd say, better hurry up we're leaving soon. Then he vanished behind a door, it didn't swing shut, it was just there. Came down fast, like a portcullis." My eyes were heavy and I rubbed the heel of my palm across my face, feeling my skin move over my cheek-bones, the sensation oddly distant as the old dream bloomed in my mind. "He didn't return, I didn't follow him either. I didn't even look at the door, just the coat hooks.

"Coat hooks?" His eyes had sharpened, searching me, as if trying to discern the truth of my story. He had a curious stillness, his hands clasped and immobile as he leaned over his knees towards me, as though his body slept until it was needed. I gave a small nod in answer to his question.

"Always the same coat hooks. Brass, slim and elegant, like vines, and above them the snarling face of a lion. I had that dream for about a month, I think." I couldn't remember exactly when it had stopped, just that at some point in my childhood I had felt its absence. "I saw it again, years later, but this time I wasn't dreaming."

"You saw your dream?"

"Yes. I was eleven, maybe twelve years old, on a trip with my youth group. We were staying at some sort of retreat, maybe it was a monastery." The old man nodded slowly.

"You're a Christian then?"

"I was back then."

"Not anymore?" There was no disapproval in his voice. I shook my head.

"It didn't seem to fit as I got older. I suppose I miss it some-times, it gave me something to be for awhile." That was honest enough, though under his gaze I began to feel uncomfortable. There was a question hanging in the air, unasked, but I couldn't discern it. I looked past him to the dark windows, polished brass rings set in the rich pine-wood panels. I could hear the storm outside, the constant splatter and hiss of rain on water, but the windows were matte black. There could have been sol-id rock behind the glass for all I could see.

"Nothing to see out there lad." He hadn't bothered to look at the windows himself before he spoke. There was a queer certainty in his words that went beyond experience of life on-board, he knew there would be nothing to see. "Did you see many of the order?"

"I'm sorry?"

"At the monastery, did you see much of they who lived there?" I tried to retrace the words of the conversation, maybe it was the tiredness or the drink but my memory seemed deter-mined to elude me. I took a swallow of the now lukewarm tea and somehow managed to inhale some of it. I sat there cough-ing and spluttering while the man sat there patiently, waiting for my story to continue and plainly unworried by my antics.

"No," I said at last. "There were parts of the building we had to keep away from so they must have been in there. I don't think they were interested in us."

"Makes sense, those who seek a peaceful life aren't likely to find it in a room full of children." He wasn't wrong, we might have been a church group, but that didn't make us quiet. Most of the days we spent outdoors; hiking, climbing, I even used an air rifle for the first time. The nights were solemn, as the adults did their best to inject a little religion into an otherwise bois-terous trip, but that didn't mean I enjoyed it any less.

"It was for the best, I think the group leaders were tired of us by the end. One of them, Shawn I think it was, he was fed up with me. I've never been good in the mornings, always running a couple of minutes late." He was the only adult leading the trip that had stuck in my memory, a stocky man with short, dark hair and a meticulously trimmed moustache. "I made it out of bed on time on the second to last day, that just seemed to annoy him even more than being late." It was strange how that still annoyed me, I had thought he would be pleased, but perhaps he was annoyed that my punctuality had taken a week to surface.

"Shouted at you did he?"

"No, he was just a bit short with me. He saw me by the door with a can of drink in my hand and told me to hurry up, even though I was ready with ten minutes to spare. He opened the door to the courtyard and looked back at me. Well, he said, you'd better hurry up, we're leaving soon." My voice was quiet now, confessional. My mind had begun to clear and the boatman was so still he seemed to fade into the furniture. It seemed that I spoke more to myself, my words barely rising above a whisper.

"He closed the door behind him then, but I didn't hurry. I just stood there, staring. A boy hurried past me down the stairs, but I barely noticed him. I was staring at the coat hooks beside the door. Four elegant brass coat hooks, and above them the face of a lion."

"Must have felt strange."

I jerked as the words intruded on my reverie. I blinked slowly, as though waking, suddenly aware of the boatman who had listened to the end of my tale in silence. He smiled patiently at me as I stared back at him, confused.

"To watch your dream played out, it must have felt strange."

I nodded my assent. The tea was tepid now but I drank it anyway, my throat dry from the telling.

"Where were you going?"

"Sorry?"

"On the day you saw the lion, where were they taking you?"

I thought for a moment, but came up blank.

"No idea." I gave what I thought was a rueful smile. "I don't think I ever asked." The old man nodded, somehow pleased with my answer.

"Do you remember how you came here?" I began to nod, then caught myself. I remembered much of the night; the party, the path beside the canal, the sudden rain, but after that it was all blank. The old man was still smiling. "There's those who ask for the arms of the angels, some for the fields of Elysian or the cave to the realm of Annwyn. Some want only darkness, some to return and live their life anew. I could ask where you want to go, but I think I know your answer."

He rose from his chair, and the room began to warp. The lion-crowned coat-hooks melted and retreated into the wall, the rich brown of the cabin walls draining away as the room filled with light. The shape of the room grew indistinct, reduced to wispy lines as though sketched in pencil. The old man stood tall, his features dark and shadowed beneath eyes that glowed like white fire.

"Who are you?" I whispered, as he took the mug from my nerveless hands. He knelt before me and laid his hand on my chest. His fingers were warm against my bare skin, and I could see that the deep wrinkles on his face were now flat against the skin like the grain of an oar.

"The boatman lad, just the boatman, and you'll know how to find me when you know where you want to go." There was no threat in his voice.

"What should I do?" I whispered, my voice choked and shrill. He just smiled his same sad smile, revealing white teeth beneath the slate-grey lips.

"I could tell you not to walk beside the canal when you're

too drunk to stand, but we both know it's too late for that."

He gave a single hard push against my chest. The world around me stretched and I fell backwards onto a bank of gravel and grass, my eyes staring up into a clear night sky. I groped my way to my knees and crawled to the canal to stare into the water, searching for my face among the ripples, but there was only the shimmer of reflected moonlight. Slowly I sat back on my heels and looked out to where a graceful vessel slid into the early morning mist, black and silver above the murky water. Dry-eyed and numb, I watched as the ghost of a narrowboat drifted through Jericho.

None who live saw it pass.

GHOST

Catherine Farfan

Who was the man
who ushered us together
to talk in haunted Oxford pubs.

He was, you said, like a photocopy of a photograph
that pressed its graven arms around our day
and walked us through the furrows.

Ghosts, we decided then, are memories etched on places
— steps on stairs, scrawls on walls and rattling trees,
planted by hands long gone.

(Later you showed me the bird that printed itself on your window.
A snowy owl, I imagined, although more likely the wood pigeon
that gently haunts your garden.

Flight grounded, it left its phantom imprint,
white-washed wings on nothing,
a memory out of time.)

As we talked — fingers barely curled on glasses —
we left marks on the sticky surface,
sinking into printed varnish.

We sketched out memories of our own that day,
just us three.
You and a ghost and me.

WHEN INVISIBLES COLLIDE

Abigail Vint

It was the first time she'd worn shoes in weeks. They felt thick against her skin.

These same shoes, and the feet they protected from the crude of the pavement, had walked past the man more times than she could count.

"Any change, sir, miss, thank you for anything you can spare, anything at all, every little bit helps, thank you sir, you're very kind miss, have a good one."

His voice was monotone, the phrases leaving his lips came out boring and lost, all meaning escaped them.

The volume was just loud enough to make it impossible to ignore and yet just low enough to allow people to pass. And pass they did, noses aloft, eyes forward, faces determined, confident that whatever task they were walking towards was worthier a quest than taking any time to acknowledge the human amongst the garbage at the corner of Walton Street and Little Clarendon Street.

Hope had been lost for many days now, but as she passed, she was drawn towards the deflated crumple of dirty clothes on the corner.

She had seen this same hopelessness before. She remembered the fear she'd felt as a young girl walking past the run-down Tobin house on the corner, recalling the stories she had heard about the angry old man who lived there. Some days, a young boy would emerge. He had looked too small for school, but perhaps his tiny frame had just been the result of malnourishment and neglect. He had stared at Hope as she passed, not saying a word, like a statue, his vacant eyes fixed on clean school uniform. She had had trouble turning away, but her mother's voice had sounded in her head, reminding her that it was rude to stare so she had continued, head down, towards home.

She recognized this look now distinctly in the man on the corner repeating lines and pleading for help that fell on deaf ears. The thought of his loneliness was too much for her broken heart to bear.

Her lead-heavy feet came to a stop on the tiny, boutique-lined street, her left arm straying absentmindedly to her stomach. The midday wind was blowing hard, but it did not move her. She found herself solidly standing about a foot from the man who sat, cross-legged, with hat in hand, repeating his lines.

As Hope approached, his voice trailed off and he locked in on her gaze. He pleaded without words, just as the small boy had done decades ago.

She couldn't walk past him. And so, remembering that sad boy outside the Tobin house and, reminding herself that this man was once someone's small child, she opened her mouth to speak.

"Uh, hello."

He smiled, stunned into muteness by her approach. She smiled properly for the first time in weeks. Never mind that it was a reflex; it was genuine.

"Um... yes, hi, well..." she managed. The words would not come but she was trapped to move anywhere. It was like stage fright, her mind wanting to flee but her body frozen in place, betraying her with lack of mobility. She had a purpose in mind but everything else pushed her away from it and the words, those stuttering, failing words, were the only thing she had to rely on.

She gave a half smile and this time, he was the one to save her.

"Hiya. Y'alright?"

His eyes looked up at her from under a dirty woollen hat. A tag "You're knot alone — Knitters for Love" was sticking prominently out of the side.

Was she alright? Was she? Minutes before this, she would have answered an honest no, an uncharacteristic response to the pleasantries of the question. But now, faced with this man, sitting amongst what could only be all his belongings in the world, she had never been more unsure of how she was than right now.

"I'm, well, I'm..."

The words would just not come. Just like an immobile actor on stage, she was struggling against an opposing force and her energy was fading. She had been proud of herself when she put her shoes on this morning and managed to step out into her terraced house street. Standing here now before this man, unable to communicate, she wasn't so sure this had been a good idea.

Then, out it came.

"Are you hungry?"

His face froze, even more than it already had on the chilly December day.

"When am I not?" His sarcasm lifted the corners of Hope's mouth.

"Fair enough", she replied.

The ice broken, Hope's words came more easily. "Well, I've not had any company for a few days and I'm dreadful at being alone," she said, clutching her elbows into a self-hug. The man did not speak, but just waited, eyes wide.

She paused, turning to look up trendy Little Clarendon Street for the right spot. She had been up and down this street so many times and yet with the turn of events over the last weeks, it all seemed so unfamiliar.

Over the years this street had become a backdrop to her life. The cafés, the cheese shop, the trendy fashion boutiques, including the bridal shop, had become like familiar rooms. The cocktail bars mingled with the chain restaurants created a diverse space that always made Hope feel right at home.

But the last few weeks had done something to the world around her. The lens she saw her backdrop through had shifted subtly, bringing some things into clear view while blurring others. It was a whole new world and now this man, with his woollen hat, had made everything around her sharper.

"Well, it's just, would you join me for some soup?"

His face dropped and he looked at the pavement near his feet. He opened his mouth to speak but hesitated to offer a response.

"Well, yeah, sure, OK." Turning from side to side, his eyes were darting around the circumference of his life, his belongings, encircling him like a cozy protective blanket.

"Oh, here." She bent down. "Let me help…"

"NO!" he barked, instinctively his sad eyes turning dark and vicious.

She pulled her hand back, as if avoiding a hot iron. Their eyes met again, his in the throes of survival, hers in shock.

"Oh, look, I'm sorry…" she jumped in.

"No, no…" His tone shifted. Now he sounded apologetic, almost defeated, but she could still hear a note of defiance there, something that made him more than a faceless voice on the corner of the trendy Oxford street.

"Force of habit. Anyone touching your shit on the streets is looking to keep it. I ain't got much so I gotta be alert."

They both let a deep breath out and nodded, acknowledging their crossed meanings.

"Lemme just do it. I got my own system," he said, gathering his things.

He began to sweep up the blankets around his ankles and stack the books he had been hiding in a winter coat.

Once he'd gotten his world packed neatly on his back, he stood up, ready to follow Hope. She led him to a bakery café.

The windows sparkled with condensation, indicating the warmth awaiting them inside.

She opened the door and he gestured for her to go before her. She thanked him and leant her head forward before heading into the cafe. For a moment, it felt as though they were just two friends headed out for lunch.

She stepped into the warmth and he followed, the sound of the bell on the door tinkling and the wave of cool air bursting through the entrance, drawing everyone's attention and swiftly bringing their eyes too. Typically, it was a simple reflex head flick, up and back down to plates of food and steaming cups of warm beverages. People did not turn away when Hope and her companion entered.

The woman behind the counter immediately spoke up in a sing-song voice.

"I'm so sorry sir, toilets are for customers only."

Hope's mouth fell open and she turned to look at her lunch-mate. "Oh, um, it's OK. He's with me."

The woman's expression widened, replying in an even higher pitch "Oh sorry right OK..."

The man, who Hope now realised must have a name she hadn't asked for, was looking at his hole-ridden shoes. She pursed her lips, inhaled deeply through her nose and tried to move things forward.

"Let's get a seat first, shall we?"

He nodded obediently and looked up at her to follow as she headed towards the two-seater right at the back of the café.

She started to take her winter layers off, piece by piece. Her pom-pom-ed hat, her gloves, her long knit scarf, mechanically removing each item without thinking. All this normalcy stopped her for a split second and she paused before sitting down. I can do this, she thought. I'm now in a café. I'm now out of the house. I am putting one foot in front of the other just like last time. I am surviving.

She managed to forget about her table-mate entirely until she caught a glimpse of him as she went to sit down. She paused for a breath and then opened her mouth to speak.

The man (she must find out his name) had sat down already, layers still intact, eyes closed, inhaling what seemed like all the warmth in the place.

Still standing, she parted her lips and luckily the words "What would you like?" floated out.

"I, uh... well..." and then their eyes met. He let out a short huffy laugh, involuntarily. Hope waited. "Like... anything... not out of the bin."

Hope appreciated the smirk that appeared across his face. He seemed proud of the clever way he had answered. His humanity was coming to the surface.

She lost it too, into a nervous, short burst of hysterical laughter that she wasn't sure was appropriate but which she couldn't contain all the same. It felt good to laugh.

People had just managed to turn away from the couple after their entrance but this excitable energy drew them back. The joy in the corner of the café was hard for the other diners to ignore. Many jerked their heads round to see where the laughter was coming from, others, attempting to be subtler, slowly turned their heads in the direction of the noise. Hope and her companion did not acknowledge any of them.

"Right," she said after she had caught her breath. "Right, OK. How about we shoot for something even higher, like something warm?"

His hands raised with thumbs up and he gave her a grateful nod. Hope turned slowly away from the table walking towards the counter. The lightness of their moment had slipped from her slightly. Everything about her was still heavy. The weight of her broken world seemed to drag around with her like a dark aura. It was only when she started towards the counter that she noticed not only the number of patrons in the shop but also the number of eyes that had turned in their direction. As she walked towards the cashier they quickly turned away, as though unaware of the fact that she could see them staring.

Stare if they like, she thought. They had no idea.

The passive-aggressive worker smiled brightly at her as she appeared at the register.

"What would you like?" she said, wiping her hands on the back of her apron.

Hope inhaled. Her eyes squinted up at the sandwich board.

"Um, so..." What did she want? It certainly wasn't listed on this bakery menu.

The cashier waited, neutral faced, unaffected by her hesitancy.

"Um. Soup,"she blurted. "Just let's just have two soups."

"Right, sure thing, cream of chicken or potato and leek?"

Choice — Hope's eyes widened. She just stared blankly. The cashier didn't seem to sense her hesitation and simply waited. The answer sprang out of Hope's mouth.

"Um, so, potato and leek. Oh, and two black coffees." She'd take a chance he liked the stuff. If it came to it, she could always add milk and sugar later.

The cashier obliged, and headed off to grab the bowls and

big mugs.

She took another deep breath, soaking in the smell of strong coffee and fresh bread. It made her think of home. She was subtly aware of someone waiting in line behind her but kept her vacant gaze forward, focused on the next task at hand — successfully ordering a meal and bringing food to her lunch-mate.

As Hope approached the table, he only raised his head slightly when she appeared. She set the tray down and went to lower herself into the chair across from him before absentmindedly rising again.

"Potato and leek," she offered hopefully. "I wasn't sure what you might like but I know it's hearty. Plus, a black coffee. I wasn't sure if you drank it or wanted milk or sugar or..." Her voice trailed off, and he waved his hand at her in dismissal.

"No, no, black is good. Wakes you up." He wrapped his hands immediately around the steaming cup of black stuff that she had set down in front of him.

"My coat," she muttered, "I'm just finding it warm in here." It was lost on her that her companion probably would need a few hours before he had thawed out but he politely nodded and thanked her for the soup and hot drink.

"This smell..." His eyes widened and he dived into the soup, plunging his spoon in and just as quickly thrusting it back up to his lips and mouth. The first mouthful was hot and it burnt the roof of his mouth, but he only paused briefly before scooping another mouthful in.

Hope paused briefly to watch him dig in, and then carried on herself. They ate in silence. Him, unable to take a break from dipping the bread in the steamy soup or shovelling spoonfuls past his chapped lips and into his mouth, her, like a robot, going through the motions of daily survival. Everyone kept telling her she had to eat something; that she needed to take care of herself. They wouldn't understand; all the while, food was the last thing on her mind.

Halfway through the soup, the man emerged and looked up at Hope.

"Thank you, really just thank you very much."

A small smile grew on Hope's face. "You're welcome. So very much."

The eye contact gave her an opportunity to take them further. "I'm sorry, I didn't catch your name," she said.

He paused before quietly saying "Ben", his face softening at the mention of his name.

"Ben. Well, nice to meet you, Ben. I'm Hope." Her hand stayed perched above the soup bowl, holding her half-filled spoon.

The energy around them softened. They were now acquainted.

Ben finished his soup before Hope, though not simply due to his own speed. She had started well, but slowed after a few slurps. She quickly became distracted by a table with a young family — the father and mother watching their little everything bang a spoon against the tray of her high chair. Hope forget he was there.

A loud crash in the kitchen forced Hope's attention back to the table and what appeared to be an endless bowl of soup. Embarrassed, as she was unsure how long she had not been present, she inhaled and went to speak.

"I'm just not actually that hungry." She paused. "Would you do me a favour and finish it for me?"

Ben's face showed appreciation of her effort to make it as though he would be helping her. Even proud men feel hunger.

"Sure," he said. "Yes, sure, of course."

She slid the bowl over towards him then placed her hands in her lap. His famished state had subsided a bit and he was able to enjoy the soup at a more typical pace. Hope felt like she should say something. She did not.

Instead, she wrapped her hands around her hot mug of coffee and raised it towards her lips to keep her mouth occupied so she wouldn't need to speak. Ben seemed content to just eat his soup, coming out from the dirty shell of his clothes to become a man eating lunch with a friend. From the outside, through frosted glass or inside amongst all the café-goers, this meal might even have been mistaken for a date. Feeling more like himself than he had in days, it was he who spoke up.

"Did you know leeks cure you of the common cold?"

Hope couldn't help but smile. "Well, no, actually, I didn't know that."

Ben's expression brightened at her interest. "Yeah, and if you put a leek under your pillow on St. David's Day, you'll see your future husband in your dreams."

Hope deflated and sank back in her chair as he finished his sentence. She thought he might not have noticed her change in mood, but Ben stopped mid-soup sip.

"I'm... um... sorry 'bout that one..."

She shook her head and cut him off. "No, no, it's fine. It's not you. It's..." She shook her head and trailed off, turning towards the young family again.

Ben set his spoon back down in the bowl and sat back in his seat. He tried again.

"You know, during battle, Welsh fighters put leeks in their helmets so they could recognize a fellow soldier?"

That got Hope's attention. "What? In their helmets?"

She appreciated the distraction.

Hope raised her mug to her mouth and drained the rest of the coffee. Ben continued through the soup, scraping the bottom of the bowl with his spoon to gather up the remaining dollops of creamed potato and leek.

She was expecting him to raise the bowl to his mouth and lick it clean, and then she winced at the thought. He wasn't a wild animal.

Ben pushed the empty bowl away from him and wiped his mouth with a napkin. He looked directly at Hope.

"My mum used to make potato and leek soup. Said it was good for your blood. Kept it clean."

Hope raised her hand to tuck her hair behind her ear and let out a small chuckle.

"Food from Mum is the best," she said and Ben nodded.

She felt the need to offer something intimate about herself. They had now shared a meal and Ben appeared to be opening up.

"My husband used to put leeks in everything." Her fingers rose again to her hair, automatically twirling through the auburn strands at the mention of Peter. "He said it was the Welsh blood in him that made him do it."

Ben's eyes brightened. "Aya, a fellow Welshman. Me, I grew up in Cardiff. Tho' don't have much of anyone left there." He fumbled with his used soup spoon and set it in the empty bowl.

"Family is important," she said, and their eyes met.

There were a few seconds of silence for what felt like minutes. They focussed in on each other, hardly noticing the bustle of the café swirling around them. Boisterous booms of laughter from the far corner and a child somewhere pleading "Muuuummmmy" on repeat. The clash and clang of the cutlery and dishes from the kitchen, the clunk of the till and muffled voices of "What would you like?" and endless requests of "I'll have...", the words seemed to drift into the air the same way Ben's pleas for help did.

They kept each other's gaze for a length of time which, during a typical lunch date, would have been uncomfortable. But Hope and Ben were coexisting in parallel life fogs, realities that were outside of the typical norm. And perhaps that's why what Hope said next seemed to make sense only to both of them.

"Ben, I've not been out of the house for days and this is my first outing. You are the first person I've spoken to in so many of those days." She inhaled before she went on. "I'm not certain I can really be out in the world right now, but, I'm not certain I can leave you out here either."

He had not moved. He had not shifted. He just looked at her and let her continue. Hope was opening up to a stranger in a way she never had before, and she could only hope that his stillness was a sign he was moved inside.

"Would you like to come back to my house and have some more coffee?"

It was out there. She could hear her mother's panic and her father's worry at the thought of her inviting a complete stranger, a homeless, desperate man no less, back to her home. At least she had never entered the Tobin house as a young girl. It appeared the adult in her had become more reckless. But, she had done it.

"Um, yeah, thank you." It wasn't Ben who spoke, but rather some small voice within him that he thought had been long lost. "Yeah, yeah, that would be really nice."

And so, they had decided. Or perhaps it had been decided. They both stood up and headed towards the door.

The stares did not stop as they made their way through the maze of small tables, but the pair didn't notice. Hope held the door open behind her for Ben and he nodded in thanks as they walked out. It took Hope a minute to be sure which direction they needed to go in. She looked left, and then right before turning and taking a step.

"Please," she said, "Follow me."

Her pace was the same as it had been when she originally decided she was going to go for a walk. Ben shuffled along behind her, his hefty bag weighing his shoulders down, creating the slumped hump walk he had. He was careful not to meet anyone else's eyes as he followed her.

"It's just down here," Hope offered, aware Ben carried his world on his back, as she led them across Walton Street and down Walton Crescent.

This is happening, she thought to herself. I've now invited a stranger back to my home. And, she didn't care. Her worst nightmare had already come true. Whatever came next was going to be out of her hands anyway.

As they approached her front door, she reached into her pocket for her keys. Fumbling at the door, Ben stood behind her, raising his head only to look around at who was watching them.

She managed the key and turned to him. "Please, won't you come in?"

He nodded kindly and stepped across the threshold, the warmth waving over his still-chilled body. Hope closed the door behind him, and gestured for Ben to have a seat on the sofa.

The room had high ceilings and two large windows. It was an end unit that faced east, perfect for catching the morning sun, and it kept the room bright right up until midday. It was a decent sized room, for Oxford, with a sofa against the wall and two lounge chairs across from it. The coffee table was strewn with magazines, picture books and a half empty tissue box, the remaining used tissues and empty boxes scattered around the room. Three lone candles sat in the middle, pristine and never lit, purely for show.

Ben noticed a small kitchen to the right of the door, a c-shaped counter against the wall, dry, clean dishes airing out in the rack beside the sink. Hope opened what appeared to be a cupboard but pulled out the milk. She saw from the corner of her eye a look of wonder from Ben at the size of the full fridge freezer in such a small home. She closed the door and walked towards the other side of the small kitchen to turn on the kettle. As it bubbled and ssssshhhhhed, she pulled out a canister with "THE BLACK STUFF" on it, only to find it was empty. What a host, she thought. She had no idea how long the coffee container had been empty.

"I've just realised I don't have coffee." She turned to Ben. "Would tea do?"

"Sure, yeah, of course, whatever you've got will do me just fine, thanks."

She reached for the other canister on the counter, this one with "UNIVERSAL FIXER" on it, and placed a few teabags in a teapot.

The wall behind the sofa was lined with photos of Hope and a man, with kind eyes and a welcoming smile. Ben was drawn to the photos before he took a seat on the sofa. Many snaps spanned a number of years, in what looked like university pictures, young couple snaps on holiday, house parties with friends, and close ups on tanned faces and tousled hair.

As Hope poured the hot water into the pot, she caught him looking at the photos. A pain burst through her abdomen.

"That's Peter," she offered, pouring two hot cups of tea. "Well, that's me and Peter. My husband... well, he was my hus..." Her voice drifted off.

Ben turned to face her.

"Peter. That was my father's name. He died before I was born."

Hope inhaled, walked back towards the coffee table and set the cups of tea down. She managed a small smile.

"Guess we've both suffered loss," she offered. She wanted to hear more, but as a fellow tragic figure, she knew not to push for information.

"Ta," he motioned at the tea. "Mum always said there's nothing that can't be fixed with a cuppa." His face beamed bright at the memory of her.

"Wise woman," Hope said as she raised the cup to her mouth and gently slurped her first sip. She winced at the heat of it.

Ben leaned forward and placed his hands around his warm cup of tea, slowly heating away the bitter cold from the outdoors.

Hope needed to share more. "Peter, my husband, we were together for over 20 years. Uni sweethearts," she offered. Ben nodded, still holding the mug to thaw his hands.

She paused before she went on. "He got sick quite quickly. One day he was complaining of a bit of fatigue, the next he was being diagnosed with terminal liver disease."

It had been some time since she spoke of Peter's death. Those close to her were still working through their own grief; it was hard to find someone who could listen with unbiased emotion.

Ben's face was still but intent. "You must miss him," was all he could offer.

Hope appreciated the clarity of his statement. She paused and looked directly at him.

"Yes. Yes, I do," was all she could manage.

After a few moments, it was she who broke the gaze and looked down towards her mug. She had been so focused on her most recent loss in the last few weeks that the pain of losing Peter seemed like a lifetime ago.

"He actually wasn't a tea drinker," she offered, filling the silent void with facts about her late husband.

"Oh, yeah. Never met my dad but my mum was always telling me stories, like how he was never one for anything warm either. Just water and his nightly drink." Ben mimed bringing a glass to mouth and taking a sip. Hope knew what he meant; something stronger than cocoa. "Never did like to mess with the routine."

Hope's face recovered from the sadness of bringing Peter up and nodded, knowingly, happy to have the subject shift away from her for a minute.

There was another lull in their conversation; they not entirely uncomfortable in each other's presence but not necessarily at ease. They were in limbo.

Limbo. The word had never really struck a chord with Hope before. Funny how quickly things can change. She was not a religious person, but she could not help but think about the possibility of lost little souls, drifting round an empty space. No heaven, no hell, just a void.

"Don't get much routine these days," Ben said, speaking to her but also into the air. "Could live without the routine, it's being invisible I can't stand."

Hope looked up from her tea. "Invisible?"

"Yeah," he said back. He shifted his weight slightly towards the back of the couch. "People just walk right by, you look 'em right in the eyes and they look right through you. It's like we're ghosts. We might as well be dead, no one sees us anyway."

He turned to look out Hope's front window, his eyes sparkling with moisture, his expression a mix of frustration and sorrow.

Hope set down her tea on the side table and leaned forward.

"I see you," she said. "I. SEE. YOU," she said again, this time her voice rising with conviction. "I haven't always seen you but today, something changed. You were right there today, clear as day, plain sight."

He turned back, grateful for her words, and faced her once more.

"Gettin' seen one person at a time." He smirked. She offered a short noiseless nose laugh and smiled brightly at him.

Ben broke the silence this time.

"Look, hate to ask, but do you mind if I use your toilet?"

She transformed into Host, jumping up with a "Yes, yes, of course, please, it's just down the hall" type of reply. He had stood and begun to walk down the hallway as Hope turned to set her tea down. He was ahead of her as he walked, and instinctively grabbed the knob of the first door on the right.

Hope's world was going in slow motion as she barked "NO, no, not that door." But it was too late.

Ben looked back at Hope, shocked, and dropped his hand from the knob. The door swung open.

Light burst through the other side of the room, filling the hallway with a golden glow. Ben stared into the room and was only able to mutter an "Er, sorry" before Hope managed to reach his side, getting a perfect view of the exposed room.

A rocking chair in the corner. A small set of oak drawers beside the window. Stuffed animals piled up on a stool in the corner. The blue elephant border circling the top of the room. Neatly folded onesies and baby jeans atop a changing table. The baby crib.

Hope stared into the room. The last time she had opened this door had been to put away the baby shower gifts. Her mother had been kind enough on the day of the incident to close the door before she had arrived home. Now, here she was, standing staring into it, with this man she just met.

Ben stood solid beside her, his journey abandoned, his head down, eyeing her from the side, looking for some clue as to what to do next.

She had not moved. Her chest did not even look like it was rising with air. She too, was solidly still.

"It's not this door," she said, her voice in a far-off place. "This is not the door you wanted." Shock or fear prevented her from bringing any emotion into her words.

"Right, OK," said Ben, reaching for the handle and slowly closing the door before turning to go to the end of the hall.

Hope stood at the closed door for a moment before looking at Ben.

"Look, I'm so sorry," he said. "If you could just tell me where the toilet is, I'll get my stuff and get out of your way. I've taken up enough of your-"

She interrupted him.

"He was all I had left of him," Hope spoke in a soft apologetic tone.

Ben just stared at her, frozen in place.

"He was all I had," Hope said again, turning back towards the living room and to the armchair she had just been sitting in, drinking tea and sharing cordial stories about the man who spent more years in her life than out of it. As she went, she turned to say, "Ben, the toilet is just at the end of the hall," her hand giving a weak, flailing wave.

She disappeared around the corner to the living room before Ben could answer, open-mouthed yet silent. He turned towards the end of the hall and saw the toilet, door open, plain as day.

She sat back down in the chair opposite the couch where Ben had sat, wrapped her hands around her tea and stared into the milky mug. Still numb. She could have been there for hours.

Ben re-entered the living room, head down, walking at a slow pace. He returned to his seat on the couch, sitting gingerly and clasping his hands before looking up to face her.

"When he got sick," she spoke, her voice wobbling, "They offered us an option of saving his..." she paused, trying to find another word before abandoning the effort "...sperm."

Ben's face remained neutral, fixed on Hope.

"I've had three miscarriages in the last two years. This was the last sample, and it took," she smiled, remembering the day she passed the 12-week mark.

"I was going to name him..." She stopped. "His name was Jacob Peter..." Her voice broke. "He was born two months early. He just didn't..." Tears were streaming down Hope's face and now, she could not go on.

Ben sat across from Hope, did not move, but was present, holding the space for her grief. He didn't stop her. He didn't try to make it go away.

Hope's whole body began to shake. She put her wet face into her hands and sobbed and gasped, her broken-hearted energy filling up the room. Ben sat, clasped hands, staring down at the tea she had made for him. They both sat there, for many minutes, before Hope's face appeared from behind her hands.

"I'm sorry. I'm just..." She wiped her wet hands on the front of her dress before clasping her elbows and hugging herself. "I'm just... sorry..."

"Me too," Ben offered. And then there was silence.

Ben lifted the tea mug to his lips and sipped. He turned his head out the window.

"They don't teach you in school how to get through life when everything goes wrong," he said.

She shook her head. "They certainly don't," gasping out a few more sobs, dropping her head and heaving a great sigh.

Ben turned back towards her.

"Best to let it out," he offered. "Don't keep that shit stuck inside."

She wailed, appreciative of his permission and consumed by sadness.

"I'm... just so..." she spoke through cries, "... so very... heavy..."

"You'll feel light again." He reached for her and placed his hand on her knee. "Won't always feel so suffocating."

She nodded, exhaling out, closed her eyes and lifted her head to face him.

As she opened them, she saw him there, suddenly more

than a man who she had just met that morning. The light shone through her living room window, bouncing off the back wall and illuminating the space around him. It calmed her.

"Thank you," she said, looking him directly in the eye.

"I should be thanking you," he said, bringing her back even more into the space.

"The company has been good for me," she said, again, making it a favour he was in her home.

"I've not always been like this." He motioned to his tattered clothes.

She simply nodded, partially emerging from under her armour of grief, partially unsure how to respond.

"My mum and I were always close. She raised me on her own, for the most part, until Derek showed up. I was 12." His face dropped and his attention was drawn to the view out the window.

Hope squeezed herself a bit tighter.

He shrugged. "He never did like the competition. Guess my mum loved me too much."

"I can understand." She nodded.

He looked back to her, checking to see if he should continue. Hope was now the one sitting still, looking on, eager to hear more.

"When she died, he and I tried to get on, but some things are just not meant to stick."

Hope's face grew more concerned.

"Your mom died?" she posed the question, checking if she had heard properly.

"Yeah," Ben dug his left thumb into the palm of his right hand. "Car accident," was all he offered.

It was Hope's turn to wait. Her hand brushed away the remaining tears on her face, and she used her other hand to cradle her chin.

"Must've been only a few weeks after the funeral when I just couldn't take the punches anymore," he said. "By that time, I was 16, probably old enough to be on my own anyway. A few of my mates said there was good work to be found on farms here in England so we headed to the countryside, just outside o' Didcot. Moved in with a bunch of other guys, five of us in that place. Farming was good in the summer months but things dried up a bit. Tried to get some proper work and I did, for awhile, kitchen stuff, construction, that sort of thing."

He shook his head. "My temper was always getting the best of me," he continued. "My flatmates got fed up and kicked me out. It's hard to get work without an address.

"So here I am," he said, turning back to Hope and staring her in the eyes. "Here I am."

Hope let his last words just sit in the air. So, here they both were, she thought, shells of the former people they had been.

"Where do you sleep?" Hope asked.

"Depends on the day," he said. "There's a shelter nearby, but it's usually full. Sometimes, if I get enough cash, and I want to skip a meal, I'll treat myself to the hostel on George Street." He smiled. "That's always good on a cold night. Plus, showers," he added, pointing at his clothes.

Hope nodded in understanding and only took a few beats before offering.

"Ben, did you want to clean up or..." He stopped her.

"No, you're alright." His eyes widened in embarrassment. "You've done enough, really. I haven't felt like a human being in a long time." He paused. "Lunch and a drink, being in a real home, the conversation..." His voice trailed off, thinking of how much they had shared.

Hope acknowledged his unfinished sentence with a knowing nod. She rose from her seat and walked towards the small kitchen where she had set her handbag down. She opened it and pulled out a £20 note from her wallet.

"Here, look, here's just a little something..." She started towards him.

He raised his hands in opposition. "No, no, look, that's too much..."

"Please, just take it, so I know someone's boy is safe and warm tonight." And she pressed the £20 note in his hand.

"Thanks, really, I mean it." His face was solemn as he stood, gathered his bag and headed towards the door. Hope stepped towards the entryway to see him out, pulling the door open for him to leave. As he passed through the archway, he turned.

"He was seen, you know. Your boy was seen in this world. He brought your kindness to me. He had a purpose."

Hope's eyes streamed, and, as she couldn't speak, she simply nodded and closed the door.

ANNUNCIATION

Sam Derby

The sound of wings woke her. That skit-patter-fluttering sound that a moth makes beating against a lampshade or a blind. She turned over and tried to go back to sleep, but the sound was loud in the dark in the way that the sound of dreams is loud. She couldn't bear it. Lurching in and out of sleep, her dreams were full of wings. Birds soaring through blue skies meant peace: the whirr of air being thumped and pushed around was horror. The moth in her room did not rest, it seemed, the little morsels of silk cutting the dark around her ears, landing on her hair and mouth. She woke.

"What is it?" said a voice.

She didn't answer, ashamed that she must have cried out. The light was on, disturbing her brother in the room across the cold hall. The moth had stopped moving.

"Go to sleep, you baby," he moaned.

He used to find moths and bring them to her, fluttering and terrified, or drop them down the back of her shirt until she screamed and burst into tears. They went to the zoo and he shut her in the butterfly house, holding the door shut while she banged and banged until the banging stopped and when he then relented he found her crouching on the floor and holding her hands over her ears. In the winter, when the geese from the lake flew low in formation, pulverising the air so that you could feel it as the skein swept over you, he laughed at her when she ducked and squealed. She was a baby.

Once asleep, she dreamt of live birds trapped in museum display-cases, their wings pounding on the glass. Eventually she woke.

On the way into Oxford she passed gowned figures striding in small groups down the High Street. There were crowds of tourists taking photographs blocking the pavements, and she headed across the road to cut down Magpie Lane. One of the dons must have broken off from the main group for a cigarette, for a figure stood in the shadows of the crooked alley. He watched her as she passed him, his eyes hooded, an occasional point of flame visible.

The morning was clear and the early December sunlight struck the golden stones obliquely, casting a honeyed glow across the city. There were rooks on the bare tree beside Merton Chapel as she passed by, their wings rustling in the breeze like autumn leaves. She reached the tiny medieval hall in which she worked. The outside walls were blackened by soot and there was never the money to clean them; against the rest of Oxford they looked decidedly neglected. Inside, a tiny quadrangle formed of the church itself, an annexe, a gatehouse, and the library made up the entire estate.

She was cataloguing the books. It had been a temporary job, a year ago. Books about St Joseph of Cupertino, who could fly when the spirit of God so moved him. And Saint Gall, who caused a demon in the form of a crow to fly out of the mouth of a possessed woman. There were paintings of saints and miracles all around her as she worked, most of them worthless, all of them black from centuries of oil and candle light. There were — so far — a hundred and four books about Our Lady of Loreto herself. Or rather, about the holy house at Loreto, transported by flying angels from Nazareth to Italy, out of the hands of encroaching Muslim armies and into the heart of Europe. The holy house where the annunciation took place, where redemption started.

At the end of the day, in the early dusk, she walked across the cobblestoned quadrangle and pushed awkwardly through the small door that opened within the great oak gate. The tourists were gone and the town was quiet, the tolling of bells irregularly punctuating the silence. She passed beside Merton Chapel, where a few black feathers were all that remained of the rooks in the bare tree, and looked up Magpie Lane towards the High Street. Near the top of the lane she could see a gowned figure, in the same place as this morning, almost hidden in shadow. She stopped moving and stared. The street was empty of traffic: just a few students and town residents walking to and fro, paying her and each other no attention. The figure didn't move. Perhaps it was just a shadow — had it been a shadow this morning? She was sure she remembered those eyes, dark pools in an oddly long face. And then something moved just above and behind her head, grabbing at her hair: she screamed.

"Are you alright?"

She had her eyes closed and was shaking.

"Uh — I'm — no -" she gasped at last.

"What's the matter?"

"Something — hit me on the head, I think," she said.

"Let me see."

A firm hand pulled hers aside, and slowly she opened her eyes. It was the gaunt face of the senior choral scholar at Merton, the neighbouring college: she had seen him a few times. He was young, compared to the rest of the staff. Not bad looking, though there was something unusual about the way he looked at her across the quad: something wrong with his eyes, perhaps.

"Something has scratched you," he said.

"Oh, goodness," she said.

His eyes — they were arresting — unusual, even.

"Look, I wonder if it was a bat, or something? There's one that whizzes around that lamp every night while I practise my scales. Maybe it blundered in here somehow."

"I don't know. I — I just felt something coming for me. How did you...?"

"Let me get you a coffee or something," he said.

They walked across the road to the cafe on the High Street and drank hot chocolate. She brushed her hair across the scratch on her face and let it hang down slightly over her eyes as she looked at him through the steam, and he looked back.

"I can walk you home, if you like," he said.

"No, I'm fine, I'm — thank you."

"I insist," he said.

How old was he? It was hard to tell. She didn't want to lock eyes with him. They were deep set anyway, almost sunken. She didn't want to give the wrong impression. He had held her hand for longer than was strictly necessary. She wasn't sure she liked that.

"No — no, thank you, I — I'll get a cab."

The cab came quicker than she wanted; she sat back in the leather seat, thinking about him. She shook her head. Something odd about him. She thought about *The Annunciation*. She looked it up when she got home. It was the scene in the bible where the angel Gabriel visits Mary and tells her she will be with child; with the child of some holy thing. She had seen the scene painted many times: the angel rushes in through a doorway, towards Mary, who is seated. The angel holds out a hand to signify a message. In some paintings Mary is joyful; in others, in awe at the power of God; in some, afraid. There was a mediocre one, a copy according to the catalogue, in the library, but she didn't recall where. She slept that night, and dreamt of angels. In the morning a moth fell out of the blind, dead, onto her face, and woke her.

On her way into town the next day she avoided Magpie Lane and walked down the High Street. On the pockmarked stone walls she kept seeing brown-black-silver markings like those on the wings of moths. She kept hearing that persistent flut-ter-skitter, or the flap and whirr of take-off. Everywhere she heard the sound of wings and their movement of air. She kept her eyes down and her hands in her pockets, tilting her head downwards so she could not see the sky, walking headfirst into the breeze. In the periphery of her vision were hooded crows and death's-head moths.

At the college gate she noticed an odd gargoyle that she hadn't seen before. It happened from time to time, in Oxford: the continual decay and restoration of the place meant that ancient figures faded into oblivion over the centuries, only to reappear suddenly one day when their turn came for renew-al. This one was perhaps angel, perhaps demon: a man-like face but with something of the satyr about it, the suggestion of horns, and horned wings, glowering out of the arch above the gate. As she walked past the chapel she caught sight of some-thing dark ahead of her, heard something fluttering like a flag in the wind. She stopped, her pulse racing. This was stupid. It was the chaplain, or the reeve, or maybe the strange choral scholar. The breeze pushed dead leaves across the stone paving around her. She turned back, looked around the corner and through the stone arch of the doorway in the wall, and saw signs of no one, not even a closing door.

That evening she stayed later in the library than she had intended, distracted by her discovery of a treatise written by a midwife in the sixteenth century. The frontispiece, for some reason, showed the author holding an open book, its pages ruffled, and behind her a cloaked figure. Damage to the page twisted its features, made them bestial and strange, as if transfixed with rage.

Walking across the empty quad, watched by the gargoyles and the statues of long-dead benefactors, she heard the sound again. Heard more clearly, it was a tapping, no — a scratching. It was somewhere between the two: like something light fluttering against glass. The sound of wings, trapped, desperate, pleading for admittance. She shivered and walked towards the real world beyond the walls. As she walked beneath the tower over the gatehouse she heard the sound again and looked up to see something moving. She stood still and craned her neck, forcing herself to look. There was the statue of an angel, as always. Its shadow was deeper and darker than usual. It seemed to move. She shook her head. The sound of wings buzzed and flapped. She looked around for someone who might help her, or might tell her there was nothing there. The porter wasn't in his office and the gate was closed. The sound got louder. She looked harder. It was as if there was someone hiding in the niche behind the statue. Someone or something with the odd proportions of statuary: huge hands, an elongated face. She looked at the face, looking for the cold, dead eye-sockets of a statue. She saw a beast's eyes instead: she saw them flicker. She saw the wings of the creature emerge from the darkness, heard them stretch for flight with a weird creak. She ran beneath the tower towards the great wooden gate, holding her breath and looking wildly around for the porter, for someone. She heard the sound of wings and something descending behind her. She tried the gate but the handle was stuck, or broken, and it wouldn't open. Something touched her, clawed and rasped at her, and she screamed.

"Wait — wait — it's just me — don't scream — don't."

It was him. Her heart thumped. Fly, it said, fly.

"Don't scream — I'm not — I won't — don't scream."

The next thing she remembered she was running blindly for home, through the stone maze of the city.

"You're such..."

"Don't — don't -" she sobbed, and her brother didn't. She was shaking, her hands were shaking, so he didn't say it. They were in the pub across the road, where they never went, and he'd bought her a brandy to calm her down, though it made her sick to her stomach to taste it.

"What happened?"

She wasn't making sense.

"I — it was really, oh — he was there, the same guy, and I think he was the man in the black gown I saw too — but this time he was really there but he wasn't really moving — so I thought, he's just a shadow then, and I was about to turn home, or I had already turned maybe — and I saw the black feathers on the ground where the rooks had been, and suddenly, oh, it sounds stupid, but I knew there was somebody behind me. You know? The feeling on the back of your neck, like it's breath or something, only it's more like a cold breeze, like someone is fanning cold air against you."

"Go on."

"Then — then — I'm not sure. It sounded — ugh — it sounded — you're going to call me a baby..." She started sobbing again, and he stroked her hand.

"No, no I'm not, I'm not."

"It — sounded like wings — like a flock of birds just took off right behind me, like a soft clapping sound, ugh; you know how much I hate that sound — and I turned around, and I saw — and I felt him — I don't know what it was but it *grabbed at me — you know? It hurt me*. I don't know what it was. But I'm sure, that he was there, and then he kind of said — as if he was trying to say — and that's when I started running."

The sobs subsided, the brandy vanished, her hands stopped shaking.

"You're not a baby," he said.

"I'm not a baby," she said.

That night she dreamed that a black-winged moth the size of a vulture was chasing her almost silently down the cobbled street, its wings stretching out with each beat to surround her like a cloak, and she was running before it with her hands stretched out as if she were blind. In the morning, as she looked out on the early mist of the day, beneath a lamp-post on the street outside their house was a black-gowned figure.

A few hours later and the fog covered everything, and Oxford had its ancient look about it: an island rising out of a low, foul marsh. It could have been a day in any one of the last eleven centuries, at least. She passed the day at work in a dream, listening out for footsteps, ignoring the cloud of moths in the library window which looked like dust come to life, and the migratory birds assembled on the dead apple tree. At lunchtime she wandered down among the dusty, chained books at the far end of the library. She turned the pages of a book of hours listlessly, and paused at an illumination showing the Annunciation. Mary wore a blue cloak and a blood-red dress. She had a solid-gold disk of a halo, and sat beneath a painted blue ceiling set with gold stars. The angel knelt outside the room, its eyes not meeting hers. The angel wore a gown the colour of a shady lawn. Its wings were slender and partly folded, pointing straight upwards. She couldn't tell if the angel were happy, or angry. She went through the art history section and found more, going back in time starting with da Vinci and Botticelli, through Fra Angelico and Fra Lippo Lippi. Da Vinci had Mary in control, receiving the angel calmly. For Botticelli, Angelico, and Lippo Lippi she was defensive, moving away, arms folded over her chest or pushing the angel back, concern on her face.

The angel's movement was determinedly towards her. Further back, in Byzantine frescoes and illuminations, the angel became predatory. In one, the angel hung in the air, poised to dive like a raptor. She found the earliest known image — a second-century icon carved into the ceiling of an early Christian burial cave. A stark outline showing a winged figure, reaching out irrepressibly towards a woman who appeared to be tied to a stake.

When it was long dark and the library was quiet, and she had finished transcribing a long passage from the book, she thought she heard singing from Merton Chapel. Was it tonight that he practised? She listened a little longer, straining her ear so that the background sounds of the library came into focus; the shuffle of pages in an unseen alcove, the tread of feet on the floor above, the buzz of the lightbulbs and the tick of the radiators. She walked over to the window and looked out. A light was on in the chapel. It must be tonight. She gathered up her things and bundled them into a leather satchel. She was about to leave when she looked up and saw the painting, the copy of *The Annunciation* which hung apologetically behind the library door, which was usually held open by a doorstop, obscuring it. It was a copy of a fourteenth century work by Simone Martini, the original of which hung in the Uffizi. It was more horrific than she remembered but she was drawn towards it nonetheless. The angel was scowling, arrogant, thrusting its neck forward towards Mary who drew back in undisguised horror. A nasty tangle of birds crowded the ceiling above her. The flowers borne by the angel were thorned. The message he brought was not welcome. She shuddered, moved through the door and closed it behind her.

As she walked across the quad she started shaking again. She couldn't face the cobbled street and the shadows of the lane. There was a shortcut through Merton, through the doorway in the old stone wall, and she took it. As she passed Merton Chapel she saw the light go out and there was a gowned figure walking away from her towards the rose garden. She stopped for a second. She couldn't hear the music. Or perhaps — could she? Was that someone humming? It was the same tune — coming from the rose garden. The moon was dark. Don't be a baby. Come on, then.

She followed the figure across the neatly laid path through the trim lawns, past the chapel with its gargoyles and statues. In the rose garden the figure was nowhere to be seen, but there was a cigarette butt and there were some markings on the ground. There was another exit from the garden: that was it, perhaps, just a cigarette and then walk back past the white rose and the yellow rose, do a little circuit of the gardens in the silent darkness, then go back to his lonely recital. Something flew past her, quite close, and she cried out. The sound echoed across the garden. No one came.

Starting to feel frightened she looked round for the quickest way back to the main gate. She had just started walking when the sound of wings brought her up sharply. She turned around slowly, and saw only the flicker of a shadow in the corner of her eye, as if someone had just moved out of sight, and behind the wall. Someone tall and thin, and cloaked, or gowned. Or winged.

"Who's there?" she said, though her voice turned out quieter than she wanted. There was no reply. *I'm not a baby*, she thought.

"Who's there?" she said again, and walked towards the wall.

When she turned the corner, she saw the strange figure moving away along the path, away from the chapel and towards the little gardener's hut at the edge of the deer park. It was fringed with some straggly daffodils born too soon, but the door looked new and the roof was sound.

She saw the figure go in. She followed it, like in a dream. In the trees of the deer park's edge she fancied she could see roosting birds. In the black sky above her she could feel thousands of tiny wings beating, and she kept her head down and walked straight, looking at her feet and the solid ground. Outside the door she stood, listening for something human, the sound of humming, or the strike of a match: she heard nothing but the rustling of the living undergrowth, the sound of night. The door handle was stiff but it turned, nevertheless, and she opened it.

In the dark hall, across from her as she burst in, was the tall thin figure. His bestial face was tilted down so that she could see that there were small horns just breaching his scalp. His eyebrows were arched sharply and his eyes, clearly revealed now, were like a goat's eyes: long thin ovals that both fixed her and looked beyond into the world that she had left behind her. There was a flutter, louder than her dreams, and an almost imperceptible movement behind his head. Then she saw them: huge, shaped like the windows on a Norman church, and shaded the brown and silver colour of a moth's wings. They shivered, and the terrible sound came again, like shards of glass against sandpaper, like the sound of nerve-endings being slowly diced. He was looking through the shadows, directly at her, stood in the doorway poised to — what? To ask: why have you led me here?

Then there was another sound, as if he were clearing his throat of nectar, or blood. She saw in his small mouth a tiny thin black tongue. She heard the sound it made, a leathery rasp behind his whisper, against a weird clicking and a quiet howl, as he spoke.

"I have a message for you," he said.

THE HAUNTING OF HANGMAN'S HILL

Sophie Watson

Help with Mary Blandy | SpookyGal98

Has anyone been able to summon Mary Blandy? I've been trying on the castle mound for months but no luck. Any tips would be much appreciated!!

RE: Help with Mary Blandy | IAintAfraid

What sort of equipment are you using?

RE: Help with Mary Blandy | SpookyGal98

I've got an EMF app, but it's a bit hit and miss. I've read about using an IR beam. Do you think it's worth investing in a kit?

RE: Help with Mary Blandy | IAintAfraid

Are you thick or what? IR beams are the biggest scam out there. Complete waste of time.

How could a spirit set off a beam when it's in a transparent state?? Bloody amateur.

RE: Help with Mary Blandy | MB_Fan

Hi SpookyGal98,

An excellent question. I myself have been to the mound

numerous times and have been fortunate enough to find my-self in the presence of Miss Blandy on several occasions. The most memorable of which I will now detail.

It was a frosty April night. I remember it well for my dar-ling Morgana was quite unwell and I had spent an upsetting couple of hours at the local veterinarian's. A particularly nasty bout of Haemorrhagic Gastritis I'm afraid, but thankfully she made a full recovery. You may not think this relevant, but re-member — Mary poisoned her father! In some way I think she was trying to send me a message, though why poor Morgana had to suffer I do not know.

I read on the <u>Sympathetic Magic Forum</u> (a most illumi-nating place) that they can supernaturally control people by using a representative object (think: voodoo doll). This got my cogs turning and I thought I would test this theory on the astral plane and lo and behold — success!

While I was unable to summon a baying mob to chant for her death, I was able to bring along some items she would recognise. Below is a list of what I took along, and a star rat-ing out of 5 as to how she reacted:

▶ Rice * I read online that rice has high levels of arsenic, but evidently not high enough as Mary barely made her presence known.

▶ Mutton chops and apple pie ** Her last meal. She didn't respond well to these. I might try M&S next time.

▶ Prayer Book *** This was held in her hands before her death. More of a reaction than the pie, but I wasn't able to find an original 1752 edition, so she may have disap-proved of the colour images.

▶ *Miss Blandy's Own Account of the Affair between her and Mr. Cranstoun* ***** At last, a success! I should have known it would be her own words that drew her spirit near. If you'd like, I will PM you the resulting photographs. Even when I watermark them, they still get stolen by some ignoramus, so I'd rather not upload them publicly.

Do not listen to the detractors. Mary is there and she wants her presence known. You simply have to know what to do. I am happy to share tips regarding other objects.
MB_Fan

RE: Help with Mary Blandy | IAintAfraid
This place has gone downhill ever since the new mods took over

RE: Help with Mary Blandy | SpookyGal98
Thanks @MB_Fan. Please could you PM me more details?

Nina looked at her watch and sighed. He was late. She had been waiting so long the courtyard had completely emptied out. The last of the school trips had departed hours ago and it was too dark for busloads of tourist to tread the cobbles and place their heads in the stocks for a photo opportunity.

Her phone buzzed in her hand and she opened the EMF app. The needle that pivoted at the centre of the semicircle stayed in the red zone — low chance of paranormal activity. She held it aloft, stretching her arm up towards the top of the mound. From down here she could just see the shadow of one of the trees, silhouetted against the charcoal sky, but it was difficult to tell whether there was anyone, or anything, else up there. The further she stretched her arms, the further the needle edged closer towards the orange zone. Good, she thought, tonight might finally be the night.

Nina's head twitched at the sound of footsteps. But it was only a family walking across the courtyard, children skittering towards the bright lights of the Castle Quarter. Nina watched as they slalomed across the courtyard, screaming and whirling as if tugged by some playful gale.

She turned her attention back to her phone and refreshed the Paranormarax forums.

No new posts. No new messages.

Nina opened her messages with MB_Fan and read:

>Thank you SpookyGal98. If you bring the necessary equipment I can certainly help you to reach Miss Blandy. Message me when everything is set up and I will tell you what you must do next.

Nina's fingers hovered over the keyboard. Was it too keen to message back now? Maybe she should wait until everything was ready.

>Will do x

She pressed send and cringed. A kiss was definitely too keen. At least it was only one.

"S'up Spooky Gal?"

Nina jumped, but it was only Denny. He slunk towards her, wearing his signature leather jacket.

"You're late."

"Close enough." He shrugged.

Nina sprang from the bench and they walked towards the fence that encircled the mound, where large banners advertised an outdoor performance of *Twelfth Night*. She clambered up the lip to the metal gate and beckoned to Denny.

"Do you know what the code is?" he asked.

She clicked her teeth at him, and then promptly hopped over the fence.

"Nina!" He looked over his shoulder, but the courtyard remained empty.

"No one cares about us going up here and even if they did, what are they going to do about it?" She beckoned to him. "Come on!"

With a last, lingering look around the courtyard, Denny clambered over the fence, dropped to the other side and followed Nina up the winding path.

"Remind me again why I need to be here?"

"You've got a dictaphone."

"Right. And you couldn't have just asked to borrow it?"

"It's more fun this way." She illuminated the rocky path with her phone, swinging it like a divining rod. "And it'll look good on your CV."

He scoffed, but said nothing more.

Nina marched upwards, feeling her muscles burn as she broke the crest of the hill. From the top of the mound, the traffic trundling down New Road looked surprisingly small — the steep angle transforming the bobbing rows of headlights into dainty strings of fairy lights. Straight ahead, Nuffield College's spire thrust into the heavens, dominating Oxford's skyline. She closed her eyes and breathed in. She could smell wet grass and a faint hint of thyme.

She turned around and surveyed the mound — there was no other living soul here. Opposite, the hill's famous trees spidered out towards the sky. To think that hundreds of years ago, this would be the last thing prisoners would see. She turned back to the picture-postcard skyline.

"Hurry up, slow-coach," she called down the path to Denny. She couldn't see him from where she stood but could hear his slow, shuffling footsteps and laboured breaths.

Nina shivered. She must have left her coat on the bench below. It was colder up here than last time. Open to the elements, the wind seemed to relish in whipping the grass into a frenzy and she pulled her cardigan tighter. One forum post had said that low temperatures were a good sign when ghost hunting, but without a thermal imaging camera she couldn't be certain whether the cause was paranormal or meteorological.

Her phone buzzed in her hand: medium chance of paranormal activity. She opened the EMF app and tracked the needle as it swung into the orange zone.

Nina grinned, and set off towards the trees, crossing the short distance in a few strides. She placed her hand on the bark, feeling the rough texture under her palm. With her eyes closed, she strained to sense any psychical energy. Nina peeked at her phone, but the needle stayed firmly in the orange zone.

"Is this where it happened, then?" Denny had caught up with her, his breath rickety.

"I'm not 100% sure. Some sources say she was executed down there", she pointed towards the nearby Hotel Malmaison, "and some say up here. There's a picture — see?"

She pulled it up on her phone and Denny leant in to look. A grainy scan of a woodcut showed a primitive gallows constructed between two spindly trees. A woman stood at the foot of the platform, head bowed with prayer book in hand, while a large crowd pressed into the right of the frame, their faces twisted and eager.

He took her phone and held it up to the trees, comparing the past and present scenes.

"It doesn't seem very plausible to me. They're too far apart to support a beam."

"I thought you failed GCSE Physics?"

"Well, you don't need an A* to know it's impossible for those trees to support a beam."

"There are plenty of primary sources." She snatched her phone back. "And anyway, there's activity here right now."

She pointed to needle in the EMF app, which edged ever

closer to the green zone.

"Even if it she wasn't executed right on this spot, it's clearly significant."

Denny opened his mouth to speak, but then shut it again. He rooted around in his pocket for the dictaphone.

"So you want me to turn this on now?"

"Can't hurt. We should probably start, anyway. Before we miss the window of paranormal activity."

He nodded and switched on the tape recorder.

Nina sent a message to MB_Fan:

>Ready when you are

She rifled through her bag, drawing out a square hand mirror and a silver pendulum tied to a long piece of string. "Let's try the ghost mirror first. Bought it on eBay especially."

She ignored Denny's expression and lifted the mirror up. It was about the size of a ping-pong racquet and had a thick plastic casing. The red frame had a hairline crack running down the right hand side, but the mirror itself was intact. She held it out at arm's length, testing the best angle for maximum visibility.

"What's meant to happen?"

"You're supposed to be able to see spirits in the reflection. The seller said it had been particularly useful in exposing poltergeist activity in Abingdon." She pivoted on the spot, staring at the space behind her shoulder. "It's like a portal to the astral plane."

No matter how she angled it, she could only see the distant winking lights of Oxford's buildings. Nina drew the mirror closer, staring intently at the reflection, then started to spin, slowly at first but getting faster and faster until she tripped and stumbled to the ground.

"Are you ok?" Denny held out his hand.

She brushed him off and stood up, careering slightly. Pointing to the mirror, she asked him to try. He shrugged in agreement and took it from her.

"I think you're going about it the wrong way," he said. "Shouldn't you be looking between the trees?"

With his back to the trees, he raised the mirror up and stuck his tongue out.

"The only scary thing around here is this ugly mug," he smirked, extending his arm as far as possible and looking in the mirror. It slipped from his hand and hit the ground with a thud.

"Denny!" Nina scrambled to pick up the mirror, which had landed face down on the grass. "That cost me fifty quid!"

She looked at him and even in the half-light she could see that the colour had drained from his face.

"What? What is it? Did you see something?"

He pointed to the looking-glass with a shaking hand. Nina grabbed the mirror and held it out in front of her. She scrutinised the dark gap between the trees.

"There's nothing there!" she whined. "What did you see?"

"I think there was a face," Denny whispered.

"What sort of face?"

Nina held the mirror back up and peered into the blackness.

"A woman's face. In between the trees. Coming out of the darkness."

Nina flung the mirror on the ground in frustration. She opened the EMF app — the needle hadn't moved from the orange zone.

"That can't be right. There's only a medium chance of activity."

"I only saw it for a second, but it was definitely a face."

"The mirror must have broken when you dropped it on the floor. That's the only explanation."

Nina grabbed the pendulum from where she'd left it and pinched the very tip of the string, the way she had seen it done online. She steadied herself, still dizzy from spinning around with the mirror. She closed her eyes and balls of light burst behind her eyelids. If she concentrated, she thought she could hear a faint ringing noise.

"Mary if you're here, please make your presence known by making the pendulum move."

The string stayed stock-still.

She shook out her shoulders and tried again.

"Mary Blandy. If your spirit is present tonight please give me a sign by moving the pendulum."

It stayed immobile.

Nina groaned and flung the pendulum towards Denny.

"Oh you try it, since she likes you so much."

Denny picked up the string and spoke, haltingly: "Mary if you're here give—"

Without warning the pendulum started to career wildly, rocking back and forth, tugging on the string. It bucked and whirled like a kite caught in high winds. Denny's eyes grew wide.

"Ask her! Ask her!"

The ringing noise grew louder, filling Nina's eardrums.

"Mary, are you with us here tonight?"

The pendulum flew from his hand in a preternatural arc, landing high in the tree. The string snagged in the branches on the way down and the pendulum hung, twitching, in the gap between the trees.

"Did you throw it?"

"Of course I didn't!" Denny stared at his palms. "It was like it was wrenched from my hands."

The ringing reached an unearthly pitch, like metal scraping. Nina clamped her hands over her ears.

She looked up. An orb of light hung between the trees, growing brighter and brighter as the scraping noise pitched higher and higher. Nina opened her mouth to scream but she couldn't make a sound. Her chest felt tight. Her palms were hot. Her head was going to crack open.

And then it was over.

"Did you hear that?"

He nodded.

"I can't believe our luck."

Denny's voice was very quiet: "I think we should go."

"And quit while we're ahead? Are you crazy?" She picked the mirror back up. "Mary's here and she wants to tell us something.

Nina's phone buzzed.

>Have you found my gift yet?

Nina frowned and showed the message to Denny.

>What gift?

>Look behind the right hand tree

Denny looked like he wanted to do anything but. They crept around the tree, Nina's grip growing tighter and tighter on her phone. She could feel Denny's arm trembling next to hers. She held her phone up to the branches, blanching them with blue light, but there was nothing there.

Her phone buzzed in her palm: high chance of paranormal activity.

"Look!" Denny pointed at the ground. He'd spotted a silver flask nestled at the base of the trunk. It was half-covered in dead leaves, but still shone in the light from Nina's screen.

>You've left us a flask??

>Drink it and you will understand

They stood, shoulder to shoulder, and stared from the message to the flask. Nina could feel Denny's arm shuddering, as if he were being electrocuted. It matched the arrhythmic beat of her heart.

"What should we do?"

Denny's mouth kept twitching at the corners, like a fish

caught on a hook.

"We should go."

"But what if –?"

He took her by the shoulders, his grip ice-tight.

"Have you lost your mind? Who knows what's in that?"

The phone buzzed again and they both yelped.

>What are you waiting for?

Denny made a wailing noise like a wounded animal and kicked the flask. It rolled down the hill, picking up speed, before it careered over the edge, diving down into the darkness. Nina thought she could hear it make a dull *thunk* against the railings below.

"I can't believe you did that."

"I can't believe you were considering drinking it."

From down where the flask fell, Nina could hear a scrabbling sound, like dirt being clawed from the side of the hill. It was growing louder.

"We're leaving. Now." Denny grabbed her hand and they tore across the top of the hill, kicking through grass to reach the path down to the gate. Nina stopped at the edge.

"My bag!"

"Forget it Nina."

She turned back and there, between the trees stood a hazy figure. It raised its hand to her and dropped something to the ground.

"Denny! Look!"

"It's not worth it, Nina." He dragged her down the path. "We'll get your bag in the morning."

They scuffed down the hill, stumbling over their feet. Denny refused to let go of Nina's hand until they were in the courtyard. Once he finally let go he doubled over, hands on his knees, breathing hard.

The castle quarter was quieter than earlier. All Nina could

hear was Denny's laboured breathing and the distant rumble of traffic. She walked over to the bench where she had sat earlier.

"My coat's still here!" She pulled it on. "Oh." The right sleeve had ripped, leaving threads hanging over her wrists.

Dennis walked over and tugged on the broken sleeve.

"Come on, let's get you home."

Nina looked back over her shoulder at the hill, where a purpling dawn was beginning to blot the sky, silhouetting the spidery trees that stood, stalwart, on Hangman's Hill.

A PIGGYBACK ON PUCK LANE

'Doc' David

1.

The first to arrive was a man called Mitchell, and he clambered down toward the well-maintained garden through the gate marked private. The family who owned the house also owned the toll bridge. If they were home the incident unfolding did not disturb them.

Past the house Mitchell saw the man in the blue suit. He didn't appear to have moved a muscle; he was still on his back, still in the garden facing the toll bridge above him, every inch a man who had just fallen off that bridge. At least he was in the shade, thought Mitchell, who picked up his pace a little as he headed over to help.

It was a strange sight, this man who might be sunbathing, except for the suit, flat on the ground and yet proud against the landscape. He was a striking counterpoint to the lawn, and the lawn's tidy mower tracks sweeping round the apple tree at the centre of it. It looked as if, this Saturday morning, a modernist painting had collided with the world.

But Mitchell wasn't one for art.

"Hello, mate," said Mitchell, crouching down at the side of the snappily dressed man to check for vital signs. He didn't really know what he was looking for when he was checking for vital signs, but he patted down the man's arms, legs and chest with the discipline of one who had seen it all before on television. Nothing appeared to be broken and there was no bleeding that he could see. "You're okay, mate," deduced Mitchell, loudly, as if addressing a dead man.

The man on his back opened his eyes. "I've had a strange accident," he said, puffing up his cheeks for a weak smile. "I had everything planned out. But I'm afraid this accident has scuppered my plan." The man's gaze wandered, and he puffed up his cheeks again. "You're my Good Samaritan," he said eventually, looking deeply at Mitchell and grabbing Mitchell by the hand.

At this point some of the other people from the bridge arrived in the garden. They stood looking over Mitchell's shoulder at the fallen man. "I've phoned for an ambulance," one of the new arrivals said.

"I saw what happened," offered someone else.

Mitchell didn't know what to do about a man holding his hand, so he patted the hand like he would his nephew on the head and sprung to his feet. He reported cheerily to those around him that there were no bones broken. Then to the small crowd still on the bridge he gave an a-ok hand signal. "No bones broken!" he shouted up at them.

Saturday was Mitchell's day for drinking. Each weekend it was the same story. He drove into town early, parked up at his mate's house, walked into town, got steaming drunk with his mates, ate a burger he couldn't remember and then on Sunday drove home again, at some point, nursing a fuzzy head. He behaved like he was still a teenager. But because his wife had left him and he lived alone, that didn't matter much.

Mitchell was aware the clock was ticking on his drinking time. Valuable drinking time. He was aware of something else, too, something familiar about the man in the blue suit. In that face and in that manner was a song from long ago.

The general consensus was that a man who falls off a bridge should not be moved. He should remain where he landed until the paramedics arrived. "Fourteen feet," said a lady confidently, referring to the drop. Mitchell was torn. In a hurry to head off, to get to drinking, he also felt duty bound to stay and help the familiar stranger. As first on the scene of the accident, it was his responsibility to get the man up on his feet again, walking about. He believed that. Shake off the cobwebs, so to speak.

Mitchell pulled the man off the floor by the arm and encouraged a few diligent steps, watching with the others as he made his way halfway to the apple tree and back. There was the hint of a limp, but Mitchell said that was only to be expected.

Then it hit him. Who the man was.

Mitchell hadn't seen him in donkeys' years, since school, and here he was now at the foot of the Swinford Toll Bridge, staggering about. "Hey, mate!" said Mitchell, a grin wide across his face. "Remember me?"

The man's expression betrayed him. It was slow to form, surveying the scene like it was a ridiculous Where's Wally? picture puzzle. Wally was nowhere to be found and then suddenly there he was. Mitchell laughed heartily and placed his arm round those blue suited shoulders, shaking those shoulders fondly and then helping his old schoolmate out of the garden with the small entourage in tow. He wanted to know all about it. How did it start? What had happened?

Tim-Tim resigned himself to the telling of the tale.

2.

It was a Morris Marina. Not what he had expected and not what he wanted. Morris Marina was only his second favourite type of vintage car. He grumbled to Nan when it pulled up outside the house. "That's not what I wanted," he said, arms folded at the bay window like he owned the place. "If I wanted a Morris Marina I would have asked for a Morris Marina." It was a Mark I no less, likely one of the last to roll off the assembly line. The colour was harvest gold, bright and unusual next to modern cars, but little compensation for the overarching blandness of the thing. The wedding ribbons only seemed to make matters worse.

Nan told him enough of his noise and she reached up to straighten Timothy's tie, which was straight enough, and she found other things to fuss over before they headed off.

Timothy. Tim-Tim, she called him.

Tim-Tim had hoped that Nan's eyes might fill with tears of pride and joy at the sight of him in a suit, on this day of all days, but that was too much to ask. If not for the neighbours who came outside for the spectacle of a vintage car on a wedding day, Tim-Tim might simply be making a trip to Aldi for the big shop as he did each Sunday. He snapped the front door of the house closed. Nan checked again, rattling the door to make sure he had closed it properly. It didn't feel like the biggest day of his life.

The morning in Witney was warming up. The sun found the tall chimney of Waterford Mill that had so excited Tim-Tim when he was a boy and it cast a shadow over the small town. Once the chimney had been used in the manufacture of the blankets for which Witney is famous, and in his dreams as a boy a cyclops lived inside it. (He had no idea why a cyclops.) Now it wasn't used for anything, the mill closed down years ago. But it remained a fixture for the apartments that lay on that side of the meadow, a talking point for those who liked an echo of the past on their doorstep.

Tim-Tim admired a big chimney, as he admired many things that are old. But he did not admire the Morris Marina Mark I, whose open doors beckoned at the end of the driveway. It was a bland car Nan had hired and he couldn't help but think she had done it on purpose.

The driver in his white shirt and red tie opened all the doors to let some air in, standing beside the car with his fingers knotted as if he had all the time in the world. Even halfway down the path, Nan clutching his arm, Tim-Tim could smell the plastic seat covers waiting inside.

"Not so fast," said Nan, snapping at him like an arthritic ferret. "Stop walking so fast. You're walking too fast."

The wedding was scheduled for 11AM in the St Aldate's Room of the Town Hall, the smallest and cheapest of the rooms. Tim-Tim was in a suit that fitted just about right and yet somehow still managed to be uncomfortable, which is why he kept pulling on the sleeves. He wasn't used to a suit — he didn't wear one for work — but tradition dictates that the groom ought to wear a suit on his wedding day and so he got himself a blue one from Marks & Spencer's, in a style they call modern slim. Modern slim made him itch and pull on his sleeves. He didn't feel particularly modern or slim, nor did he feel the million dollars the elderly floor manager said he looked when he tried the suit on. Tim-Tim was a man of forty-seven going on seventy-seven, because that's what living with Nan did to him, raised as a child in a house of books and cats.

Another thing tradition dictates is that the groom should arrive early for the wedding. That almost didn't happen when the Morris Marina broke down. The car first made a circuit of the town centre, Nan and Tim-Tim on the backseat like royalty, before heading up the A40 and onto the B4044 for Oxford. Tim-Tim didn't like to attract everyone's attention but the driver, a man called Dave, who knew a lot about everything, road directions in particular, said that people generally liked parading about in a vintage car because it made them feel like kings and queens for a day.

The smoke from the engine appeared on the High Street, Eynsham, shortly after passing the shop that sold buckets and grass feed. The Morris Marina lurched forward in fits and starts. Tim-Tim felt entirely vindicated by the turn of events, reminding Nan (out of earshot of Dave) that the Morris Marina was not what he had wanted. She clucked harshly.

It was a good job Tim-Tim factored in plenty of wriggle room. Had he known he was getting a Morris Marina he would have factored in more. But he reckoned they could still make the Town Hall in time, and he looked out the back window of the car, hoping to see a bus on Eynsham's thin corners.

Nan thought it absurd that a groom should catch a bus to his own wedding. She told Tim-Tim to stay put, unless of course he had come to his senses and was going to go home. There was, she said, still time for an about-face, a change of heart. He could forget all about the wedding. "This nonsense," she called it. She never wanted him to marry, because no woman was good enough and certainly not some slapper from a supermarket checkout, as she put it.

The word slapper horrified Tim-Tim. Dave the driver did his utmost not to listen.

When the Morris Marina finally gave up and came to rest it was in the worst place possible: next to the toll booth on the Toll Bridge. This Grade-II listed structure, the Toll Bridge, in need of sprucing up, or knocking down, according to the local community, was a particularly bad spot for a breakdown because the road here was even thinner than the High Street and there was no lay-by. A breakdown was exactly the sort of thing to agitate the locals, as typified by the Morris Marina that Saturday morning.

Sandwiched between the low wall of the bridge on one side

and the toll booth itself on the other, the Morris Marina created an impasse. A lad in a high visibility jacket leaned out from the booth, his hands filled with loose change — five pence for cars and ten pence for lorries — to say "no stopping here." But traffic was already backed up. Soon angry horns would sound and men in white vans would have something to shout about. Tim-Tim did not want to be the centre of attention. He couldn't bear the thought of anyone but Nan shouting at him. His was a life in equilibration, the way he liked it, passing through without so much as a ripple.

It was different in Eynsham. On the B4044 he became a bottleneck because of a Morris Marina with wedding ribbons.

Might he simply give up and go home, as Nan suggested? To his electric recliner from DFS, and a nice cup of tea and whatever happened to be on the box at this time of day? Likely one of those nasty squabbling daytime talk shows, featuring families on benefits in meltdown. The stuff Nan liked but he didn't. Perhaps if he went home he could use the time constructively, doing the things he had been meaning to do for ages. Joining a gym, for example. A procrastinator by nature, Tim-Tim found it all too easy to hijack one good intention with another. In the end nothing got done, unless of course Nan was sniping at him to do it. Yes. He would join the Windrush leisure centre and take up studio cycling. Not only would it get him out of the house, but it would also equip him for his modern slim style suit when next he needed it.

But gym was too much like being at school and he shuddered at the thought of it — school, the gym, exercise, Nan, the books, the cats. (He plucked a cat hair from his sleeve.)

The memories came flooding back, a tsunami of memories laying waste to his mind. He saw himself as a small boy again, wearing short trousers on the back seat of Nan's car, a Morris similar to this one. Her seat covers had been plastic, too, and they aggravated the eczema behind his knees. Consequently he smelled of aqueous cream through much of his early teens, which had to be applied twice a day on account of the itching. At school he foolishly confided this to his pal, Mitchell, and promptly fell out with Mitchell after word got round and some pretty nasty tricks were perpetrated at his expense.

The Morris Marina was not as modest and homely a car as the Austin Maxi, which was Tim-Tim's number one favourite vintage car, the one he had wanted in the first place. Dave the driver couldn't apologise enough about the breakdown. He tucked his red tie into the front of his shirt and stepped purposefully from the vehicle, mindful not to bang the vintage door against the vintage wall of the toll bridge as he did so. Cars supplied by the Vanguard Vintage Car Hire Company were regularly serviced and generally reliable, he said. Popping his head through the passenger window, he then explained how it might be the alternator because sometimes it's the alternator.

The wall on the bridge was low, and on the other side of it a drop into a large and well-maintained garden. A plaque on the wall called this the Swinford Toll Bridge, one of the last toll bridges in private hands. Very old. Having been mindful not to scratch the door on the wall, Dave the driver was equally mindful not to fall over the wall into the garden or indeed the River Thames, which adjoined the garden, and he made his way cautiously to the front of the vehicle to fumble with the clasp for the bonnet. He opened the bonnet — without looking, so familiar was he with the process — and out came a puff of smoke that rose over the bridge and disappeared in the blue warm sky.

Tim-Tim wanted to see whether he could help, but Nan wouldn't let him. He might hurt himself. They sat there together on the back seat for what seemed like ages. It was awfully cramped and Nan was pressed way too close, still gripping his arm. She had on a long silver dress with a nipped waist and a bonnet to match that only served to accentuate her frailness. This was clothing she had owned forever, from before the time of even the Morris Marina, and he was certain her bones were visible through it.

The dress was for best and didn't come out often. Nan kept it at the top of the wardrobe in her room, along with some other stuff, wrapped in yellow tissue paper and mothballs. The box was labelled Boswell & Co, and was the same box the dress came in when she bought it in 1949. The fug of mothballs hit him. He was aware of the odour before, but it seemed absolutely pungent now, sticky sick like old sweets and chemicals. It was a smell much worse than the smell of aqueous cream. Tim-Tim instinctively gripped the plastic seat beneath him, elevating himself from it should his eczema come back. His trousers were long now but behind his knees he felt the familiar prickle of discomfort.

When he said mothballs, Nan mistook it for something else and told him to stop it. Stop saying it. Stop saying mothballs. He slid himself away from her as far as he could on the backseat, bending his neck into a corner of the car. But it wasn't enough. Nan was too close. Her grip was like the black clumps of tree branches, fidgeting on his arm as so many dead-alive moths in a mothball forest.

"I can't breathe," gasped Tim-Tim, and he released his tie an inch in a theatrical way. He pulled himself up into the driver's seat and stuck what he could of his head out of the driver's window. The air was fresh and dizzy. "Is it the alternator?" he asked Dave the driver, more of an apology than a question. Then he pushed open the passenger door to escape and, intoxicated by mothballs, fell promptly over the toll bridge wall.

3.

Yes, Tim-Tim remembered Mitchell. Arms round one another's shoulders, the two of them made their way past the house,
through the gate marked private, and back onto the road where
more people waited. A fresh chorus of concern greeted the fall-
en man now that he was back on his feet.

Tim-Tim looked round for Nan. She was on the back seat of
the Morris Marina, feeling tired, and was still tired when the
broken down car was pushed out the way by some of the men
in the crowd. Dave the driver steered it carefully backward to
the parking space belonging to the family that owned the toll
bridge. Dave applied the handbrake and Nan got out, feeling
much better now. She thanked Mitchell for helping to push the
car.

Tim-Tim still harboured a grudge. He had been betrayed by
Mitchell, because of what had happened at school, and he felt
it even now. He wished he hadn't called him a Good Samaritan.
Resentment was a bird too fat to fly away.

If Mitchell was aware of this betrayal, the hurt and pain he
had caused Tim-Tim, he didn't show it. Mitchell was probably
a bit thick, someone who went round saying things like schooldays are the best days of your life. Tim-Tim was dismissive
of people who said things like that. They had failed to apply
themselves as an adult, that's what he thought. Likely they had
done nothing since leaving school, except owning a house and
having kids, so of course schooldays were their happiest days.

"I hated school," Mitchell announced solemnly.

It came as a surprise to hear it. More of a surprise was the
apology for all the nasty things he had done.

"That's interesting," said Tim-Tim. He hadn't meant to say
it out loud and he knew what would come next. Mitchell was
a little rusty, a lot of years had passed, but he found the pat-

ter eventually. Tim-Tim was in the habit of saying interesting. Mitchell laughed. "Yes, very interesting," he said. "You haven't changed much, I see."

Sometimes Tim-Tim wasn't really listening, that's why he said interesting. He was listening now.

He accepted Mitchell's apology. He also accepted the lift that Mitchell offered into Oxford, and off they went in a brown Audi to the pub together. Even Nan.

The pub was at Mitchell's insistence, for old times' sake, but also because he was aghast to hear Tim-Tim had not had a stag night. Libations before marriage were an absolute necessity, said Mitchell, understanding the matter well. He said it was important for a groom to go out and get pissed before a wedding. Therefore, in order to make amends, Mitchell decided this would be Tim-Tim's stag night. Today, now. A stag morning. On the day of the wedding itself.

The prospect amused Mitchell and Nan more than it did Tim-Tim.

Having parked the Audi, the three of them piled into the boozer opposite the town hall where they stayed for a good forty minutes. The place was almost empty. They found a table close to the bar and Mitchell got all the beers in, downing one pint in the time it took the others to raise their glasses. Tim-Tim did not think it possible for a person to drink as much as Mitchell was able. But one drink led to another.

"It's my fault-line," said a happy Mitchell on his third pint, before heading off to buy another. "On me," he said over his shoulder.

"He's a nice man," observed a convivial Nan. She watched Mitchell, money in hand, go at the bar like a hungry wolf in a chicken coop. "Strong arms."

Tim-Tim pulled a disapproving face.

Mitchell set the latest round of drinks on the table, throwing in a packet of pork scratchings. A meal he called it. Something to line the stomach. Then he reminded everyone how he could never miss out on a stag do. Nan nodded. She was up for it after a white wine spritzer.

The final year of school was worse, the year the other boys made a game of his underclothes. He couldn't remember how it started — probably Mitchell — but boys would snatch Tim-Tim's underpants from the changing room during PE and hide them in weird places for a lark. Only Tim-Tim's, no one else's. Tim-Tim tried to dismiss these episodes entirely, explaining them away as an inversion of Maslow's hierarchy of needs, kids being nasty for nasty's sake, making underpants and their acquisition a sort of civic duty.

Nan didn't see it that way. She hadn't helped when she came to school to make a fuss.

"You know," said Nan, grabbing Mitchell's arm across the table. "I don't care if we miss the wedding. He's marrying a slapper. I want to go home."

"Now, you don't mean that," said Mitchell, patting the frail hand.

"Yes, I do." Nan straightened her back. "Yes, I do mean it."

Tim-Tim thought better than to object. He knew exactly why he hadn't had a stag do. Nan would deny it, of course, but she was the reason he had missed his own stag do. Now Nan couldn't open the pork scratchings. "Do this, someone," she said, pushing the troublesome packet to the middle of the table. Tim-Tim glumly took the packet and popped it open, handing it back to Nan. She plunged her hand inside, mining a sizable deep-fried, salted unit that slipped easily into her mouth.

"He's got no friends. And now he's getting married to a slapper," she announced. She was sucking on a pork scratching. Nobody wanted to watch Nan suck on a pork scratching. "He doesn't even have a best man."

For a moment Nan was angry. Pointing a finger back at her-self, as if she had done all she could, she said to Mitchell, "I'm the best man. Me."

Tim-Tim announced that it was time to go. He stood up at the table, almost knocking the drinks over.

Mitchell stood up as well. It was obvious. He had the answer.

4.

There are many things haunted in the city of Oxford and its en-virons. Sightings of the Devil in North Leigh, for example, the legend of Sir George Cobb of Cobb Hall, Adderbury, whose spec-tral coach is drawn by fire-breathing horses, the shifting ghost of Burford — these and many other folkloric tales befit a city as ancient as this one. But this story, one that nobody knows, is a more recent story. It concerns Tim-Tim, a man as plain as he is true. Tim-Tim is approaching middle-age. He happens to be reasonably intelligent, has a job he considers boring with the local authority, and he lives in Witney, a town twelve miles west of Oxford, in a house he shares with his grandmother. Theirs is a relationship that transcends logic, being neither good nor bad. By rights he should have moved out years ago and would have done if not for her manipulative ways. But that's how it is in this story. In this story there is no traditional haunting, no ghost to speak of. And yet, for the sake of argument, we shall give it one; the good readers of a book of ghost stories ought not to be disappointed.

So, a week before he was to be married, Tim-Tim woke to the distant sound of a train. He wondered where the train was, or what it might be, because there was no train that ran nearby. The station that had once existed in the town was long gone, and so too were the tracks. He found a book about it in the local library, where he spent most evenings (except for Tuesday and

Sunday, when the library was closed; and Wednesday when he took Nan to her social circle and listened to the old biddies chat about immigrants and the NHS as they would upside-down cake).

On his way home from the library, getting dark, he first saw them: two people, one carrying the other on their shoulders. The piggyback couple crossed the road and headed toward the shopping arcade, the same way he was headed. At this time of the evening all the shops in the arcade are closed. Even so, Tim-Tim was surprised that no one else was about and it suddenly seemed much later than it was. Having passed through the shopping arcade the couple continued onto Puck Lane, a small passage that would eventually bring them to Waterford Mill and the meadow. The same way he was going.

The piggyback continued. Tim-Tim had no idea how long the piggyback had been going on, but he had seen at least five minutes of it and there was no sign it would be stopping anytime soon. The couple remained oblivious to Tim-Tim as he approached, preparing to pass them by. Halfway down Puck Lane he was close enough to hear snippets of conversation, some of it was playful and intimate, so he coughed to make his presence known. Still the couple did not acknowledge him. He was now close enough that he could see the figure being carried was an adult male — tall like himself — while the person doing the carrying — most peculiar — was a frail old lady. She wore a long silver dress, nipped at the waist, and dance shoes.

The man on the shoulders was berating the frail old woman for her poor grammar.

"Charles's and Edeltraud's book," he snorted. "Not Charles and Edeltraud's book. I should know."

The old woman did not know.

Tim-Tim was puzzled. He thought that maybe the piggyback was a sort of penance for poor grammar. Maybe a new incentive for the students at the college. But he was denying himself the actual facts. He felt then very weak. Sweat on his brow and down his back signalled another one of his turns. The smell of mothballs filled the night air.

As he reached the couple and walked past, Tim-Tim saw what he otherwise could not. The man wore Tim-Tim's face, and the frail old woman was Nan. He heard again that very moment the sound of the distant train. A sound, which, as it got closer, he recognised was his own scream.

5.

Mitchell did not arrive on time, having promised with all his heart to arrive on time.

He appeared at the open door of the St Aldate's Room, knocking twice and asking if he was in the right place. He had got lost, he said, on his way over from the pub, and then had trouble with the stairs. Beautiful stairs, mind.

Waiting at the front of the room was Tim-Tim, along with Nan and Tim-Tim's bride-to-be. There were guests, too, none of whom Mitchell recognised, of course. Mitchell ambled in. "I had time for a couple more slurps," he announced, hiking his thumb over his shoulder in a way that intimated there was still time for a couple more. The reaction of the room spoilt that idea.

"But here I am," Mitchell conceded.

His eyes fell about the place, approving of the wood panel walls and the ornate desk surrounded by chairs. These were the sorts of chairs good for stacking when not in use. Beige chairs. He counted many more chairs than there were people. Only eight people to be precise, the majority resembling the portraits on the walls, smiles so awkward they might be frowns. "This is nice," Mitchell said, and he sat down in the chair next to Nan, because she was pointing to it.

On the other side of the aisle to Mitchell was Tim-Tim, resembling a ship lost at the edge of the world, ready to fall off. Had he the means to reset the day and start afresh, he surely would. That's how it appeared to Mitchell when he leant forward in his chair with a cheery thumbs up sign. He got up and made his way over to another chair, the one next to Tim-Tim. Nan was sorry to see him go.

Tim-Tim was not accustomed to people asking about his wellbeing, yet it was happening a lot today. He itched beneath his blue modern slim suit, scuffed now because of the fall into the garden, and nodded when Mitchell asked how he was holding up. Mitchell gave him a manly squeeze, as he would his oldest and best mate. "That's the spirit," he said.

Mitchell, who wasn't one for long pauses, rubbed his hands up and down his Abercrombie & Fitch t-shirt. He had something to say.

"Best man," he said, a smile for the impromptu decision, and for the many things he would not remember because of booze. "I'm your best man. Who would have thought it, eh?"

"Indeed," said Tim-Tim. "Best man."

That was Mitchell's idea, and Nan was only too eager to accept it. Who ever heard of a best man in jeans and a t-shirt?

Tim-Tim reappraised his mental itinerary of noxious smells, added Mitchell's overbearing deodorant and booze breath to the list. Still at the top of the list, however, was Nan, smelling more and more like a mothball.

The service at last was starting.

There was only one interruption. A passage from Vivaldi's The Four Seasons, which was a ring tone playing loudly. It took a while for the owner of the telephone to turn it off. Other than that, the service went without a hitch. At 11:30AM, Timothy Hopkins and Sandra Setters were officially pronounced man and wife, kiss the bride and all of that. There was a smattering of applause, a glass of buck's fizz, and then everyone was ushered out of the town hall to the pub across the road, where, upstairs in the Blue Room, the wedding reception was held.

Mitchell is at the bar.

He is sampling the different cask ales in the little taster glasses provided for that purpose. Three of the glasses — the size of shot glasses — are lined up and he knocks them back, one after another. "I'll have that one," he says to the barman, pointing to the last glass. The barman hand-pulls one of the locally crafted icons — Marston's Brakspear Oxford Gold — into a pint glass with a handle.

Mitchell is looking at the badge on the pump. The Oxford Gold is a zesty pale golden ale. Then he turns to Tim-Tim, like he hasn't seen him in a while. "Hey!" he says.

And to the barman: "And another one for my friend here."

Mitchell bends toward Tim-Tim. Sampling beer in taster glasses requires an explanation. "Excuse me for being such a pretentious cunt," he says. The emphasis is on the word 'cunt' but he whispers it in Tim-Tim's ear because there are ladies present.

"Not at all," says Tim-Tim. "Nothing to apologise about."

"Mm," says Mitchell.

That Mitchell is thinking makes a shape in his brow. He leans on the bar with both hands.

"You look like someone who's seen some interesting times," he decides.

Tim-Tim blushes but mostly agrees.

By now other people have arrived for the reception. Some are milling about at the far end of the room, friends of Nan who compliment her like it was her big day. What a lovely silver dress and bonnet. Others are standing at the bar waiting to be served. They engage with Mitchell when he talks to them, but on realising how drunk the stranger is, they back away and wish they hadn't bothered.

"I've seen some hardship," says Mitchell, returning to Tim-Tim. "But you know what the difference is between you and me?"

Tim-Tim hasn't a clue. But it's likely something mean. "Seven pints?" he says, making light of the question.

Mitchell is running on fumes and the quip is wasted.

"The difference between you and me," he says, "is that I've got an eye-patch."

Eye-patch. Tim-Tim frowns.

Rummaging through the pockets of his jeans, Mitchell does indeed have an eye-patch. He pulls it out, a black old fashioned one, which he places on his head. He straightens the elastic with beer-fingers, until the patch sits squarely over one eye. He looks like a drunken Patchy the Pirate.

Tim-Tim wonders why Mitchell is carrying an eye-patch. Does he always carry an eye-patch? He evidently doesn't need an eye-patch. Is it an ice breaker?

Mitchell cautiously carries the drinks to an empty table, his two pints and Tim-Tim's pint, setting them down without spilling a drop. "Not very good for hand to eye coordination," he says.

Mitchell is still wearing the eye-patch when called to give the best man speech. It isn't a rehearsed speech. He'd quite forgotten all about being a best man, let alone knowing what a best man does. Despite Tim-Tim insisting that a speech isn't necessary, Mitchell wants to have a bash at it.

"Give me a minute," says Mitchell, ensconced in the gents, facing a urinal like it isn't there and blowing wearily at the wall.

Several minutes pass before he reappears in the Blue Room.

The projector screen, normally used for sports and Power-

Point presentations, has been rolled up in its cradle. Mitchell thinks that a man giving a speech should stand where a projector screen would be, and so that's where he stands. He pulls a chair over, too, and climbs up on it. But the chair wobbles and he carefully climbs down again. Every action is now measured and considered, including the gulp from the pint of Oxford Gold, which finally leads Mitchell to a story about how he doesn't know Tim-Tim at all well, not having seen him since school.

"I have no anecdotes about our adult lives together, about how we grew up together and how we got drunk together." Mitchell pauses and grabs the air as if that's where inspiration lies. "Actually, we have got drunk together. This morning. Before the wedding. In this very pub."

Mitchell scans the faces before him, still not a lot of them. Cold dead planets, he sniffs. He's got his work cut out.

"This morning," he says, "I had the pleasure of re-acquainting myself with the man before you now." He points toward Tim-Tim. "He had fallen off a bridge. He's had two of his teeth replaced with" — Mitchell can't remember the name of the thing that replaces teeth and so says words that sound like they might be right — "lapis lazuli." Then he says them again to be sure. "Lapis lazuli. I hadn't heard of it before, either. A Latin compound. Anyway, when our friend here fell off that wall" — Mitchell points again to Tim-Tim — "all I could see was his lapis lazuli."

At this point in the story Mitchell realises he isn't talking about Tim-Tim at all, but mixing him up with someone else. He makes a face of benign contemplation and comes clean. "Wait a minute. Wait a minute. That's not who I'm talking about. Tim-Tim doesn't have lapis lazuli. That's someone else."

Mitchell can't think of another story to tell for the time being, so he continues with this one. He takes another glug of Oxford Gold and insists it's a good story.

"The physicist asks whether I have met this man he calls Parker. He is not in the queue. No, not the queue. What is it? That other thing? Anyway, he wants to get on the boat that takes him to Camden in London. Not the boat, I mean the bus, to where Parker is. He says he has not met Parker in years, and he takes a folded photograph from his pocket that is ten years old and shows it to me. The photograph is creased down the middle. The man I am talking to is on one side of the crease and this fella, this Parker fella, is supposedly the fella on the other side of it."

Mitchell needs another drink. Expressions of abject fear and horror follow him to the bar. At the bar he necks a large Jameson and, boasting another pint, returns to the space where the projector screen was.

"That was Parker," he says. "I have no idea whether the physicist found him or not. The end."

Only Nan applauds.

Sensing he's on the right track, Mitchell relates some stuff from his schooldays. He is oblivious to the fact that none of it is in Tim-Tim's favour. It begins with an explanation of how Tim-Tim got his name.

"It's because he had this habit of saying 'interesting' all the time. He might still say it. Hey, Tim-Tim! Do you still say interesting all the time? Mm. Anyway, some kid would explain what had happened in last night's episode of *The Sweeney*, or that Spike Milligan show, the one with all the naked boobies in it, and Tim-Tim would go, 'Oh, that's interesting.' Which we all thought was pretty lame, because what does it mean exactly? Interesting?"

Mitchell looks back over at Tim-Tim as if he might furnish an answer. He is pale in his blue suit on his big day.

Is it good interesting, or bad interesting? Or inconsequential interesting? That's what Mitchell wants to know, but he doesn't quite get the words out.

"Know what I mean?" says Mitchell ruefully. "Tim-Tim said interesting all the time. But he himself was not interesting. He was like the polar opposite of interesting. A real smart arse. Oh so bloody boring! Tim-Tim — so boring we named him twice!"

He remembers the time Nan came to school to complain about Tim-Tim's missing underpants. Mitchell is going to relate that story, too, another fond illustration, but he feels he ought to say something about the bride. He knows even less about Sandra Setters than he does Tim-Tim and yet he has a stab at it anyway.

"Sandra Setters. That's a funny name. All the S's."

Stony silence. He needs more than that. He needs to say something nice about the bride.

Mitchell lifts the eye-patch from his eye and raises his pint in a toast.

"Nan thinks Sandra's a slapper. I don't agree."

SUNDAY

Sarah Milne Das

It is Sunday in the attic, and a girl lies on the bed, weeping. Her sobs are desperate and noisy, unconstrained as an infant's. She is scared to look up, scared to know what is happening around her. She whispers, "Am I mad?"

It is Monday, and there are people I do not know inside Iremonger House. It is not the first time — people come and go and live and die — but the first time in a long time, I think. I have been almost sleeping, almost dreaming, almost forgetting the house around me; now I am jolted back into such consciousness as is allowed me.

Three voices. Two girls, a boy. They clatter and call to each other like squawking birds. Perhaps they will not come upstairs.

I hear clambering and perhaps, after all, I am not sorry. It has been a long time. A girl pushes the door first and sneezes as dust swirls around. Then, as her features uncrumple, I look at her face and I see his face.

It unguards me, seeing those bones, that jaw and brow and temple. In that moment she sees a flash of me and she reaches out, entranced. Then there's nothing again in front of her and she crinkles her small nose. I know she smells lye.

Footsteps, light and heavy. Voices, male and female. They're here now, the other two, with faces their own and not of the past.

"Mummy, Daddy, a lady a lady..." The girl babbles and is indulgently ignored. They are not two girls and a boy then, but mother, father, daughter. They all look like children to me.

They talk like babies playing grown-up: investment, refurbish, gut the place. Rental markets and nest eggs.

Inheritance.

It is Tuesday and it is quiet. The men have melted away until the next time, the next day. They come, they carve up the house, they shout, voices blaring and boots stamping. They go, I suppose they sleep, and slowly their comings and goings transform the house.

I have forgotten how to measure the distances of time. What is a day among so many days? What is a second, a month, or a year? The men have been coming for minutes or centuries. Weeks, it must be, though. Weeks.

Sunday, Monday, Tuesday, Wednesday, this I remember, this is my almanac. Thursday, Friday, Saturday, Sunday again and again and again. When the rhythm of days is lost, the rhythm of syllables makes my anchor.

Still Tuesday, and I am wrong. The men are not all gone; two sets of footsteps are left. They are climbing up to the attic, and this is new — the men never come here.

The first to enter is a beautiful boy, he walks as if he has never been troubled. His loping stride reminds me of a young man I once admired.

I will not think of that.

He walks like a prince in his ugly boots, though his hands are calloused and he's dusted all over. He looks up to the skylight and down again, pulls a forgotten old trunk from a corner, and settles it below.

"Sure that'll take you?" the other man says. He has been standing, silent and watching. He is trying to sound impatient, but I am old now and I know the sound of yearning.

A flashing, dashing smile, and he's up, hauling his body with muscled arms til he's sitting on the skylight edge, shins swinging inside the attic.

"Well?" says the man inside.

"I can see it! By the church. That's my mum's house, just there — I know the chimneys, I'll give them a wave."

The other man barks a laugh; he wants to be gruff but his eyes are light, and his lips curve into a secret joy.

"Pass my phone, could you?" the boy calls down. "I want to take a picture, show her what the view from the big house looks like."

A throw, a click, and that's it — he leaps down and is inside the attic again. But his careless words have made me remember, made me feel things the long-dead forget to feel. I had a mother once, and I miss her I miss her I miss her and how she was proud of me then, so long ago. I hope she is dust now, her heartache ended. I hope that she does not remember.

"I'd best lock up now, come on then," the older man is saying. But neither starts to move just yet, the attic has bewitched them.

"It's a nice house, this," says the boy with the mother, a wistful note in his voice.

"Lucky for some," the man agrees. "Old family property."

The boy nods absently, but his attention is elsewhere. "Do you hear church bells?" he asks.

A pause.

"No, I don't hear anything. Anyway, it's not Sunday."

It is Wednesday, and today the girl with his face comes to find me. I have been waiting for her since they came to live in Iremonger House. Her mother and father I have seen often: they bring boxes and cases up to the attic, but they never bring the girl.

She comes because she remembers that fleeting glimpse of a figure. She remembers the lye.

Tentative but determined, curious, not frightened, the girl creeps in like one who knows they are somewhere they have been forbidden. "Hello," she whispers cautiously. "Hello, are you there?"

The girl gazes around her, searching for a clue. Looking up, she sees the skylight, sees the sky and this inspires her. "Do you live on the roof?" she says. Unanswered but undaunted, she sets to childish work. She makes herself a shaky ladder of the detritus that lives here. She stacks a box on a chest on a chair and then hauls herself up with chubby hands, certain she's found the way.

Childish plans are mother's fears and as if she knows that harm is near, the woman's footsteps are audible. They quicken, then they run. "Elsa!" she cries, as the girl's foot slips, as the tower topples and she's falling. Uselessly the woman's arms stretch, she is not nearly close enough, but then in a heartbeat she's across the room, faster than nature and not her own impetus.

Improbably, she holds the upright girl by her legs, from below. She lifts her upwards, propelled by something unseen. The girl rises up like an angel.

Then the spell is broken and the girl's lowered down, scolded, enfolded and held so tight.

As her mother carries her away, the girl looks back, lingering. I see her lips mouth words. I think they are, "Thank you, lady."

It is Thursday and I have not been expecting any company. But laughter and tiptoes are nearing and I am curious to see my visitors. They talk in hushed tones but jump as the door creaks. Laughter again, a little nervous perhaps, I hear a girl or a woman and a man or a boy.

"It's so dusty!" says the girl, and "What did you expect?" the boy. They skirt the walls together, almost touching arm to arm.

I know that face, it is her again, but this time she is not looking for me.

"Servants' rooms once, do you think?" the boy says. "This house is big enough to have had them."

"Yes, yes I think so. But I'd forgotten they were so small... I haven't been up in here in years..."

"Why ever not? It's the perfect hideaway."

"Oh really," says the girl, and her voice is heavy now, older and rougher. "Tell me why I'd need a hideaway..."

"I think I'd rather show you."

And then they are hands sliding down limbs, breath and whispers and sound and heat and it's like I'm held captive in their intensity and I can't bear it, can't bear it.

They are so tender, but so *wanting*. I didn't know it could be like this. I could swear I feel a hot tear running down my living cheek as I see the joy on her face and on his and I learn at last what I should have known then.

Perhaps I am jealous or sad or angry or shy but suddenly as their gasps swell I am there where she is and I feel what she feels and I glow and I'm warm and her body shudders.

Afterwards, I watch them from back across the room again. They are curled where I left them and the girl is shivering still. He covers her and holds her, and I almost cannot watch. "Are you ok, Elsa? You're shaking really badly."

"Yes," she murmurs, "yes, yes, yes, I'm just... I'm cold."

It is Friday, and Elsa is painting the wall when the doorbell rings.

The man who bounds into the attic lets out a whistle of

admiration. "Classy loft apartment inhabited by gorgeous girl about town," he grins, catching her by the waist.

They kiss, long and deep, and then she pulls back and dots his nose with paint. They laugh and she hands him a roller; he loses jacket and tie, rolls up his sleeves.

"Seriously," he says, "it looks amazing, you were right."

"The house is too big for anyone, nowadays. It should have been converted years ago, but mum and dad loved it, so..."

"Flat 7, Iremonger House," he proclaims. "Now that's an address with a ring to it. But the stairs! Elsa, my darling, my love, are you trying to give me a heart attack?"

"I told you, Toby, there's a friendly ghost here. I needed the top floor flat." She smiles at him, then turns back to work, and his smile turns to a frown as he stares at her back.

They continue in silence until he cannot keep the question inside him any longer. "Elsa... you didn't actually choose the flat because... because you believe it's haunted, did you? I know that's a stupid question, you just sounded like..."

She stops, and I can tell — perhaps Toby can, too — from the set of her shoulders that she is serious. Elsa turns to face him, and her face — it is *her* face now — transfixes me.

"Yes, Toby, I did. I really, truly, honestly believe that there is... *something*, up here, in the attic of Iremonger House. Something *good*. Something supernatural. It saved my life when I was a little girl. I *saw* her the first time I came to the house. I know it doesn't sound rational, but yes, I believe it, I do."

Toby is silent, and Elsa faces him defiantly. Eventually he shrugs with a rueful smile and turns to continue painting. Elsa relaxes, finally, and moves towards the kettle in the new kitchen.

Soon after they are sitting and laughing again, warming their hands on mugs and sketching out plans for the attic.

"Perhaps the ghost is your ancestor," says Toby, when the

conversation lulls. "The house has belonged to your family forever, right?"

"Right," she agrees. "Mum's side. Her granddad's granddad built the house and it's been ours ever since. We were the "family at the big house," once — funny, isn't it, to think of? There are no actual Iremongers left, that's something I do know. The name died out a generation ago."

"Iremonger." Toby rolls the familiar word in his mouth. "It's a good, solid, powerful word. Maybe we should adopt the name, bring it back, what do you think?"

Elsa smiles, "It sounds steeped in anger, I always think. Ire-monger: dealer in ire. I'm not sure that's the name for me."

They continue to bat words back and forth, and I watch them and I think I'm envious. But something else is making me thoughtful.

A friendly ghost, a something good. Is that who I am to her?

It is Saturday, and Toby fights his way across the attic's threshold. Leaning against the door's inside are boxes, chairs and a heavy chest.

He stumbles through, looks at the fallen blockade and sighs. His face is angry but his eyes are sad, and his voice is level as he calls out, "Elsa!"

She appears in the bedroom door and stops still as she takes in the mess and Toby. Now, she looks frightened.

"Toby," she begins, but he interrupts gently.

"I'll pack my things and go, Elsa. I wish you could just *talk* to me instead of, this –"

"Toby, I swear –"

"You swear what? That it's a *ghost*? A phantom is barricading the door to our, *your* home? Elsa... this is crazy. You know, god I *hope* you know, you could never have anything to fear from me. I don't know why you're doing this, but I know that if I need to force my way in then I shouldn't be trying to get through the door. I'm packing a bag, and I'm going."

Elsa watches him leave in silence then walks slowly to the bedroom, throws herself down. "Am I mad?" she whispers to no one but me, and starts to weep.

It is Sunday and I am a living fourteen. We have come from the Church in bonnets and boots, trooping like truculent school-children back to Iremonger House. My head is slow and sticky as treacle, and so must be my feet — I feel Elsie's nudge at my side and her whisper to "*hurry up, she's looking at you.*"

I look up blearily to find her there. It is Mrs McCabe, the housekeeper. "Run along, Elsie," she says, but her eyes are on me and I know what she sees. Purple smudges beneath my eyes, reddened lids and dull doughy skin. Shoulders slumped and dragging feet; I am so wretchedly tired.

"You're looking peaky," she says. "What a sight to be seen in St John's — what's wrong with you, my girl? Now stand up straight and fix your collar. Try to look like a good girl from Iremonger House should."

I try, I pull my shoulders back, I look Mrs McCabe in the face and wish myself smart, neat, pleasing and bright. She sighs. "Get you to bed, then. Clearly you're taken ill. Tomorrow I shall talk to the Mistress about calling in the doctor."

She sweeps away in her long black dress, not knowing she brings my doom to me.

The doctor will come and the doctor will know and what comes next is too big and too terrible for a small mind like mine to grasp. I will be sent packing, everyone will know, and they'll talk of me — all of them — as just another bad girl, a wanton. And the thing — the thing inside me, it will grow, insistent, un-stoppable. When I close my eyes I can almost feel it clawing, wanting to be known. My hands go to skate across my belly and then they're claws, too — my fingers pinch, trying to grip the creature, squeeze it away, make it gone.

I'm sweating, panicked, heart swooping, and yet still my body's weary. I cannot think, I am trapped like a fly in the treacle of my mind and the treachery of my belly. I slowly climb the stairs to the small attic room that I share with Elsie. I stand at the top and I try again to summon the courage to jump, to fall. If I were just a little braver I could kill it or me or both of us here, escape the fate that is given me. But I cannot, I am a coward.

Still, cowards can find a way.

In the attic, all I can hear are the distant bells of St John's. With the small strength I have I pull my trunk and Elsie's against the doorway.

I sit quietly on my bed and tear the sheet into strips.

Tie the knots, test just one. It tightens when I pull at the loop. Vomit leaps into my mouth and I force it down in painful swallows. Acid, tears, and then, unbidden memory, his hands on the back of my head. He pushes, insistent, my eyes stream and throat gags, and I hear him, strangled sounds and breath.

Throw my rope over the beam and catch it. Knots again, pull them tight.

Kneel by the bed, say a last prayer, I forget all the words I know and all I can find is, "Mother, I'm sorry, I'm sorry."

Feel under my bed for the small jug that I secreted away on laundry day. Scrunch my nose and stow it in the pocket of my dress. A coward always needs a choice to run away towards.

Stand on the bed, catch the loop, bow my head like a mockery of worship. "I am sorry for my sin," I whisper.

I jump.

It is Sunday and Elsa still weeps. She sinks to the floor from the bed, covers her eyes with her hands, but then opens them again, surprised. There is something...a smell. It is familiar, but from a long time ago. Her eyes widen in realisation and she starts to drag herself in a half-crawl across the floor.

It is done, I think, it is done, and there is nothing left for me to face or choose. Seconds feel like minutes as I wait for the peace of darkness.

But there's a sound. Crashes, thumps, and I start to flail and turn in the air as my peace is shattered. It's Elsie, she's through my poor barricade, she cries out and stumbles towards me. Grabs my legs.

She lifts, I rise like an angel.

Then she's walking me back towards the bed, she's sweating and red with my weight, but determined. She looks up, her face is tearstained.

My arms are free. I reach down into my pocket, and grasp the jug. Nothing seems difficult now.

"I'm sorry," I whisper, to Elsie or anyone, before I throw what is in the jug down my throat.

Elsa is in the kitchen, on the floor, under the basin. Her face is still wet and ugly with sorrow as she scrabbles her fingers down the cupboard door until she finds and grasps the handle.

Pipes, plumbing, cloths and sponges. Her fingers range with purpose until she closes on a bottle — it's bright with gaudy colour and embellished with warning symbols.

She unscrews the top, breathes in and smiles an unhappy stretched smile of recognition.

I watch her and I know now, what I have done, or almost done. Just one moment and the circle closes, the last of his kin will die just like the girl he hurt. All I must do is wait and perhaps I will have my peace.

I am not conscious of moving but now I am down there next to her, and for the second time in our lives but the first time of my choosing, I am there for her to see.

The girl looks up.

It is Sunday, and the attic smells of lye.

RETURNING

Thomas Benson

'The place is habitually almost deserted, except by ghosts
of the dead. Returning to it, when friends are gone, and
every one is a stranger, the echoes of our footsteps in the
walls are as the voices of our dead selves; we are among
the ghosts; the past is omnipotent, even terrible. Echoes,
quotes Montaigne, are the spirits of the dead, and among
these mouldering stones we may put our interpretation
on that.'

—Edward Thomas

For the longest time after I left the university, Oxford was
fraught with recollections. Returning to the city for the day, a
stranger's particular stride, perhaps a certain angle of expression, would inspire a memory of a former friend or acquaintance; sometimes, seeing a person cycling in the distance in the
same clothes and outline as a former coursemate, I would hover in the brief moment of doubt whereby it seemed, against all
rationality, that friends I knew to be outside Oxford had nevertheless rematerialised on its streets. At such times Oxford
seemed to have become a dream, unreal, wavering between the
present moment and the past, as if the city itself was a mere

illusion: a recollection made vivid.

Thus did Oxford assume a certain chthonic aspect, flickering with shades from the subterranean ground of my own memory. Yet it was not oppressive. To visit old haunts was not painful; to retrace my past steps, or to see old friends, pleasant. Perhaps my former life did not seem so very distant; perhaps it seemed too distant to matter any more; it was hard to say which. At any rate, I felt comfortable whenever I returned, and when I returned to start a new job in the old city it did not feel, at first, like I was descending into my past.

It was perhaps this initial ease with being back that meant the visions did not start right away. Perhaps at first I dismissed them as mere flukes of psychology, the pareidoliac impulse that lead me to double-take at strangers. I was, of course, unwilling to admit to them being anything more for the longest time. It was only after a while that I had to concede that these were not comparable to the quick flashes of recognition or recollection, the brief tricks of the mind that I have already described. Quite what they are, or were, remains a mystery to me. I do not wish to know, in some ways.

The first vision I can remember seemed innocuous enough, if strange. It occurred as I was walking through the parks in the north of the city, stalking hurriedly against the cold. It was a route I had taken before to walk to lectures: a route I perhaps had not taken as frequently as I should. Dead grass lined the banks of the river, frost catching on the stems. The air itself seemed grey and hard. Far-off details were jagged by a thin haze. Nobody else was walking through the park: and then, thin and wavering, a figure appeared coming the other way. The figure was black, indeterminate, and faintly... vague, as if printed hastily on the backdrop of the park. It was difficult to place him in relation to the space around him. As I got closer details began to fade in: a young man, books tucked under his arm, face partially obscured behind thick coat and scarf. It was only when I got close that his scarf blew away from his face — though the day was windless — and I halted, caught once more by the sense that the world's usual reality was fast receding.

The young man was me. Or at least, it appeared to be a younger version of me. Drawn, harried-looking, familiar messy hair and long sad mouth. He gave no indication of having seen me- indeed, of taking notice of anything. He strode past with his eyes fixed ahead, staring at uncertain distance, the earth rolling underneath his disregard. When I looked over my shoulder I saw nothing, as if had vanished... or perhaps I saw a far-off smudge of a person in the distance. It was difficult to say.

It was curious and a little unsettling, this first vision, but not the first time I had seen a stranger strongly reminiscent of a familiar face while walking through Oxford. It was therefore easy to rationalise as mere coincidence, a resemblance made striking only through eyes squinting with cold-pricked tears. And yet, though I told myself it was something-of-nothing, I couldn't help but return in my memory to the stranger's — my — vacant gaze, his — my — purposeful but forlorn gait. How had it seemed so like me, so uncanny? How had the aura of unreality, of shifting and wavering solidity, attached itself to this figure?

It was a little over a week later that the next vision occurred. I had buried myself in my work to distract myself from a vague but growing sense of dissatisfaction with Oxford. I was increasingly irritable with old friends; I now avoided old haunts that reminded myself of my university days. I was uneasy in the presence of nostalgia, discontented with the samenesss and familiarity of the place. If the present seemed discoloured by the past, the same was increasingly true of the inverse. My memories of university were taking on an increasingly sour note. I picked over my university years in a discontented, disgruntled way, ruing opportunities I hadn't taken, chances I'd missed. Occasionally, in these bitter moods, my thoughts would drift inexplicably to the solitary, wan figure in the park. I found the memory of him unnerving, and thus I tried to forget about him, and university, and to remove anything that reminded me of the place.

However, trying to avoid Oxford while in Oxford is patently impossible. Memories of the university rose unbidden in a constant stream. Then it happened: while walking over Magdalen Bridge, a recollection formed in my mind's eye of a girl that I had dearly loved some years ago, a girl I had, by chance, bumped into on this bridge, a girl I'd pined for unrequitedly. I smiled slightly, and then, the smile dying on my face, looked straight ahead at a figure that was moving through the crowds with a molten ease. The resemblance to me was undeniable this time: a dark, thin version of me, younger by some years, moving not so much around people as among them. At first his stare seemed as vacant as before, but as I gazed at him in slight apprehension he slowly turned to look at me, ignoring the crowds around us. He stared unblinkingly. His face was a mournful cast, sorrowful lines hard around his youthful mouth, his expression unchanging and deeply etched like a greek mask. He did not look away, nor move: nor did I. I stared at him until, with the vague reassertion of noise and light that marks waking from sleep, I dimly became aware that I was no longer staring at a boy, or anything, but had been fixed for some uncertain period of time on a patch of sky, gawping into mere nothing by myself on Magdalen bridge. A couple of passers-by, tourists, looked at me curiously. Suddenly self-conscious, I moved on.

After his silent reappearance, the figure of the boy was ever-present in my mind, creeping into my more nervous and solitary moments. He had seemed both more and less real in his second manifestation: increasingly immaterial and vague in

his relation to the world around him, but also increasingly undeniable as a phenomenon. I could not mark it as a mere quirk
of recognition. The boy had stared at me, and me specifically,
and he was me, no doubt about it. It was like looking at a dark
pane of glass. The prospect of further reappearances filled me
with a vague sense of unease and nervousness that made me
edgy, somewhat jumpy. A dark movement in the corner of my
eye, a silhouetted stranger, a reflection in a pane of glass: I was
constantly guarded against such things, eyes flickering suspiciously. I cut down on smoking weed and drinking alcohol, in
the vague hope that maybe sobriety would reassert normality
over the streets of Oxford. But I had never been particularly
intemperate to begin with, and even at the time I knew my
actions were symbolic, an attempt to assert control by doing
something. It was an unsurprisingly futile gesture.

The visions continued with greater frequency. Sometimes
they would be mere glimpses: the figure batting through
crowds on Broad Street, lurking in cloistered shadows along
St. Giles, always indefinite and murky, like an inkblot on wet
paper. Sometimes he — this figure that seemed so much to be
I — would manifest in front of me, staring listlessly, face always composed in a rictus of apparent misery. After a while,
the shock of seeing him began to wear off, to be replaced only
by a hopelessness at the idea of ever being free of the stalking figure and his motionless stare. He seemed embedded into
Oxford. The city had become stained by his constant presence,
this shadowy blot, and, increasingly, my memories of the city
had become tainted also. I could not think of the university
without his skulking outline making itself apparent; within
the sanctuary of my head, I could not think of my past without
invoking him in my recollections. The boundaries between us
became elided. To picture myself at university was increasingly to imagine this funereal, pale manifestation, his tragedian's

mouth and dead eyes.

My memories of university grew accordingly distressing. Repeatedly pursued by this younger, ghostlier incarnation, they seemed unreal, ominous, marked by an overcast sense of doom. Increasingly I began to seek refuge from my own recollections, wondering on what I could have done at university, what other things I might have accomplished, seeking to avoid the dissatisfactions of my own spectral past by assuming the dissatisfactions of speculation and potential. It was in these new imaginings that my own image could dwell without interference from my sad-mouthed interloper. Yet they were painful in and of themselves, these imaginings of could-have-been and should-have-been. I began to measure up my university recollections and find them wanting. How much had I enjoyed university? I seemed to remember that I had done, at the time. Yet in the bitter, nervous mood inculcated by my own pale likeness and his lurking presence in my head and on the street, it no longer seemed that way. Oxford was no longer a place of cheery reminisces: increasingly I dived into my memories of the past as a fount of grievance, not nostalgia.

Indeed, now, as I walked the streets, they seemed a constant reproach for the past. The brute solidity of Oxford's heavy stone seemed a reminder of the fixity of history; the colleges seemed to draw away from me, unwelcoming, as if to remind me that I no longer belonged there. I no longer saw glimpses of friends and old acquaintances in the street: the crowds had reverted to the simple, unfriendly faces of strangers. Oxford seemed newly alien to me, possessed of a hostile past, an attenuated present. It was as if my own shadow, my pale interloper, was deliberately bleeding my memory of whatever enjoyment or pleasantness it once had. I was obsessed by old remorses, filled with new regrets. I unhappily revisited failed love affairs, failures of nerve, failures of initiative, old complaints or resentments about my study, my friends, my college, myself. Everywhere the past taunted me with its obdurate unchangingness. Everywhere the faint ghoulish image of myself would flicker into being, stalking amid the crowd or haughtily alone, whenever I had cause to remember the past.

In an effort to rid myself of Oxford's stone walls, I walked through the city and headed north to Port Meadow. The dreary flat fields, grey-green and marshy, were hardly beautiful, but they did at least afford some semblance of openness. I walked to the river's edge, where the bridge lay low across the water, and gazed upon the water. It was a muddy, miserable afternoon. Alone among the faint brutish noises of the cows and the solitary caws of the birds above, I attempted to assemble my thoughts. I reflected on the last time I had come to Port Meadow as a callow, overworked undergraduate: I had walked through the fields then also to clear my mind, to forget the constant looming threat of exams and deadlines. I had been similarly haunted, worried, and alone. Nothing had changed much. I reflected on my studies, and the trouble it had caused me... the long nights, the stress, the intermittent boredom. Why was I back here? It suddenly seemed ridiculous to have returned to Oxford. The past offered me no solace, my memories no comfort. As I recalled it now, I hadn't enjoyed my time here as a student. I hadn't done particularly well: I hadn't got a First, I hadn't joined a sports team, I hadn't appeared on stage, I hadn't much luck with girls, I couldn't even say I'd had a particularly fun time... Now I had returned, and for what reason? Why return at all? My resentments and regrets bubbled all at once to the surface and I felt almost nauseous, my stomach tightening in impotent and anxious distress.

And then, as I stared balefully across the grey meadowlands, consumed by unhappy thoughts on the past, a now familiar blur appeared in the distance almost as expected. I watched as the vision of myself came closer and closer, the fixed expression of misery, the empty eyes, the hunched-over walk... and looking down at the water below me, I noticed with a dull shock that my reflection had begun to take on the same mournful rictus, the same paleness... I looked back at myself with the same vacant gaze I'd first seen on the face of that strange apparition in the park.

I looked at myself, then at myself again, gaze sliding from the reflection in the water below me to the ghostly caricature in front of me. I had begun to understand, with a sinking sense of hopelessness, that as long as I was in Oxford, I would always be dogged by memory of the past. I couldn't escape from it. The past was still here, stalking among the towers and lecture halls: if not a living thing, then close to living, enough to infect the present. My undergraduate self, all that he was and could have been, all that existed in recollections and imagined speculation, was still here, staring back at me in every instance of the present. I couldn't escape from it, nor could ever hope to change it: the past was implacable, out of reach, forever scornful of any human wish to alter or redress. I stared at my adversary, my friend, my semblable, my self, from across the water. I understood that he belonged to this place, more than me: I would never free myself of him while I remained in the city.

Yes. Some part of me had never left Oxford. Some part of me had remained, lurking and forgotten, bound to the earth by Oxford's ever-present history, its constant reflexive turn to the past, the insistence of its libraries and scholars of constant and exhaustive record. Yes: just as the past was constantly dragged to the present for re-evaluation by the university, so it appeared that I, too, must go through this process of resurrection, rousing the past in reverberations of the present. I was among the ghosts, and it was to them that the city belonged.

And yet the most unsettling feeling of all was that I could not decide who, truly, was haunting the ancient city. Was it these shadowy glimpses, these echoing recollections, these fragments of a former spirit? Or the man who walked the streets of Oxford alone, more solid and yet still fleeting, caught up in regret and remorse... was he not equally a mere ghost of the dead?

THE GHOST HUNTER

Ian Robertson

On Holywell Street a bicycle bell rang a warning that drifted through an open window and into an over-cluttered office. Professor Anthony Eldridge sat behind his desk, smiling weakly beneath unkempt greying hair. Tufts of it stuck out from behind his ears at strange angles, and from these ears a pair of glasses emerged and fought with two bushy eyebrows for dominance over his face. Julia thought the professor could have been handsome once upon a time, but now he had a certain deflated quality, the sense of someone who knows they are past their prime and can see little point in making the effort.

"Can you give a date estimate as to when the full procedure might be completed?" asked Julia.

"Oh one can never be sure how long these things will take!" mumbled the professor. "The situation you describe sounds especially difficult. It would help a lot if there was a more complete history, perhaps a family genealogy to go along with the property? You're sure all records were lost in the fire?"

"Yes, I'm afraid so, and the records office has drawn a blank too," Julia repeated patiently.

Unlike the professor, Ms Julia Appleton's appearance was crisp and professional. Her dark blue suit was lint free, her black hair was freshly straightened, and her fresh white shirt had been steam-ironed into creaseless submission.

"Seems mighty strange for a big house like this, but I trust you lawyer folks know your way around the paperwork a lot better than I!" Professor Eldridge got up from his desk and went over to a filing cabinet that did not contain files. "In that case we will have to rely on science and gizmos!" he declared, and out of the cabinet produced what looked like an electrician's amp meter with a few coat hangers soldered onto it. He waved it about dramatically and Julia forced her lips into a smile, reminding herself that she was getting paid by the hour. She did not believe in ghosts but she did believe in con-men, and to her Professor Eldridge seemed like a bona-fide example of the latter.

"Well I have instructions from our clients to proceed as soon as humanly possible," said Julia. "Are you free today for a pre-liminary investigation? I have the keys to the property with me and my car is parked just around the corner."

"Oh I'm afraid you'll have to make a future appointment," replied the professor. "I do have other jobs I must attend to, and an awful lot of research and paperwork to address, as you can see!" The professor indicated the room; the dust on many of the stacked papers suggested they had not been attended to for quite some time.

"I understand you're busy," said Julia, her patience un-strained, "but if you make this case your number one priority the client is prepared to pay double your usual fee..."

The professor's face visibly lightened and his smile became more genuine. "Oh well, in that case I'm sure I can move some things around! Just give me a few moments would you? I'll need to change and gather a few things." He opened another drawer in the filing cabinet and lifted out a pair jeans and a slightly yellowing t-shirt, which he unfolded with a grin. *I ain't afraid of no ghosts!* read the t-shirt's caption. "This is my work outfit you see, I can't be wearing this suit crawling around dusty attics and goodness knows where!"

"Of course," replied Julia, even though his suit looked to her like it had already seen a few dusty attics in its time. "I'll wait for you in the car"

Receding glimpses of the dreaming spires danced between the trees as they climbed the A420 and left Oxford behind. Professor Eldridge decided to make a second attempt at car conversation. "So do you have to sell many haunted houses in your line of work?"

"No, this is the first," replied Julia, "and actually our firm deals primarily with inheritances. Property conveyancing is dealt with by a different type of solicitor."

"I see, I see. Never seen a ghost yourself then?" asked the professor, playfully.

Julia allowed herself a quick laugh, "No, I can't say I have! I assume you've seen a fair few?"

"One or two. One or two..." the professor seemed to drift off, then his eyes widened with a question: "I say, how did your firm find out about me? Was it my website or a referral?"

"Neither. You're a condition of the will."

"I beg your pardon?"

"It's a condition of the will that your services be employed before the property is passed on, though why the deceased couldn't hire you while they were still alive is a mystery to me."

"Well I am intrigued! Can you really not tell me anything about this deceased will-maker?"

"No I'm afraid not. All I can say is that the family came into possession of the property fairly recently and are not relevant to its history."

"My, my, the plot thickens!" quoted the professor and Julia winced imperceptibly behind the wheel.

The gravel in the drive leading up to the manor house was puckered with weeds and clumps of grass, but it still crunched beneath the wheels of Julia's car as she drew up beside the front steps. The building was not vast, and seemed to blend in well with the broad-leaved woodland that surrounded it. Sandstone battlements edged the roof and a few square turrets gave the manor a castle-like appearance. Tall lead-lined windows emerged from the ivy that coated the walls and a few panes of glass were broken where vandals had thrown rocks at them.

"Do you need a hand with anything, professor?" asked Julia

"No, no," he said, lifting a hastily packed bag out of the boot. "Oh, and please call me Tony!"

"Ok Tony, I'll go up and unlock."

Julia took the keys out of her purse and climbed the steps to the arched double door. The new steel bolt and chrome-plated padlock looked out of place against the dark wood and rusting hinges. Apparently they'd had to install it as the old lock had jammed and the door was refusing to close. She unbolted the doors and pushed gently against the rough oak grain, bracing herself for a flock of bats or some other silly fright to emerge, but nothing stirred inside the house except the stale dusty air.

"I'll just do a preliminary walk through and check for any spurious electromagnetism," said Tony, waving the device he had shown off earlier in his office. "I've got a spare one if you'd like to give it try?"

"Sure, why not?" replied Julia, briefly imagining herself getting into the ghost hunting racket.

"Excellent! It's fairly self-explanatory — you point the antenna in the direction you want to scan, and if this needle here moves up then that's a good sign of supernatural energy."

Julia looked at the needle. It sat firmly on zero and did not show any signs of moving.

"First we need to switch it on of course!" Tony reached forward and flicked a switch on the side of the device — the needle swung across to the top of the scale. "Sorry, it must need calibrating." He took the device out of her hands, held down a button and adjusted a couple of knobs. "There you go!" he said, handing it back to her, the needle back on zero. "Don't wander off too far. And if you see a ghost just scream."

Julia laughed. It took a lot to make her scream and she tried to remember the last time this had happened. On the rare occasions she wasn't working late in the office, or out running errands like this one, she liked to go in search of adrenaline boosts. Horror movies in the dark were quite fun, and death-defying roller coasters were up there amongst her favourite activities, all of which she enjoyed with barely a gasp escaping her lips. The last time she could remember almost screaming was when she went to open her curtains and a particularly big spider had fallen out of them... but that was more of an 'ughh!' noise followed by a decisive stamp of her foot.

Tony smiled as she laughed, but there was a strange worry in his eyes that made her doubt whether his comment had really been intended as a joke after all.

In less than ten minutes, Julia had 'wandered off too far'. Old empty houses were exciting and Tony seemed to be painfully slow about things. *Probably putting on a show in order to justify his outrageous fee,* she thought, waving the ghost detector around here and there. The needle lay flat, which did not surprise Julia in the slightest.

She explored the kitchens — someone had clearly begun the process of updating them but not finished. A modern electric cooker sat gathering dust beside a grand fireplace with a fantastic open range. No food in the cupboards though, which was disappointing as she'd had to grab a quick feta salad for lunch. *I think I'll order Dominos tonight,* she decided, giving up on the kitchens and heading for the next door.

Julia entered a parlour full of furniture covered with white sheeting. She went to pull back one of the sheets to take a look beneath, but first glanced over her shoulder; she couldn't shake the unsettling feeling that someone was watching. Her thoughts kept getting sucked towards the back of her neck with the clichéd sense of eyes boring into it. *Damn my imagination,* she thought, pushing the sheet back and feeling the softness of the red velvet chaise longue beneath. She imagined owning something like it, perhaps in green, and began to construct her perfect living room in her mind's eye. *Clean whites and greens... elegant, but not overly ornate... nice, tall windows... a town house with a parkland view, perhaps...* The thought of her current savings balance flattened this fantasy like a bulldozer. *Still, I'm a fully-qualified solicitor now,* she consoled herself, and made a mental note to check ebay for green chaise longues when she was next on the internet.

Julia's next discovery was the library — a grand affair with two levels of book clad walls, a thin balcony, and a circle of free-standing book shelves that radiated out from a central study area like spokes on a wheel. Julia closed the library door behind her, hoping to shake her figmental stalker that lurked back there, disrupting her train of thought. She strolled through the shelves, running her finger over some of the old and dusty spines. *I could always do some reading while I wait for the mad professor,* she thought, and sat down at one of the central desks. She stared around the books and papers scattered there, and on some parchment in front of her she noticed something scratched in ink: "*LEAVE MY HOME*" was written alone in violently capitalised calligraphy.

Julia scanned the parchment with the ghost detector, refusing to be rattled: the needle did not move. Still sitting, she rotated the chair slowly around in a full circle, checking each avenue of books for those imagined eyes she could not shake, but nothing was there. She wondered if books might start jumping from the shelves as a ghostly warning, but nothing moved except motes of dust, which danced in shafts of light from the high windows. All was silent aside from the creak of her chair on its spindle. *Time to move on,* she decided.

The door on the other side of the library opened into a hallway, which was windowless and saturated with a thick blackness. Only the light that came through the open library doorway penetrated this darkness and illuminated a small patch of dark wood panelling on the opposite wall. Julia extracted her phone from her bag, poked her head into the hall, and shone the phone's flashlight into the void.

The void appeared mercifully empty of phantoms, but a small desire to go back to the car was starting to work its way into Julia's mind. Ahead she could see that the hallway turned a corner, around which something glinted in the torchlight. She couldn't pretend to herself this wasn't scary anymore. There was something primally terrifying about the darkness — it exposed her to a million unseen evils and left her clutching at this single source of light, lest blindness take her. Still, fighting this fear was like a sport for Julia. She loved the tenseness in her mind like a weightlifter loves the burning in their muscles or a runner loves the stinging of cold air in their lungs. However, she felt compelled to check for phantoms behind the library door before pressing ahead, waving the ghost detector as she did so, but there was nothing there. And so, feeling her back was relatively secure, she pressed forward through the doorway, into the darkness.

The unknown flowed around Julia's body as she stepped out into the hall, and her pulse quickened. The blackness caressed her face and soaked her hair, it trickled down her neck, flowed under her collar and pooled against her warm skin. The darkness penetrated every crevice of her being. She might almost merged with it, were it not for the small array of light-emitting diodes in her hand and the rapid beating of her heart. Her rational mind fought hard with an imagination that kept suggesting what might lurk around that turn in the corridor... Lurching zombies that would clutch at her with their rotten arms... A giant spider that would leap forward and ensnare her with its long legs and hooked fangs.... She gritted her teeth. It would be an empty corridor she was sure... well, almost sure.

Julia held her phone protectively in front of her and focused it on the corridor ahead. She rounded the corner and there in front of her was the unsettlingly anthropomorphic sight of two full suits of armour, one holding a spear and the other a sword. "Nothing to worry about," she said out loud to quell the suffocating silence. "Just two empty... OH FUCK!" Julia had lifted the ghost detector into the torch light and could see its once lifeless needle was dancing wildly up the scale. "Fuck! Fuck! Fuck!" she yelled, jumping backwards and pressing herself against the wood panelling.

The metal beasts shone motionless in the torchlight and Julia watched them, transfixed. After staring at them wide-eyed for a minute or so they still did not move and she began to gather her senses. *It's ok, it's ok, must be something to do with the metal,* she decided, and moved the detector closer to the first suit of armour. Sure enough, the needle swung higher. A spider's web had been spun between the helmet and the breastplate, and a thick layer of dust dulled the armour's shine. Closer still, every muscle in Julia's body was taut, ready to fight or run if the armour produced the slightest movement. Moving closer, the detector was approaching the top of the scale now. She held it alongside her phone in her right hand and reached out with her left... closer... and closer...

TAP TAP TAP

She knocked her fist three times against the metal and its hollow echo was somehow reassuring. "That trickster has got me wandering around with a fucking metal detector!" she grumbled, a semblance of poise returning.

Resolving to get this all over with as quickly as possible, Julia strode over to the second suit of armour, which looked identical except that it held a sword rather than a spear. She confidently lifted the detector in front of her and angled her phone to illuminate the needle. It had returned to zero. The bottom fell out of her world.

A couple of seconds later she found herself pressed against the nearest door, at the furthest end of the hallway, her hand desperately rattling its handle. The door was clearly locked but she still rattled it for several more moments in the hope this situation might somehow change. It did not. She was stuck there in that pitch black hallway and her back kept screaming under the glare of those once imagined eyes. Eventually she accepted this was all really happening and turned back to face whatever her imagination had desperately warned her against.

The suit of armour with the spear had moved. It was now standing in the middle of the hallway, blocking her path, and visible as a silhouette from the faint light escaping the library door at the other end of the hall. That light represented her only sure escape, and the way was barred. Julia did not know how the armour had moved so silently, but there were many things she did not know at this point, so she discarded this thought along with the others she no longer had the serenity to consider.

Julia swung her phone's light onto the armour's static form and summoned her shredded nerves. "Professor, I'm sure you think yourself very funny, but this is extremely unprofessional and if you don't take that thing off this minute I will give you an extremely negative review!" she shouted, her voice past strained.

The suit remained silent, but then it suddenly moved, thrusting its spear arm out sideways so as to further block the hallway. The awful truth of this motion broke something in Julia's conscious mind. Hell hath no fury like a lawyer who's been fucked with. "That's it!" she yelled, marching forward. With her heart pounding in fear and rage she grabbed the helmet's visor and lifted.

Her whole body went rigid. There was no one inside.

After that moment's pause she suddenly felt the weight of the helmet in her hand and shrieked as the whole suit of armour collapsed around her with an almighty crash. She jumped backwards as the breast plate fell towards her and dropped the helmet, which clattered down onto the metallic pile below. Her mind reached desperately for explanations. *Magnets? Strings? More damned gadgetry?* Yet nothing could quell the terror that burned in her. She reached for the 'ghost detector' that still hung around her neck, seeking her world's salvation in its coat-hangers and circuitry. Calming her desire to flee, Julia waved the detector frantically around the iron helmet, gauntlets, breastplate and other parts, desperate for an explanation, but the needle now sat stubbornly back on zero.

Giving up, she straightened her back, moved the detector sideways to sling it over her shoulder, and saw the needle twitch. She turned slightly more, now acutely aware of the cold sweat that hung about her. The needle twitched further up the scale.

She turned fully and the second suit of armour was there, standing not more than a metre behind her. Julia finally screamed with all the air that was left in her lungs.

The scream reverberated throughout the house, dancing with the dust grains in the library, vibrating the empty glasses in the parlour, even disturbing the bats that roosted in the attic. Tony heard it where he was scanning some suspicious jam jars in the pantry and looked up, alarmed.

Then the scream stopped while still at full volume, as if a sound cable had been suddenly unplugged, or the screamer suddenly muffled. Back in that dark hallway a quiet hiss of air could still be heard escaping from Julia's lungs, but it was coming from a wind pipe that was no longer attached to vocal chords. Her severed head rolled backwards along the carpet and came to rest against an armoured glove that had previously clutched a spear. Her lifeless body collapsed onto the armour pile with a heavy clatter.

The phone torch now shone fixedly on the ceiling, its dimly scattered light illuminating a murderous phantom, which lowered its bloody sword and maneuvered itself back into position against the wall. The sword's tip pressed down into the ruined carpet, and all was motionless once again, except for the red drip-drip-dripping of a body draining of life.

The ghost of Oakleigh manor possessed many common features of evil, but paranoia and ruthlessness were perhaps foremost amongst them. Whatever remnants of humanity this spirit had emerged from had long ago been sloughed away by the erosive forces of time. The rich vocabulary of words and ideas that once swirled between the manor walls had worn away to a single violent notion that whispered down chimneys and under doors. "*MY HOME!*" it called in dimensions where few could listen. These remaining syllables hummed through wood, stone, tile and glass — even the ivy trembled with them, and turned brown and died when it tried to grow out of place.

The manor had been a happy place once — too happy perhaps, since the bitterest darkness may feed on kernels of the brightest light. First a favoured child was taken from them, and in their grief, the family closed themselves off from the world, but the world could not yet let them go. The royalists would not tolerate this neutrality, not so close to the new seat of the king, but the family ignored the calls to arms and the royal summonses until, finally, the soldiers came. It would not have mattered if they had angered King or Cromwell — the tragedy played out like a boulder rolling down a hill, where the stone was the armed bodies of insulted soldiers and gravity was the hatred in their hearts. Hearts immune to those black robes of mourning — hearts that saw only bright silverware, decadent furnishings, and insolent defiance that had to be extinguished. They made the father watch it all, his anguished cries reverberating in the porcelain teacups, a man twice-broken, the words *"THIS IS MY HOME!"* escaping in fear and anger, and etching themselves into everything they touched. The words found purchase in the steely hearts of the soldiers that sliced the family's throats — none of them would survive the coming war. The ghost of Oakleigh Manor was not simply the spirit of a man who had lost it all. It was the coalesced energies of the whole murdered household, their stories, their echo, their love and loss sharpened to a piercing hate of anyone who should invade these memories.

Once again this spirit was being invaded, not by soldiers this time but by two people carrying strange electrical boxes. To the phantom these boxes made irritating humming noises that could not be endured. It knew of the deed-owner's last will and testament, and that some form of exorcism was on the cards. The phantom would soak these walls with intruder blood before it let this place be destroyed. To us mortals exorcising a ghost might not seem like destroying a place, but a ghost considers *itself* to *be* the place. The walls and land that contain it are merely insubstantial vessels that its memories must cling to, like we the living cling to air.

The ghost could sense Julia's malignancy the second she had unbolted the door. Like a parasite she had crawled around under its skin, nibbling at its spirit with her thoughts and footsteps. The phantom had merely waited for the right moment to cut out the wriggling cancer, and it was a brutal surgeon. It knew there would be trouble over this of course, more irritating people would come and fuss over the mess like ants swarming to protect their nest... but some itches just needed to be scratched. The consequences could be endured.

The second itch was in the library now, trying to follow the scream. *Perhaps make this one look like a suicide*? the ghost considered while its voice scratched "*MY HOME*" on the pages of closed library books. The professor's device seemed to grow louder, hissing ethereal, maddening. *Cut him to pieces,* came the decision as the ghost condensed itself inside a metal shell once again.

Tony opened the side door of the library and there stood the armour, its blood-soaked sword held by both hands and pointing towards the heavens.

"Ah," he said, and looked down at his ghost detecting device where the needle waved manically. "Well this is a new one..." He stepped backwards away from the door and the suit of armour lurched into the room. "Oh, Jesus Christ! Erm, terribly sorry to disturb you, I'll leave right away!" He stepped back further, then behind him a book shelf creaked, tipped sideways, and crashed into its neighbour. The domino effect spread around him, tumbling bookshelves into bookshelves and cutting off all possible exits. He was stranded in a book-cluttered arena with the metal swordsman still advancing.

Tony stepped backwards again and tried to clamber up onto the mess of shelves and books while keeping his eyes fixed on the iron-clad phantom.

It raised its sword.

"Please, you're making a mistake!" yelled Tony.

The swordsman swung, but the blade made a swishing noise in the air, and the professor's t-shirt and jeans flopped emptily to the floor.

If phantasmal suits of armour could display facial expressions then this one would have looked confused. The books ceased their scratching and for the first time ever the quasi-dimensional drone of "*MY HOME*" acquired a question mark at the end.

A "TAP TAP" rang out on the armour's back plate and the phantom turned.

There stood the professor, now dressed in the worn-out suit he had been wearing back in the office. "Tada!" he exclaimed, and then punched the ghost square in the mouth. His fist penetrated the helmet with a transcendental ease and the knight-like shell disintegrated as the phantom stumbled backwards, out of it, stunned by the blow.

"That's right you swine! You're not the only dead codger in the room today!"

Stepping through the tumbling armour, the professor landed another fist into the ghost's metaphysical stomach and it fell to the floor.

"You didn't give me a chance to introduce myself," announced the professor, grabbing hold of a ghostly ankle and pulling the phantom back into the room as it tried to crawl away and de-materialise. "My name is Professor Eldridge, formerly chair of quantum metaphysics." He flung the ghost down onto a writing desk which cracked in half under the blow. The physical and metaphysical were confused as the professor dragged the phantom kicking and howling through intersecting dimensional realities, thrusting it hard into whichever time-bound object happened to hurt the most. "I'm deceased, obviously, and not in a pretty fashion." The professor lifted a heavy Bible from its stand and brought it down on the phantom's head, which made a ghostly crunching noise. "And I eat spooky little shits like you for breakfast!" The pages of the Bible flopped open, and the angry ink scrawlings that had once read $\mathcal{MY\ HOME}$ were now jumbled and unintelligible. "Now sometimes out of charity I might allow a lost soul like you cling onto some minor trinket, but after what you did to that nice Julia girl I think that's out of the question." The phantom managed to scramble forwards and in a sudden burst of energy dissolved through the library walls and out into the hallway. There it found the professor waiting, a knight's helmet on his head and a spear in his hand. "Boo!" he said, and shoved the lance through the phantom's chest, pinning it writhing against the wall.

"Now obviously I can't kill you, what with you being already dead and all, but I figure I'll just make a sufficient nuisance of myself until you shuffle off of your own accord. Sound good?"

With painful concentration, the phantom managed to disengage from its impaled form and melt into the walls. "Off to hide in there are we?" cried the professor. "It'll do you no good I'm afraid!" He reached back and plunged his hand into the wood-work behind him. It re-emerged clutching a ghostly head of hair; the phantom was taking on a more human-like form as the metaphysical beat-down progressed. "Look at the damned mess you've made!" yelled the professor, forcing the ghost's head to look at Julia's decapitated body. The professor looked too, and briefly closed his eyes with repressed emotion before standing up and stamping on the ghost's spine for good measure.

"Sssttop," hissed the ghost, remembering the sound of long lost words. "Isssst nooot right!"

"RIGHT?" cried the professor, extracting the spear from the wall and jabbing it down into the phantom once again "There isn't any right or wrong about it! We're both bloody dead! None of this nonsense makes any sense what-so-ever!"

"Shstop!" wailed the phantom.

"Going to go quietly, are we then?" the professor said removing the lance from the ghost's bloodless stomach. Its face had definite features now and two blue eyes in the centre of it were wild with fear, they looked at the end of the spear and then narrowed: "*MY HOME!*" yelled the phantom defiantly and then evaporated in a cloud of dust.

"I thought not. I do wish you'd hurry up and change your mind though. I've got to figure out what to do about a decapitated body after this!"

The professor took off his spectacles and wiped them with a cloth, pondering how to speed things along. He replaced his glasses and scanned the ceiling. He did not need a torch to see through the darkness, the fearful droning in the walls was more than enough to navigate by. Sometimes, though, there were quiet patches... "Ah I think I spy just the ticket!" said the professor before vanishing. He re-materialised in an upstairs bedroom and proceeded to lift the carpet. Slipping a small jimmy bar out of his pocket he began to pry up the floorboards. Behind him was an open wardrobe and from its shadows the phantom emerged silently. Floating slowly and deliberately it lifted a coal shovel from beside the fireplace without making a sound, raised it above the professor's head, and swung.

The blunt object passed through the professor's head and body without even slowing, and then clanged loudly on the floor where his knees appeared to be resting.

"Glad you could make it!" cried the professor as he grabbed the phantom by the arm and pulled it down to the floor. With his other hand he extracted a carved wooden soldier from under the floorboards. The phantom let out a scream. "Well I can see this little soldier toy really resonates with you doesn't it?"

He flipped the phantom so that he was straddling it, one hand holding it by its screeching throat and the other gripping the toy in front of its half-formed face. "Now I know this hurts in a different kind of way to a spear in the guts — worse perhaps — but there's no use trying to fight it. I can see the memories surfacing in you even now, those entanglements to times long past..."

The ghost made a different kind of sound.

"No, there's nothing to be done about all of that now. The past is what you're made up of after all! I know, I know. It hurts, but look deeper, right at the centre of the pain, because there's something hiding there isn't there? That's it, go with that thought for me will you? Then I'll be out of your hair in no time at all."

The ghost trapped beneath the professor looked almost fully human now, and its blue eyes began to well with tears.

"That's the ticket!" cried the professor. "I don't like to get all hippy-dippy on you, but can you feel that love again? See that beautiful source of all your nastiness?"

The ghost's tears streamed downwards. It still struggled a little beneath the professor, but with a defeated futility. "Excellent," cried the professor. "Now I'll let you stand up and hold the toy in a jiffy, you just keep focusing on that love for me..."

Slowly, the professor released the phantom and it eyed him suspiciously before morphing itself upright. The professor took a step back, holding the toy soldier in an outstretched hand. "Ok you can take it now... gently..."

As he said this though he saw the hatred flow back into the phantom's eyes like a dark wave engulfing a sinking ship. "*MY HOME!*" It lunged forward,

"Bugger," whispered the professor, tossing the toy gently into the air and ducking to the side.

The phantom's human features melted away as the memory of that parental love sunk back below the milieu of pain that had flowed from it. It caught the soldier in mid-air, but in its haste to grab the toy the ghost did not see the tall mirror that been hidden behind the professor. Only when the toy soldier touched the silvered glass and slipped from the phantom's grasp did it realise its fatal mistake.

For the phantom, falling through the surface of the mirror felt like slipping into cool water, except it was only the surface it could feel. Below that surface was neither hot nor cold, just the numb nothingness of annihilation. The phantom screeched once again, trying to stop itself from being entirely submerged. It fought its ghostly momentum and the pull of the void, which draws powerfully on those who should have left the world a long time ago. By changing shape it managed to catch a hold of the mirror's frame and with gnarled grey fingers it gripped it on each side, keeping its head above the glass surface which was now sucking backwards like a whirlpool.

As it struggled against the undertow, the phantom's empty blue eyes watched the wooden soldier hit the floor, then the professor stepped forward. "Mirror, mirror, on the wall, who's the fairest of them all? The answer is: not you!" And with that he dealt a final blow, from his boot to the phantom's nose, and sent it plunging through the glass into the never-after.

The room was quiet now as the professor stared at his own reflection, contemplating what that nothingness must feel like, although he was aware of the contradiction in this query. "Right then..." he said to the empty room. "One best be on the safe side I suppose!" And with that he lifted a heavy earthenware pot from the bedside table and flung it against the mirror. The jug was not a ghost and did not disappear into the never-after. Instead it smashed the mirror into a thousand pieces and made a significant dent in the wall behind.

"Just try giving me more bad luck, why don't you!" declared the professor, waving his finger at the glass shards. "This dead solicitor business is going to be a nightmare, I can tell!" Slowly he sunk down through the floor, mumbling aloud. "I wonder if there's any bleach around here..."

The walls of Oakleigh Manor were empty of memory now. The swallows dreamed of their nests beneath the guttering, the spiders planned expansions of their cobwebs against the windows, and the mice contemplated their hidden food within the walls, but the words "*MY HOME*" no longer trickled through from anywhere at all. The place was at peace, restful, silent...

... Well, almost silent.

If you had the correct EM-interferometry instrument to hand and pointed it in the right direction you might still hear a faint metaphysical echo in the air, carefully muffled, but present nonetheless. Its source was not the walls, paintings or other scattered possessions; it came instead from the library. It did not come from the books or scattered parchments, nor from the tumbled armour, or even the bloody sword. Instead the voice came from a ragged bag of ghost hunting equipment and a yellowing *Ghostbusters'* t-shirt, and in the professor's voice it hummed:

"KILL ALL THE BLOODY GHOSTS! KILL ALL THE BLOODY GHOSTS! KILL ALL THE BLOODY GHOSTS!"

MOONLIGHT SONATA

David Olsen

Children no longer dare to play amid the overgrown brambles beyond that reluctant iron gate. Their parents claim that, when clouds in fury tear across the moon, in that unbalanced light a woeful woman's face can be seen to peer from a dormer window of that derelict house. At other times, the rare passerby on that seldom-travelled lane in Old Marston might hear familiar strains of a Beethoven sonata, obsessively played with expert skill, over and over again.

Old-timers in the pub still speak of the murder of a concert pianist during the night of the full moon many years ago. It was supposed, with near certainty, that her husband killed the woman in a crime of passion on discovering her infidelity with a charismatic violinist.

The presumed killer left town in haste. The police traced him to Southampton, but by that time a ship had sailed for Australia. The man's name did not appear on the passenger manifest, and the trail went cold. The crime remains unsolved.

On my daytime rambles I sometimes pass by that accursed Victorian red-brick house, but as a retired mining engineer recently returned to Oxford from many years abroad, I'm guided by faith in observables and reasoned explication. I'm a man of science, and give no credence to supernatural claims.

Yet, as I regard my sun-damaged complexion and full beard in the mirror, I confess to being a lunatic, in the classical sense of the term. When the fullest moon opposes the sun, in that intemperate time I avoid the house. For in those heavy hours of extreme distress, I dread descent into the web of madness. The haunting's not in that forbidding house; it's in a fragile mind that clings to the ragged edge of sanity.

OUBLIETTE

Jade Mitchell

Something like an insect, or a small drop of rain landed on the back of Sean's neck and he slapped at it, distracted. He looked into the small, dark entryway and wondered why he'd never seen it before. He was completing his second year in Economics and Management at Brasenose, and had taken this route to lectures past the Covered Market at least a hundred times. But this was the first time he'd seen the low-set entrance on Turl Street.

Sean had heard about there once being tunnels beneath the Covered Market during a particularly camp ghost walking tour at the beginning of the term. In medieval times, he remembered the guide intoning, livestock would be sold to college kitchen staff in the marketplace. The petrified pigs, cows and fowls would then be taken below the surface, where the air stank of burning candles, fresh blood and voided bowels. They would be slaughtered and butchered, their meat loaded onto wagons that would be transported across Oxford, to individual college kitchens using a networked system of underground delivery tunnels.

After the tunnels were apparently abandoned for more hygienic methods of food preparation, their shroud of darkness attracted a less savoury line of business. The network became the preferred venue for depravities that ranged from drug abuse, to everyday prostitution, to elaborate, esoteric orgies for wealthy perverts... or so the story goes.

Sean had called bullshit. If there were still tunnels under the market, he'd heckled, why hadn't anyone found a way to sell Harry Potter merchandise out of them? Kavitha had slapped his arm and called him rude, but had giggled into her scarf all the same.

He supposed he owed that guide an apology now.

To call the entryway a doorway would have been wrong, it wasn't nearly tall enough and it was blocked only by a thick, black metal grate, which had fortuitously been left open this early September morning. Sean peered into the darkness beyond, trying to use the dim glow of his mobile phone to see farther. Self-conscious, he turned to look up and around, but dozens of passers-by walked on, oblivious. The students seemed harried and the tourists seemed lost. No one was looking at him, looking into the tunnel.

Sean gripped the stone mantle over the entry, squatted, and entered. After a few steps, the tunnel opened up inside so that he could stand at his full height, but only just. The ceiling was low enough that he could still feel it ruffle his hair as he moved. The walls were rough, untreated rock, and looked as though they were formed naturally, instead of dug by human hands. The width of them was irregular. They'd come tight around his shoulders for a few steps, and then widen out unpredictably, making him lose his bearings. His phone gave him some visibility in the total darkness, but only one, blue-lit metre at a time, so he relied on careful footsteps to navigate the uneven, earthen ground beneath his trainers. Sean was no great cave explorer– he'd never been deeper underground than his Aunt May's wine cellar. But he'd read enough horror stories to know that ways in were often much easier than ways out.

For ten long minutes, Sean navigated the twisting path of the tunnel. The length and trajectory of it seemed incongruous with the size and layout of the market above, and he quickly lost his bearings. Of course, Sean reasoned, he did still get lost on his way back home in the evenings. Even when he wasn't drunk.

He started to fear that the large metal grate behind him might be shut soon, locking him in, dooming him to a life immured, and possibly even a tardiness penalty for his Microeconomics tutorial. But just as he considered turning around and going back, the walls around him vanished and the tunnel opened out. Curiosity drew him forward, but fear made him cautious.

His eyes adjusted and he realised he was standing in a vast, domed cavern, maybe twenty metres in diameter. It was curved all around, the floor dipped down and the ceiling soared up, creating a huge stone chamber. Like an amphitheatre, or a ballroom. The hairs at the back of Sean's neck rose. Before, he could hear the dull cacophony from the busy Oxford street outside, but in here it was impossibly silent. More tunnels, their presence denoted only as patches of comparatively darker shadows leading off from the walls circling the hall. Cold seeped up through his shoes, and he felt faintly nauseated.

What a find, thought Sean, his breath loud in his own ears.

What an incredible discovery, he mused, his stomach lurching and his heart pounding. His legs itched to move, and a tiny nerve spasmed in his eyelid.

What an excellent place for a party, he decided.

Days passed, and every morning the trees looked a little more barren, and a little more beaten. Dried leaves abandoned their branches easily for the merest suggestion of wind. Sean walked the same route to his lectures down Turl Street every morning, just to convince himself that he hadn't imagined the tunnel. The entryway was still there, still unlocked, and 'The Great Hall' as he had idly nicknamed it, still lay beyond.

Sean had been considered bright at high school, but Oxford made him feel like a model-C student at best. He did acceptably in all of his subjects, attended an adequate number of social gatherings, and performed passably on his projects. It wasn't that he didn't try. It's just that Sean was quickly realising a hard truth most people only learn much later in their adult lives. He just wasn't very good at anything. He tried not to let it worry him too much though, mostly by drinking heavily, and then embarrassing himself in front of unattainable young women. Women who reminded him as little of Kavitha as possible.

Kavitha was Sean's closest friend, but he suspected he wasn't hers. She was popular, bold and funny. A New Yorker with an unflappable sense of self, she made everyone feel important. Even Sean. He'd written her off at first. Her kaleidoscopic ensembles and bubbly laugh came across as contrived, orchestrated. Like something out of an American sitcom. But beneath the paisley and neon pink was a dark sense of humour, a wicked temper and an intellect sharp enough to draw blood. After months of running into her in every class and crowd, Sean was now quite inconveniently in love with Kavitha.

And while he'd been happy to suffer the pain of his unrequited affection in silence until now, fate and the ever-surprising streets of Oxford had presented him with a unique opportunity to be excellent in her presence.

"Halloween is only my favourite-ever religious holiday," Kavitha had joked at their last formal hall. They had dressed like grown-ups and were surrounded by mutual acquaintances, many of whom probably considered Kavitha *their* closest friend as well.

Their little dining group had then gone around the table,

comparing plans that included themed club nights, raucous house parties and more traditional scare-fare like the Hellfire caves and Sulgrave Manor. Kavitha had hummed, unamused, through the suggestions, until she was quickly and happily distracted by dessert.

So, Sean was right in thinking that Kavitha would immediately grasp the Great Hall's potential. He brought her to the tunnel entry at midday, while the sun was paused in its sluggish trek across the pale autumn sky. As he led her down the unlit pathway, he heard her hesitant footsteps and considered taking her hand, but quickly decided that it might be seen as making a move, and he was saving that special humiliation for his birthday in November. So he walked on, boldly, and felt like a conquering hero presenting discovered treasure to his queen.

She gasped when they reached the hall, and Sean stood back to allow her to explore it entirely. Where he had hesitated at the precipice, she surged into the centre, her arms wide to the all-swallowing gloom. God, it was dark. So dark he could feel it between the lengths of his fingers. So dark it looked like their clothes were stained with ink. She spun towards him, and her hair fanned out in black shadows around her in the unnatural light of his phone.

"It's perfect."

Sean couldn't see her face properly, but he could hear the smile in her voice, and so he smiled back.

Kavitha took control from that point. She arranged a DJ, lighting, chairs, swathes of fake spider webs and gallons of a lethal, vibrant red, vodka-based punch she called 'pig's blood'. She created a database for guests, wrote invitations and created an online payment portal to collect entry fees. She tried her best to involve Sean along the way, but he knew he'd already exceeded his usefulness. He didn't really know which songs to play, or what to charge for drinks. But he adored being invited back to Kavitha's flat after tutorials, and revelled in his new-found notoriety at the college. Students he'd never met before came to ask him about the tunnels, or the party, or Kavitha. Accordingly, he told them what he'd seen in the tunnels, what he'd heard about the party, and that Kavitha had a boyfriend.

He and Kavitha returned to the tunnels frequently. Both alone and with others. They took many strangers and potential suppliers to the Great Hall in the weeks leading up to the party. The fine veil of eeriness peeled away from the place a little more with every subsequent visit. It was replaced instead with Sean and Kavitha's more earthly, logistical concerns of how to power the lights, where to put the bar, and whether they should have sought permission to throw a party before they posted the invitation on Instagram.

When the time came to decide on a costume Sean chose to go as Jack the Ripper, agonising over whether or not to include a white mask with the top hat, tails and novelty knife. In between a last-minute DJ cancellation, and avoiding the inconvenient curiosity of the police, Kavitha had still found time to make her own costume. She fabricated grisly ropes of pink-stained intestines from a pair of old tights, which spilled from a rip in her dress, and painted a jagged line of blood across her throat to messily separate her body from her ashen, painted face.

"It looks like we've got a couple's costume," she'd teased, poking Sean in the ribs on their way to do the final preparations. Sean's heart fluttered, and he hoped that others might think so too.

They did not. He had to explain who he was meant to be several times, growing increasingly irked by every 'Phantom of the Opera' mention. The mask was clearly a mistake. Everyone, however, gushed over both Kavitha's costume and her talent with events.

She had excelled. The entrance tunnel itself was lit with fat, dripping, white altar candles, in full, tacky, Halloween tradition. The hall itself was spectacularly transformed. Sickly red and yellow stage lights were suspended from makeshift scaffolding, casting a ghoulish, florid downlight on the crowd. A hip-looking, tattooed DJ played loud electronic music in one far corner while a couple of equally hip-looking, tattooed bartenders pre-poured cups of strong, ruby punch into polystyrene cups. The whole room pulsated with the contained hum of loud music and the rhythmic jerks of a hundred sweaty, young dancers. Already there were the early indications of a highly successful student gathering. Two girls dressed in short skirts and high heels screamed at one another over the drum and bass, tears and sweat streaking and smearing their painted faces. A boy dressed as a meat pie was slumped against a wall. A delicate thread of vomit trickled from the corner of his mouth and stained the front crust of his costume. Someone had drawn a crude penis on the side of his face.

Kavitha knew many people, and she loved to dance. So, it was inevitable that they would be separated. But Sean only fully accepted this two full hours after she'd told him she'd 'be right back'.

He consoled himself by quaffing the too-sweet pig's blood concoction like it was pop. It went straight to his head, then down to his legs, and settled somewhere in the middle. He tried gracelessly to proposition a first-year dressed like an obscure anime character. She responded by tipping her cup of punch on him, ruining one of his two good white shirts. Still, Sean was not so easily dissuaded, and didn't leave the party until the early morning. He emerged from the tunnel dazed, and shuffled home quickly before dawn could catch him.

When Sean woke, his mouth felt like it was glued shut, and his skull felt too tight around his brain. He was clean, naked and in his own bed. All commendable achievements for his drunken self. His memory was a blacked-out blur. Vivid snatches of recollection revealed many cups of punch, some inventive dance moves, and a clumsy topple into the street while he was trying to take a piss on a parked car.

The mid-morning light scorched his eyes and churned his empty stomach. An hour after his alarm jolted him from a disjointed sleep, Sean finally steeled himself to stand. He made a cup of instant coffee with lots of sugar, and then threw it up twenty minutes later in the shower. He missed his Finance lecture and battled to stay awake through 'Strategic Management'.

There were very few students present in his last lecture, and those who were there looked as though they'd had a similar night to Sean's. He messaged Kavitha to ask her what time she'd got home, how she was feeling (fine, he suspected ruefully), and whether she wanted to do anything later. The messages showed as delivered, but not read. Sean wondered smugly if Kavitha had let herself get carried away at her own party.

By five in the afternoon, Sean's gloating gave way to real worry. His messages were still unread. It was unlike Kavitha not to respond quickly. Answering texts while talking was one of her least attractive habits. His phone's home screen was not empty by any means. It was cluttered with hundreds of notifications, tags, images and updates from the night before. He ignored everything as he scrolled through every feed looking for any kind of correspondence from Kavitha. There was nothing. The last picture on her Instagram account was the selfie she'd forced Sean to take with her in the Great Hall before their guests had begun to pour in. Even undead, she was radiant. He sent her another message.

'Kav — are you OK?'

The last place in Oxford, or on the face of the planet, that Sean wanted to be that evening was the college's dining hall. But after almost twenty-four hours without solid calories, a five-quid meal seemed like a positive life choice. That, and Sean knew that he might see Kavitha there. The dining tables, like the lecture hall earlier, were nowhere near as populated as they were usually. In place of the clamour and din that usually accompanied the evening meal was hushed conversation and owl-eyed stares.

Sean was painfully self-conscious in social situations. It was one of the reasons he liked a drink, or nine. But tonight, he knew it wasn't his imagination when every diner in the room turned to look at him. He must look an absolute fright, he thought, abashed. He couldn't remember doing anything exceptionally shameful at the party. Not by Oxford standards at least. He scanned the faces of his fellow students for Kavitha's. She wasn't there. And neither was anyone Sean knew well enough to want to sit with. He found an empty table at the back of the hall and poured a glass of room temperature water from the decanter as soon as he sat down. He emptied the glass in four giant swallows, and refilled it immediately.

Someone dropped suddenly into the seat next to him. Sean startled and looked to his left, his mouth stupidly open with shock. It was a girl he'd seen around a few times, but hadn't spoken to or tried to solicit yet. She had long, blonde hair that culminated in faded streaks of magenta, and a deeply distraught look on her face.

"Hey."

"Hello."

"What happened last night..."

It took Sean several moments to realise she wasn't asking a question. Even then, he wasn't sure how to respond.

"I don't know what you're..."

"I keep thinking I should call the police."

"What?"

"Or the RSPCA? I mean... That was... Jesus. I've never seen anything like that."

"Is this a joke? I don't..." Sean struggled for a path of reason in the mire of his confusion, "I don't understand anything you're saying."

The girl's face shifted from afraid to irritated. "You're Sean, right? You helped Kavitha with the party." Again, despite her inflection, it wasn't a question.

"Yes, but -"

"So you guys didn't organise the pig?"

"What pig?"

She stared down at the table in front of her and they were both silent for a long time. Her lower lip began to tremble. A tear slipped from one red-rimmed blue eye and hit the varnished wood grain. And then she stood up and left as abruptly as she'd sat down.

Sean was unable to eat very much of his college-subsidised dinner that evening. He walked home, showered for the second time in a day, and got back into his bed a scant eight hours after leaving it. He felt clean and almost well for the first time since he'd got up. With his still-tender head mercifully supported by a mound of flat, unwashed pillows, he finally had the inclination to trawl through the flood of messages that had accumulated on his phone. There was still nothing from Kavitha. But while he had expected a deluge of triple-barrelled Halloween-themed hashtags and costumed selfies, the actual content of the messages made his meagre supper sit uneasy in his stomach. On the Facebook page and WhatsApp groups, there were about two dozen threads of hysterical messages from friends and lovers looking for lost companions. There were pictures of a fight that had broken out, which had involved upwards of five different people, and close-ups of the blood-nosed, puffy-eyed aftermath. Another series of photographs showed two boys posed lewdly with a passed-out girl propped up between the two of them. The photos became more and more obscene as he scrolled until they stopped. The final image was of a young girl, with a long white wig and a short black dress, riding an enormous, pink pig into the hall.

Sean turned his phone off. He didn't remember any of this.

Sean went to many parties, drank gallons of booze, and frequently couldn't remember the things he'd said and done in the morning. But he thought he might remember a fucking pig. He turned the phone back on, scrolled to Kavitha's number and hit 'call.' Her phone rang three, four, five times, and his heart sank when he heard her recorded voice ask him to leave a message, or better yet, to send a text.

Despite his exhaustion and the strain imposed by his terrible hangover, Sean did not sleep soundly that night.

In the morning, he returned to the entrance of the tunnel. Of course, the black, metal grate was closed, and of course, it was locked. Sean had expected the worst and was unsurprised to find it. What *did* surprise him was that the 'entrance' now covered by the grate was no more than a foot in circumference. He thumbed the edges, where metal met stone, testing the newness of it. It was the same, aged mortar and crumbling plaster as the surrounding wall. No hasty post-party construction had been undertaken by market management in the wake of their soirée. Sean stepped back, looking around urgently, praying that he'd approached it skew, and was merely looking from entirely the wrong angle. But no. This was the exact position he'd watched the tunnel from for days. Only now it wasn't a tunnel. It was a hole. Smaller than the garbage chute in a block of flats. Wide enough only for a cat to pass through. From this side, at least. Ways in are easier than ways out, after all.

Shaken, and shaking, he retreated to the routine of his day, but was unable to listen or concentrate. Outside, in the corridors and along the garden paths, his fellow students acted strangely around him. On their own, they would recognise him and then give him a wide berth, or impulsively change direction to avoid him. In groups, they huddled closer to one another, eyeing him in turns and talking again in frantic whispers only when he'd passed. Sean had always thought of himself as a bit of an outsider, someone for whom common ground with others was a largely foreign country. But this was the first time he'd been actively ostracised.

That night the dining hall was almost back to its usual capacity. It made the startled silence when Sean entered even more jolting. Chris, a slight Korean boy and mutual friends with Kavitha, saw Sean and rose quickly from his seat. He strode towards him with a wide, hurried gait that would have been comic if his features weren't set with such grim purpose. Without missing a step, Chris took Sean by the elbow and, like a schoolmaster chiding an errant child, led him back down the passage, past the coat rack and outside to the garden nearest the kitchen.

"What are you doing here?" Chris hissed, his eyes dark with anger.

"I'm having supper," Sean said, prying back his arm and sounding more confident than he felt, "and I'm looking for Kavitha, have you seen her since –"

"Are you for real? Are you for real right now? You're just acting like nothing happened..."

Sean looked at Chris, who stared holes back into him. Sean's shoulders and bravado dropped.

"Chris, I got really drunk at that party, I don't remember a lot that happened and I'm just... I haven't seen Kavitha and I'm starting to get really worried. Did I say something to her? Have

I pissed her off? Do you know where she is? Do you know why she won't talk to me?"

Sean could hear his voice quaver and he felt the prickling of tears in his eyes. He didn't want to cry in front of Chris, who would surely go back inside and tell everyone, and so he swallowed hard several times to compose himself.

"Okay, slow down. What do you remember about the party?"

"Everyone was having a good time. I tried to talk to some blonde girl, it didn't go well –"

"Well, yeah..." Chris interjected. Needlessly, thought Sean.

"I drank a lot of punch, and I think I fell over at some point... Nothing distinct."

"That's really all you remember?"

"Yes."

Chris pulled his mouth in a strange way that didn't look intentional; it constructed an expression that was part anger, part pity and part disgust.

He didn't say anything else then. Instead, he pulled his mobile phone from his trouser pocket and showed Sean a series of videos that had not been shared on social media. The girl in the white wig rode the pig underground. Revellers took turns pouring alcohol down its throat. He saw himself, inebriated, crazed, lope around the pig, hit it with his fists, and take clumsy, unbalanced kicks at it. He saw himself with a knife. Bigger than a kitchen knife, nothing he had ever owned, or seen before. He heard the terrible squealing and screaming that sounded at once heartrending and inhuman. He turned away, grimacing, nauseated.

"Watch." Chris commanded, his voice unforgiving.

He saw himself covered in blood. Others too. Kavitha in the crowd, and then not. Two women kissing, their faces slick with red.

Sean had one hand over his mouth, like a pantomime of horror. The other hand trembled uncontrollably at his side. Bile rose to burn the back of his throat and the world began to dissolve around him. Only when he felt Chris's thin hand on his shoulder did he come back to himself.

"I didn't do that," he croaked in a tiny voice.

"You should think about going to the police before someone else does. You could get rusticated. But if you own up things might go easier for you."

But Sean wasn't listening.

"Where is Kavitha?"

"Listen to me, Sean. Nobody knows. Her mom called me today. She's been calling all of her friends, her tutors. She's going mental."

Sean felt dizzy again. This time Chris didn't reach out to stop him and when he fell, he hit the ground hard.

Kavitha's mother never called Sean. And he didn't have her number either. So, when, at twelve minutes past three in the morning, Sean's phone buzzed and blinked in the dark, and he checked it with first utter disinterest — then shock, surprise, elation and finally joy — he had no way to reach her. To be honest, it didn't even occur to him to try to find a way to tell her that her daughter was alright. All that mattered in that moment was that Kavitha had contacted him. Him.

'Sean, I'm okay,' she'd sent, and then, 'I found a different way.'

Sean felt such a rush of relief that he nearly forgot about the video of the pig.

Immediately he fired a half-dozen gibbering responses back at her. He asked her where she'd been, if she was alright, or alone, or in college. He asked her if she'd eaten and what she was doing. His messages showed as having been 'read', which he took as a positive sign, but Kavitha didn't reply again. So, he browsed the internet for a while, waiting for her response, but eventually his eyelids slid closed and he slept better than he had in days.

In the morning there were two new messages on his phone. One was a voicemail from the Brasenose Senior Tutor, left after Sean had apparently slept through four attempts to call him. The police had visited the college administration, looking for him. He was to report to them immediately. More importantly, there was another text from Kavitha.

'Meet me at the market.'

'Where?' he texted back, followed quickly by 'What time?'

As before, his messages went read, but unanswered. Sean showered, checked his phone another six or seven times to no avail. Feeling too anxious and fidgety to sit down, he went to the market to wait for her there.

It was busy, as per usual. Jumbled streams of shoppers and tourists dragged past one another in stilted progress. Those in a hurry cursed under their breaths when the people in front of them paused to look at something in a window. People queued at the most popular food stalls, while overworked waitresses shimmied between overly close tables in compact coffee shops and eateries. Sean walked every aisle several times, hoping that he'd look up to see Kavitha approaching him, her face plastered with a relaxed smile. Or that she'd be stood, talking to someone he didn't know, and she'd spot him and wave him over amiably. He didn't want to go and look at the porthole-that-used-to-be-a-door without her.

He almost missed her when he did spot her. She had her back to him and was walking away at speed. Her long, dark hair looked dull and dirty, she wore shabby grey jeans and an over-sized hoodie. She looked like a faded photograph of herself.

"Kavitha!"

Her head turned slightly, like she'd heard him, but she didn't stop. She cut straight through the slow-moving crowd like an arrow, leaving him to squeeze, push, and side-step his way through the crush of people behind her.

He followed her out of the market, turned after her down Turl Street, and then again into an unfamiliar side alley. Despite the thinned crowd, Sean still couldn't get close enough for Kavitha to hear him. Until she stopped suddenly, and turned in place to look at him. The contempt that twisted her face into a sneer stopped him short. Her eyes traced a disappointed line down his body, and for a second, he thought he'd been following the wrong girl.

"Kavitha?"

As Sean watched, Kavitha walked to a drain on one side of the alley, bent her knees in a crouch, grabbed the top of the drain, and then seemed to drop into the earth below. Sean bolted over to where Kavitha had stood and saw, from this new perspective, that the drain opened up beyond.

"Jump down," he heard her say, but her voice sounded flat and hollow. Like a recording of a recording.

By holding the upper lip of the drain, Sean saw, he could lower himself in, and swing out into the tunnel opening to drop down inside it. The way Kavitha had presumably done.

'I found another way,' she had told him.

He couldn't see how far down the drop was, but he didn't hesitate. He shuffled in feet first, with considerably less agility than Kavitha. The seat of his trousers dragged, ruinously, across the wet concrete. When he swung himself out, his arms didn't have the strength to hold him through the full arc of his movement, and he fell heavily, and farther than he'd expected to. He landed uncomfortably on his left ankle and careened into the side of the tunnel before finding his balance. He turned back, to look at the way in. The opening back to the drain looked minute from this angle. It was now much higher up than he could reach on his own, and there was no way of climbing back up that he could see. Ahead, there was only the darkness. And Kavitha.

Sean hurried maybe thirty paces, until this tunnel too opened out into a rounded chamber, but one much smaller than the Great Hall. It wasn't raw rock like the hall either; it was bricked over in neat, terracotta rows that could have been as recent as the last decade. He could *see* the bricks was because this dome was vastly better lit. In the centre of the domed ceiling was cut a perfectly circular opening. Light streamed in from the surface, obstructed only by a pair of jean-clad legs.

Sean's watched, agog, as Kavitha's lower body dangled through the hole briefly. Then she drew her legs up after her, as she pulled herself up and out and onto the surface, effortlessly. Impossibly. The ceiling was almost twenty feet high. There were no ropes, no ladders, no steps. There was no way for her to climb up, no way for her to reach. But she had, and now Sean stood beneath the little circle of light. Looking up at Kavitha, looking down at him. She was crouched down, almost silhouetted by the bright grey, overcast sky behind her.

"Kavitha," he said slowly, not able to articulate the full depth of his dread. "How do I get up there?"

Her expression softened so that instead of angry, she looked sad. "You don't," she said, and he felt relieved that she sounded like herself again.

Then she stood up straight, and walked away, and Sean knew — *just knew* — she wasn't coming back. He searched frantically around the room for a way to get out. He scrabbled blindly at the walls with his hands for hidden ledges or footholds. He used the light on his phone to inspect the other shadowed tunnel entrances as far as he could, trying to find anything other than stone, or dust, or darkness. Eventually, his phone battery died. He was able to find his way back to the light of the dome, but was now unsure of which tunnel he had originally entered it from.

Defeated, Sean sat on the ground and screamed. Screamed Kavitha's name, screamed for her to come back. He screamed pleas and curses to her and to God. He screamed at the people he could see moving in the periphery, while they marched on unhearing, unmoved. He screamed until his throat stung and his voice was hoarse. He screamed and screamed, and only stopped screaming when he heard a heavy, distant scraping. Fearful, he peered into the shadows and the unknowable blackness beyond, expecting a murderer or a monster to spring at him. But when the sound came again it was loud and right above him. The slow, unmistakable grating of hard stone on cold metal. Sean looked back up just in time to see the hole at the top of the dome being closed. He watched in silence as the light was quickly halved, then a crescent, and then gone.

CONCEALED

Alice Little

As a girl I lived for a time in Littlemore, on the eastern edge of Oxford, where there was, behind the newly-built 1930s housing development, an enclave of Tudor houses. The University had promised Dad a professorial residence on Walton Street, but since there was nothing available he was offered a generous housing allowance instead: more than enough to cover a small cottage in the suburbs.

The dreariness of the local area was made up for by the convenience of the branch line into the city, and the thrill in Mum's eyes as she gazed upon what would become our home was enough to persuade Dad to take the lease. This was just before war broke out in 1939, after which our future seemed less certain.

The house had been built in the mid-sixteenth century. It had a prickly thatched roof through which protruded a brick chimneystack; the walls were constructed with black timbers between white limewashed squares. It was the perfect picture-book house.

The first thing we three girls did when the family moved in was scour the house for ghosts.

"There must be something in a house this old!" Rachel complained as she crawled out of the cupboard under the stairs, twisting a piece of blonde hair between her fingers. I liked the colour of her hair: mine was much darker, like Juliet's.

Juliet, the oldest at 13, and four years Rachel's senior, replied, "you're probably scaring them off, galumphing up and down the stairs all day."

"Why would a ghost be scared of me?" Rachel replied. "Isn't it meant to be the other way round?"

"Girls, girls," Dad called us to him in the kitchen, where he was sitting in the rocking chair by the unlit grate. We stood around him. "There are no ghosts here."

"Oh John, you're spoiling their fun," Mum laughed, putting aside the box she was unpacking to join us near the fireplace. She laid her hand on Dad's arm and smiled at him fondly.

"But", Dad continued with a glint in his eye, "there used to be witches!"

We all ooh'd and then giggled.

"How do you know that, Daddy?" Rachel asked. We looked up at him eagerly.

"Because someone has carved marks into the fireplace to ward them off," he replied, indicating two rough yet deliberate round marks cut into the wooden mantel. There were several centuries of paint applied over the top, but the marks were still clearly visible.

"Look at that, girls," said Mum, tracing the circles with her finger. "Don't you think it looks like a pair of eyes?"

Juliet shuddered. "It gives me the creeps: the fireplace is watching us!"

"Watching over us," said Dad, smiling. "Or that's what they used to believe, anyway."

"I like it," I said. "I hope it works."

When Dad went off to war a year later I used to fondly recall that first day when he told us about the charms people made to stop witches and demons entering. The house certainly felt magical to me, and I grew to love it as if I had lived there my whole life and always would.

I often paused in the garden to stare up at the old chimney, or laid my hands on the low beams in the hallway. I was enchanted by our connection to the past, and liked to imagine that by leaning my head against the wall I might hear whispers of people who had lived in the house over the last four hundred years, or see the ghosts of long-dead children playing in the garden.

However, it was Juliet who first thought she caught sight of a ghost. Looking back, that was the start of a series of peculiar happenings that began to tarnish our delight at living in such an idyllic place.

One Saturday Juliet came running in from the garden asking, "who's that upstairs? Rachel, do you have a friend over?"

"No," said Rachel, "of course not, I've been helping Mum in the kitchen all afternoon."

Juliet and I ran up the stairs to see if one of the local children had wandered in uninvited, but there was no one there. Coming back down Juliet sat dejectedly by the kitchen fireplace.

"I'm sure I saw a girl looking out of your bedroom window," she said. "She was about your age, but with dark hair."

Turning her head to one side she caught sight of the old marks gouged into the mantel and gasped. I followed her gaze and a shiver ran down my spine. The deep hollows staring out from the wood seemed to meet my own wide eyes.

Rachel looked over too. "What? Do you think it was a witch? Or a ghost?" at this point she was more excited than scared.

But Juliet only frowned, then shook her head. "I don't know," she sighed, "it just looked like a little girl."

"Dad, will you tell us more about the witches and the charms?"

Rachel asked the next time Dad was home on leave. We were in the sitting room in our nightgowns, enjoying the warmth of the fire before bed.

"Do you promise not to have nightmares?" Dad replied, that familiar sparkle in his eyes as he pulled Rachel on to his knee.

Rachel and I nodded solemnly. Juliet sighed — the look on her face said she was too old for stories — but I noticed that she didn't leave the room, and even stopped plaiting her hair to listen.

"Well, it wasn't only marks that people made to ward off evil in the house," Dad began, "they also made charms and hid them in the walls, under the floors, or up the chimney."

"Like what?" Juliet asked, leaning forwards.

"It could be coins, or a shoe, or a bottle. It would be symbolic, something like an onion with pins in it, or even a dead cat."

"Urgh!" we all said in unison. Dad laughed.

"Well, yes. You see, witches were said to have familiars: animals like cats or toads that worked with them to carry out black magic. So if you buried a dead cat, or concealed it behind the brickwork, there would always be a cat on your property — and then the witch and her familiar would stay away. That was the idea, anyway," Dad said.

"Do you think there's a dead cat up our chimney?" Rachel asked.

"Well, I don't know," Dad replied. "Have you seen any witches about?"

Rachel opened her eyes wide, her mouth forming an "O" but no words coming out.

"And, I'll tell you something else," Dad continued, speaking in a low voice. "Sometimes, if an animal wasn't enough, they might find — ah! — a little girl to bury instead!" He grabbed Rachel around the waist and tickled her; she screamed, while Juliet and I laughed.

That night in bed I imagined all the things that might be concealed within our walls. I dreamed I was patrolling the wattle and daub from the inside, permeating the house with my presence so that I could see all the rooms at once, floating like air between the thin twigs and sticks that separated us from the outside world.

In my mind's eye I could see the first family who lived here. I felt I knew them: we had all lived in the same space, breathed between the same walls. Their house was my house.

I dreamed about who might have concealed the coins or the cats: had it been a naive kitchen maid, or a superstitious land-manager, hoping to end a run of bad harvests?

Might they really have buried a child, in the hope that she would protect the house? I could picture it so vividly: the small body curled up in the grave, laid down with only a wooden doll for company, and the prayer beads wrapped around her neck.

I woke up in a cold sweat, breathing heavily. I might have cried out — I couldn't remember — but Rachel was still asleep across the room. Though only just.

She was making noises, tossing and turning. She gave a whimper, then cried out "no!" thrashing under her blankets before tumbling out of bed to land with a hard thump on the floor.

Mum and Dad both came running in, Mum flicking the switch to flood the room with bright yellow light.

"What's wrong, darling, was it a nightmare?" Dad lifted Rachel back on to the bed, where she clung to Mum in a fierce hug.

"Was it that scary story before bedtime?" Mum gave Dad a pointed look.

"There was someone here, Mummy," Rachel sniffled between sobs.

"There, there, sweetheart, there's no one here, it's all over now," Mum said.

I remembered the figure Juliet had seen at the window, and

the scene of the grave in my dream flashed again before my eyes. I wondered whether that little girl might be more than just a figment of the imagination.

After Dad returned to the front Rachel's bad dreams intensified. She would wake in tears saying someone had been watching her sleeping or moving about the room, and she grew thin and pale as the weeks passed without the nightmares abating.

As for Juliet, in the end she stopped mentioning when she saw the face at the window, it began to happen so regularly. She took to scrubbing the glass and rearranged the objects on the bookshelf almost daily, in case she could stop the sightings by redistributing shadows. But then the young figure began to appear in the garden too, and at the kitchen door, and Juliet despaired of ever being rid of her vision.

"It's as if there really was a human sacrifice here", she said as she came in from the garden, "but instead of keeping spirits away she's haunting the place herself!"

I laughed, though I wasn't sure it was meant to be a joke; Rachel smiled too, despite her own despondency.

"But like Dad said," Rachel protested, "do you see any witches about? If there is a ghost in this house at least she's not attacking us or anything."

"It's just unnerving feeling I'm being watched all the time," Juliet said. "I can't relax, and you — you can't sleep. We can't stay here like this."

But Mum couldn't be persuaded. At first she had dismissed Juliet's sightings, muttering something about imaginary friends and games that went too far. And even though she came to admit that there was something more going on, not knowing what it was only set her on edge.

One evening she flew into a rage at Juliet: "What do you want me to do about it, eh?" She dried her hands violently on a tattered tea towel.

"But, Mum, doesn't Dad's college have any houses available yet? Living here was meant to be a temporary thing."

"Yes, I know, sweetheart," she said, a little calmer, "but with the war on we don't want to move in to the city, do we?"

"I suppose not. But..." She looked about the kitchen helplessly.

"I know you find it hard, love, but the problem is we don't know what it is that makes you girls so uncomfortable." She said the word carefully, to avoid naming the dread that permeated the household. "I mean, who's to say you wouldn't see things in our next house too?"

Juliet was quiet for a moment, then she looked up at Mum. "Don't you believe us?"

Mum studied Juliet's face. "I believe you," she said, "but I'm afraid it doesn't change the fact that we can't move right now."

Juliet didn't reply, but went quietly upstairs to her room in the attic, and didn't come down again until dinner time.

I often wondered when the time would come for the family to move into Oxford. It made me sad to think of leaving the house behind, despite all that was happening. I knew that Juliet and Rachel were frightened, but I wanted to stay there forever, feeling the sun on my face as I dug vegetables in the garden, holding on to the dark beams as I gazed out of the window. I prayed no bombs would fall on its picturesque thatch.

In the end it wasn't the war or Dad's job that meant we had to move: there was another disaster.

The fire started in the kitchen one night while Dad was away at the front, long after the four of us had gone to bed. Without anyone in attendance to dump sand on the ejected embers, a discarded magazine caught light. The heat rose up the leg of the rocking chair. The flames suckled on the cushions, moved on to the curtains, and gorged on the timbers that supported the wall.

I awoke with a start, sensing that something was wrong. Rachel was sleeping deeply for once, but a bang at the kitchen door woke her with a jolt.

Someone was shouting outside: they had seen the flames at the kitchen window. Neighbours ran to help.

We smelled the smoke as it tumbled into the bedroom from the corridor. Rachel leapt out of bed and collided with the armchair. "Mummy, help!" she sobbed from the floor.

Juliet's voice came from the attic steps that led to her bedroom: "are you there? Are you alright?" There was a series of thumps as she tripped on the steep ladder and landed in our bedroom doorway. She crawled inside and pushed the door shut with her foot, trying to catch her breath between coughs.

Rachel was spluttering, her eyes streaming. I got down on the floor where the air was slightly clearer. We needed to get out of there fast.

On her knees, Juliet grabbed a shirt from the chair and dunked it into the basin on the washstand, then draped it over Rachel's head and shoulders. "We'll have to go downstairs, there's no way we can get through the window," she said, looking at the narrow Tudor casement. "And we'll have to go now, before it gets worse. Are you ready?"

"What about Mum?" Rachel choked out.

At that moment there was a bang on our door, then Mum pushed her way inside on all fours, a bitter black cloud bulging above her.

Half running, half crawling, the four of us raced down the stairs in a bundle, Mum holding Rachel's hand while Juliet and I tumbled behind. Flames were raging in the kitchen, but it was the only way out. Mum moved warily forwards trying to shield us from the heat.

As I stumbled across the hall after the others I felt a hot hand on my arm, a force holding me back. I fell sideways, onto my knees.

The roar of the fire seemed to fade as, still kneeling, I placed my ear against the panel of the cottage wall: to hear its whispers, to listen to its last words. You belong here, it said.

With my head resting on the wall I watched as Mum gave a strangled scream of determination and charged through the kitchen towards the door. The wood was partly burned away and she crashed through it into the cool night air, pulling Juliet and Rachel behind her.

The Air Raid Warden hurried them away from the house, shouting, "are you three alright? There's no one left inside?"

"No, we're all here: John's in France."

Safe at the end of the garden, Mum, Juliet and Rachel watched with wide eyes as the flames grew.

Limewashed squares, blackened with smoke, were eaten away one by one. Thatch was devoured greedily with a blinding intensity of light and heat. There was a sickening crack and a roar as the central beam of the house gave way. Mum gasped and pointed up at the bedroom window, which fell inwards with a crash of shattering glass. She dropped her arm and opened her mouth, looking around the garden.

"Mum?" said Rachel. "What is it?"

"Nothing," Mum replied. "I just thought I saw a face at the window. But it can't have been: you're both here." She gathered Juliet and Rachel to her side. "Oh, my girls," she said. "I'm so glad you're both safe."

BURIED IN THE WITCH RAVEN'S BOOK

Christine McDonough

William

She shimmers.

I say 'she' because her shape is a woman, but other than that... well, I can see she has eyes... and a mouth, or actually an entire face, but I can't really *see* it. Like what the final echo sounds like compared to the original sound.

She's *almost*, this ghost who follows me.

Yes, she shimmers, with a beautiful silvery light that is magical. And I believe she truly did have good intentions, back then, in the beginning.

But we all know what part good intentions play on the road to hell.

Charlotte

He never *really* knew it was me, I suppose. I tried to show him how much I loved him, this wonderful, smart, strange son of mine. I couldn't quite deal with how he almost saw me.

Almost.

But not quite.

After I died, I followed him, I sent singing birds to him, I left him flowers. I scared away mean dogs, and I tried to do more for him, but he had to finish growing up without knowing me. I followed him everywhere, incessantly, obsessively. Where else would I go? I needed him to forgive me.

Finally, when he started his studies at Oxford, the Old Libraries let him see me. The hundreds of years they stood, silent stones holding memory, endless stacks of books... the smell of old pages. The space is full of a kind of knowledge that summons people from the far reaches to come learn so many secrets. I did not know until after I died that once inside, there is a time-worn, tenacious magic.

It is easy to bury a Witch raven's book there.

The librarians have no idea. No matter how many times they catalogue their books, there is always one more. After I died, I found it and read it. I *learned* it. Then replaced it for the next raven. And it took so long, I almost despaired that he would ever see me. But one night in the Old Library, after reading a passage aloud from the Witch raven's book... he finally saw me.

He saw me.

William

In the beginning, my ghost was sad.

When I first saw her, she was in the Old Bodleian library. In my research of old Oxford publications about the University, I often found myself in the wood-rich, creaky-chair Arts End of Duke Humphrey's library, with the high painted ceilings, massive gothic windows, and shelves upon shelves of books bound in stiff brown leather. The space felt hushed, almost holy.

That night I had situated myself with my notebook and a stack of publications. I was alone.

Almost.

I heard a quiet sort of weeping, somewhere down the corridor behind me. Ignoring it, as one does in such a place, I kept on with my notes and switched to the next publication. Catalogue after catalogue, I continued taking my notes, and heard the bell from St. Mary's Tower toll for six, then seven.

In November, darkness falls early. And hard.

Only the lamps on the tables give off any real light. The rest of the space stays quite dim; lit with a sickly yellow light. Anyone walking around while I work on a winter's evening is reduced to a dark shape shuffling in the background. Footsteps, people whispering, sometimes a stern shushing. An occasional jarring scrape of a chair on the floor.

But weeping, that was new.

I heard it again, looked over my shoulder, and she was right there. My ghost. The shimmering shape of her, shoulders slumped, her head buried in her hands. The weeping, it sounded distant, though she stood next to me. This shimmery, translucent being, with a dim kind of glow.

As I faced her, she sensed my gaze, and slowly lifted her head. The weeping stopped. That's when I saw her face was an echo.

Her mood brightened. Well, I saw it brighten. *She* brightened. She had glittering filaments of silver running through her shape, though on a small spot on her chest… there was a lack of light. A dark mark where her heart would have been.

She leaned toward me, noticing me noticing her. Her arms reached in my direction, but I felt no danger.

I wasn't quite sure what to do. But her posture, her presence was not threatening, other than she was obviously a ghost. I felt a kind of peace, if I'm honest. She was so real, I didn't question my sanity, not once.

From then on, I noticed her in the Old Library, but only when I wasn't actually searching for her. I think she tried to give me gifts, because I found flowers everywhere for a while. I spoke to her aloud once, and that's when it was certain she could hear me, through a slow nodding or shaking of her head, but it was not an easy task to be one side of a ghostly conversation.

Then, in the depths of February, I met Sheila. The love of my life.

Charlotte

So, yes, after I died, I followed him. I sent singing birds to him, I left him flowers and scared away mean dogs. I wanted him to be happy, find a lovely girl, and have my grandchildren.

But that woman, I will stop that now. She made me realise. NO.

She does not deserve him.

William

I had given up on finding someone who seemed destined for me, sort of content in living my life alone. Meeting her was an accident, somehow fated by me needing a good fountain pen at the same shop where she was buying ink. We laughed at the silly pairing, and fell into easy chatter. I was enchanted.

After that we only had uplifting conversations, we laughed constantly. And we agreed on everything. How many kids we wanted, what kind of house, how we dreamed of seeing a pride of lions in the wild, how desperately we wanted a holiday house in Florence. She had active, nurturing parents, and a younger brother just starting university up in Leeds. And so many cousins. Being an orphan, I thought her family felt like one does when someone leaves the lights on for your late-night arrival. Welcoming, comforting, pleasant.

Our compatibility had no bounds. Never a fight.

Well, *almost.*

We did have that one fight. I can't believe the sheer *fury* I felt. Over money, of course. I let her have some, and needed it back. She knew I needed it, right then. "Nothing I can do about it," she had said. "Sorry." And she shrugged.

She just *shrugged*. She acted like my mother when I was ten years old. *Too bad,* my mother had said, shrugging. It was infuriating, this dismissal of my feelings over something important. One time my mother hadn't paid the school fee, and I was kicked off the swim team. I heard my mother's words ricochet in my head, *You weren't a good swimmer anyway.* I had blushed with rage, and found both of my hands had clenched themselves into fists. I was a good swimmer, but she hated that I was good. She was jealous because she couldn't swim.

Still, it wasn't until after the fight with Sheila I realised I could have done real harm. I knew I was capable, even with such a wonderful woman.

But enough of that.

It wasn't me, it was the goddamned *ghost* who ruined everything.

That bitch ghost.

Charlotte

There are ways to tell which people are evil. You can see a Mark on the heart. It's like a brand. Some Marks just happen, but most are passed on from evil people. Like when bad men find little girls left alone. Or in war, when soldiers get bored with a prisoner, and torture passes the time... becomes entertaining.

My own mother was Marked by her cousin, Gerard. He decided that he didn't like my mother, and when they were both eleven, he slashed her face with a shiny blade. That's how she described it, "a shiny blade." Her face healed, but the scars it left became dark pink ropes down her left cheek.

When the boys laughed and pointed, and the girls giggled at her behind their hands, the Mark on her heart darkened. It got deeper as she waited for someone to see beyond her scars, think she was beautiful, maybe even love her. She got married late, to a man who did not have a capacity for love, but wanted someone to make his dinner and tidy his house, be an outlet for his manly needs. And then she had me.

People pass their Marks to other people, and children with a Marked parent rarely escape. My mother Marked me when I was a child, holding my bare arm to the stove to 'teach' me whatever lesson I needed to learn that day. The same arm, the same place. Every time. She would burn my arm, then carefully and lovingly dress the wound. Layers upon layers of dark pink scars.

Few people saw it, but if anyone did... *It's a birthmark*, she would say. She only bought me shirts with long sleeves. I was forbidden to go swimming with my class, she was too worried about questions.

I had to deliver my mother's note to the teacher myself. *Please excuse Charlotte from swimming. She has problems with her ears.*

William

She turned on me. Once she wasn't the only important woman in my life, that shimmery, shiny ghost dimmed her light, though she still showed up unexpectedly. She stopped with the flowers, and I am convinced she set the dogs on me. I think she tried to push me down a long flight of stairs once. After that, I made sure I was on my guard every minute of the day. On watch.

Nothing is more frightening than a woman scorned, and I have to tell you... nothing more frightening than a *ghost woman* scorned. She was *haunting* me.

I was worried about Sheila. Not only what the ghost might do to her, but also... how could I explain this 'other woman' to her? The story that this ghost had attached herself to me was a difficult talk, but also how could I not sound paranoid that she was also obviously jealous of my girlfriend?

I did it, though. I told her. She looked at me like she already knew, and nodded. I was so relieved. I wanted to ask if she could see my ghost.

But instead of that, I asked her to marry me. I wanted to start a real life. After consulting a lot of books and speaking 'casually' to friends about the paranormal, I thought... there is no way I am going to let this ghost control me. Not after what I'd been through.

I told her that, too, you know. I told Sheila what I'd been through. How I had watched while my mother took an axe to my father's head, how I wasn't even surprised. How I thought my mother would...

No. I can't. I'm past it. It's not important now.

It's over.

I just want to be happy. But that damned ghost made me tell Sheila everything, and now Sheila tells me she needs to "fig-ure things out." Needs time to think. I shouldn't be surprised, but I know she'll come around. She's such a generous, forgiving woman, with the kindest eyes.

And besides, it's over. It's done.

I'm past it.

It wasn't even my fault.

Charlotte

I've already Marked my child. I didn't realise my mistake. Keeping that axe hanging behind his closet door — that axe, with his father's dried scalp still attached and a bloody mass of wiry grey hair, with more dark blood staining the handle. It seemed fitting to keep something of his father's. It never occurred to me it would Mark my son, and so deeply. It never occurred to me he would bury that same axe in my forehead only two weeks later.

I still remember his murderous scream, then the strange flashes of light and blinding pain, followed by the surprise of my own blood splattering on my lap.

I cannot describe the shock I felt. I had been sitting calmly listening to the radio, darning his socks between sips of tea, and my twelve year old son — my blood child — ran screaming into the room with the face of a psychotic.

The first clumsy blow ripped at my scalp and knocked a sharp blow to my forehead. I was so surprised, I couldn't think. Or move. I could almost say his name... *almost*... but I could only manage a drawn-out, "Wiii..." He kept on, grunting and heaving the axe high above his head.

He paused only a half a breath, but in that split second, time vanished. The radio announcer absurdly described the weather. The clock struck one. I smelled the tea. Touched slick blood on the sock yarn. Noted the curious pattern of my blood spattered across my boy's face, while I felt a drip fall from my brow to my cheek. Then time returned with a gasping rush when he maniacally screamed again, bringing the axe down and lodging it square between my eyes.

He left it there, with my dead husband's scalp and wiry mass of blood-stained grey hair covering one eye and part of my face.

When I left my body, I saw my uncovered eye, paralysed and staring in shock. My jaw open. My little boy stayed frozen for only a moment... breathing hard, his face snarling with hate, his hands grasping the handle... then he let go, his expression becoming tranquil.

He blinked and sighed, wiping at the splatters of blood like they were tears, smearing them across his cheeks...

I used to fight the guilt. *It wasn't my fault*, I would say to myself, but that wasn't true. I deserved it; I had Marked him, however unintentionally.

The cycle has to end. *It must end*. Sheila does not deserve this son of mine. He would destroy her, by axe or not. And if she survived, he would pass his Mark to her. How she has escaped being Marked yet is a mystery... but I cannot allow it from my son. With it comes the certainty that my future grandchildren would be Marked twofold; they would become demons, devils sleeping.

It is up to me, I will take the responsibility where my own mother did not. Sheila does not deserve the pain, the sheer *agony* of passing the Mark to her own children.

So now, for his sake and for Sheila's... it will only hurt him for a moment, and I can finally end this twisted legacy. Then maybe I will rest, even without his forgiveness.

I've learned what I need. I know it now, the secret I found in the Old Library, buried in the Witch raven's book. I couldn't use an axe, not this time. So heavy.

But poison.

Poison is easy.

AN UNCONVENTIONAL DEAL

Elaine Roberts

Monday

The shaving mug was still curiously intact, still sturdy. Eighteenth century, Laurel reckoned, as she wiped the mud away from its rim. Probably used by a barber on a steady stream of customers back then. A tiny nick where she'd first uncovered it with her trowel — never mind, it was immaculate otherwise. She turned it over in her palm. *Not so different from Jack's old shaving mug* she thought, and immediately chided herself. There were more pressing things to think about.

It was early evening; the sun, which had been blazing without mercy all day, was finally beginning to set over the excavation site. Its rays had already seared the skin of several team members, but this was nothing compared to the prickly heat Laurel felt every time she thought about their lack of findings so far.

So it was with a tingling high that she turned to everyone else, eager to show them her discovery. But her words caught in her throat. Robert — colleague of three years, permanent frown lines and a blob of sweat currently running down his nose — was striding towards her, and his face was sombre. He had left to take a phone call some ten minutes previously.

"Interesting," he said, glancing at the mug, "but not what we're looking for." He paused, pushing his phone into his pocket. "Look, Laurel, the funders just called me. The council have been on their backs, complaining about the disruption... I mean, look at it." He gestured to the edge of the field, where the cordons for their excavation stretched onto Abingdon Road, forcing the piles of traffic into a hot, angry bottleneck. "It's not good news. They're not convinced that this is the correct site, and they're going to pull the plug if we don't uncover the friary by Friday."

The first ever excavation that she had project managed, and the funding was in danger. A swoop of panic replaced the nagging doubt which had been steadily gnawing away at her insides.

"Which Friday?" she asked, although she already knew the answer.

"*This* Friday." An eye roll, a note of condescension.

"If they do that", said Laurel, trying to keep her voice down lest the others should hear, "we'll have to tell the College. And everyone will be out of a job for the summer."

They looked over at the team: ten archaeologists of all ages and abilities on muddied hands and knees, scraping away at what could be utterly barren earth. Paula, already struggling with her rent, had comforted Laurel throughout the divorce. Tom had helped her to move all her furniture out. She imagined telling them — and the rest — that they could be unemployed by next week, and her panic increased tenfold.

"I know," Robert shrugged. "And like I said, if *I'd* been asked to project manage this one, I'd have started with a site west of the city, not some godforsaken spot going south -"

"Look, we've been over this. I'm certain the friary's here," said Laurel. But the quaver in her voice suggested otherwise.

Robert held his hands up in mock defeat as he turned to locate his spade. "You know best, Laurel. You and your magnetic heat maps." He had always been bitter about failing his geophysics module.

The team wrapped up the day in silence. As Laurel strode home, dodging the students and office workers pouring towards chattering pub gardens, she tried hard to quell her longing to succeed in this project, and forget her frequent daydreams of her trowel hitting a stone wall, or the frayed remnants of a robe…

Laurel had once been the child who never failed to express her wants with gusto. When she was nine, she had wished more than anything that she could meet her favourite girl band in person. She wrote about them in homework exercises, she bellowed her way through their songs every play break, she had even planned the questions she would ask should she ever meet them. Her dreams came true when a highly-publicised arson attack on her house killed her mother and brother, and the band came to visit her in hospital.

The perverted nature of this twist of fate was not lost on her even as a child, and for years afterwards, Laurel continued with life in a kind of numb haze: school, exams, graduation, then marriage to Jack, a classmate. Every motion of a normal life was just that — a motion. With sad resignation, Laurel no longer let herself truly or deeply long for anything. Now, however, she found herself thirty-three years old, trudging down a street in Oxford, and obsessing over a mediaeval friary and her performance as a project manager.

"Yeah mate — Rolex, *diamond-encrusted*!" The suited and booted young man didn't even look at Laurel despite nearly colliding with her; she swallowed her annoyance as he swaggered past, smartphone glued to his ear. She caught sight of a glimmering wristwatch, then he was gone. *Flashy git.*

Maybe, she thought dryly, as she picked up a takeaway pizza for dinner, *maybe the curse struck again with Jack*. After all, a year ago she had let herself wish more than anything that he would settle into the new job he had been so cripplingly anxious about, and settle in he soon did — with a colleague from Human Resources.

And now her divorce papers were waiting in her messy studio flat, pinned to a side table beneath her igneous paperweight. It was a humid evening and she would have to throw the windows open when she got in. Perhaps if a stray breeze caught those papers and blew them far away, she would never have to sign them. That blasted doubt about her chosen excavation site was beginning to seep into her divorce decision, too. The doubt and trench both grew more colossal by the day.

Laurel shuddered as she walked through her front door. An icy gust, totally at odds with the day's weather, was making her skin erupt in prickly gooseflesh. Stifling heat was all she had ever known in this flat; it was with mounting concern that she tried to locate the source of the chill.

She checked the windows, the fridge-freezer, even the tiny bathroom. Nothing was out of place, and a blade of foreboding began to pierce her insides as she climbed down from inspecting the extractor fan; the temperature seemed to be plummeting by the second.

It was then that it happened. The bathroom light bulb flickered, then died with a soft *pop*, enveloping her in sudden, oppressive darkness. She hurriedly pushed open the door to let the light from the main room flood in — there was the icy blast again, as though she were walking into a giant freezer. She had to screw up her eyes as the stinging cold hit them. She blinked and when she refocused, her blood ran cold too.

A figure with the most grotesque of afflictions was standing in the middle of the room.

Laurel whipped her face away so hard her neck cracked.

Bile began to snake up her gullet. And although she wanted to put as much distance between herself and the ghastly thing as possible, her treacherous knees buckled instead; in a split-second the floor was rushing towards her.

She lay on her side, face still averted from whatever the thing was. Now all she could see was her skirting board, cracked and yellowing, and a beetle, long since dead.

Shivering violently, Laurel squinted at that beetle, on its side like her, its stumpy legs splayed in all directions. She needed to commit it to memory, every detail of its shiny black shell and miniscule, vacant eyes, because if she stared hard enough, its image would surely replace the gore that was currently stamped to her retinas.

How long she lay there, she didn't know. Was she passing out from the terror and cold, slipping in and out of consciousness? Was she dreaming or was the thing *speaking* to her? And were its words a hissing whisper or a thunderous roar through her every synapse?

You ache to find something. The thought of it consumes you.

This was surely a nightmare, she thought, eyes squeezed shut. A pause. Then:

I know where it can be found.

Laurel's breath became deeper, more ragged; she could tell she was ingesting dust from the crevices of her unhoovered carpet. Was she supposed to reply? But that was ludicrous, how would it hear her, how could it even *speak*, it had no -

There is something missing of mine.

Laurel's eyes snapped open. Freezing terror still coursed through her veins, yet she had a sudden and hysterical desire to laugh.

"I see that," she replied at last, her voice a hoarse crackle. The beetle trembled and swayed with the movement of her breath.

Say you will find it for me. Then when you have found it, I will show you where to find what you desire.

This whole thing was preposterous, ludicrous; she was supposed to be a woman of logic, for God's sake. She did not answer. The beetle had rolled away from her now, its lifeless body feather-light, but her mind's eye still was still unwillingly stitched together with the maimed figure standing behind her.

The hours crept by, and very gradually, the chill subsided. It wasn't until birds began to chirrup outside that Laurel finally scrambled to her feet, sidestepping the forgotten, congealing pizza, and stumbled to bed.

A long look around the room indicated that she was alone.

Her last thought, before she switched out the lamp, was that divorce trauma really did mess with one's imagination. Because the figure she had seen was clearly missing its head.

Tuesday

Is this the correct site? What if it isn't? Why did I hallucinate that thing yesterday? Should I sign the divorce papers? Is this the correct site?

"Shut up!" Laurel snapped, and Paula, who was digging frantically nearby, looked around in alarm.

"Alright, Laurel?"

The rumours of being shut down had spread through the group as if by osmosis, and, despite the brief jubilation surrounding the shaving mug, there was a palpable air of desperation as everyone concentrated harder than ever on churning through their patch of earth. Even with protective gloves, tiny morsels of mud and clay had stubbornly etched themselves in the grooves of everyone's palms.

"I'm fine, Paula. Just talking to myself!" said Laurel. She could hear the thick tiredness in her voice.

Paula seemed to hesitate before picking her way across the trench to kneel next to her. "Laurel," she began, looking slightly embarrassed, "are you sure we're in the right location?" Laurel stared as Paula continued, "it's just that, well, Robert's been telling us all about anecdotal evidence from the time period, and he thinks that somewhere further west -"

"I like to put my trust in heat maps, rather than anecdotal evidence," said Laurel quietly. "And I've explained this to the team. The maps show that there's something to find *here*. I'm project manager for this one, so we're staying put, OK?"

"OK. And we're sure you're right, Laurel, we really are," Paula said, but her uncertain half-smile spoke volumes.

The end of the day loomed, still stifling and still worrisome. The group had uncovered nothing, not even a second artefact from completely the wrong century.

"Good work today everyone," called Laurel, trying to ignore her squirming insides. "We can do this!"

Robert looked over at her as they gathered their belongings. "Tick tock," he said.

The hours between arriving home and getting ready for bed passed without incident. But not long after she had fallen asleep, Laurel woke to a horribly familiar chill and oppressive, unnatural darkness.

And although the room was pitch black, Laurel sensed that her visitor from last night had returned. There was something standing at the foot of her bed. Her mind's eye unwittingly conjured up the grotesque image of the thing facing her — if *facing* was even the right word. This time it did not speak; it seemed to hover in expectant silence instead.

Lying face up on her bed, Laurel whimpered quietly, wishing with all her might that it would give up and leave. But the night marched on in blobs, then swathes, and still the darkness and iciness persisted.

Had it been half an hour? An hour? Two? "Go away," Laurel murmured. Nothing changed. "Go *away*," she screeched, and she pulled the covers over her head. But her childish sanctuary was useless; she knew the thing was still there, standing and waiting. Perhaps she could switch on a lamp, but then she would risk seeing it. That was the only thing more frightening than not seeing it.

It seemed to take aeons for Laurel to come to terms with the one impossible, unreasonable and downright absurd way to put an end to this. And when she could bear it no longer, she sat bolt upright, staring blindly into the gloom and clutching her duvet, still questioning her own sanity. "I'll help you! I'll find it for you, alright?" she said shakily. The darkness and cold immediately began to lift. "But — but –" she continued desperately, "*I don't know who you are!*"

She was met with yet more silence, but now a stifling humidity was creeping back into the room, and blessed moonlight was finally piercing her curtains. Laurel fell back onto her pillows, her mind racing. What on earth had she promised? Where was she meant to start looking for it? Was this all a highly-crafted joke by one of the team?

But the hours of tension and anxiety had exhausted her; she soon fell into a deep slumber of vivid dreams and memories which whirled through her head. Her mother lugging a picnic basket over a rolling, technicolour meadow. Her little brother scampering away across the grass with Laurel in pursuit. Then he slowly turned on the spot and she began to scream, for he had become the horrifying spectre from the night before — and this time it kept bursting into flames. Then she was Alice down the rabbit hole, tumbling down a muddy tunnel that was writhing with maggots and beetles. But through her fear, one thing was certain: she was pretty damn sure she recognised that meadow.

Her dream rolled towards a close with the striking image of a corpulent town crier pacing the cobbled streets by a partially-built Bodleian library. Ringing his bell hard, he was bellowing an unfamiliar name over and over as the jeering city folk gathered around him: this name apparently belonged to a violent criminal who had been apprehended whilst masquerading as a barber. *"Caught, jailed, will suffer the severest consequences,"* he roared. *"Caught, jailed, will suffer..."* But Laurel's consciousness was trying to punch its way to the surface and the crier's bell soon mingled with the church bells by her flat striking six.

Wednesday

Bleary-eyed, bleary-brained, and not quite believing that she was going along with this, Laurel rushed to the College to catch Robert before he could leave for the excavation site. She had barely entered his office before she spoke.

"Let's move the search to Port Meadow."

Robert's face split into a wide grin. "Yes! I knew you'd come around. What made you change your mind?"

Laurel hesitated, then took a seat. "I ran some heat maps on the Meadow last night. There's something else down there... beams... walls... something," she said, lying through her teeth. Robert's eyes widened.

"I *told* you. What are we waiting for? Let's go!"

"Well, there's the problem of permission. We don't have it." This obstacle had been tormenting Laurel ever since she had reluctantly decided to move the search. "Maybe we could phone the funders, beg them to extend the dead-"

"No! No need for that," Robert suddenly looked sheepish. "Actually... I was sure that I'd be asked to project manage this one, so I did some paperwork weeks ago, and, well, we have the permission for Port Meadow." He pulled some papers from a drawer and tossed them across the desk. "Total go-ahead to start excavating at any time."

Laurel didn't have the energy to be angry at his arrogance. "I'll just read through these, then call the team to let them know," she murmured. She glanced sideways at him as she left; he looked like the Cheshire Cat again.

As she strode towards her own office, Laurel pulled out her smartphone and navigated to the web page on 'Paranormal Oxford' which she had visited maybe twenty times since 6am. She wasn't sure why she was doing this yet again; she already knew the crucial bit of text off by heart.

Found guilty of heinous crimes in the eighteenth century, the highwayman George Napier was executed and his body cut into segments which were scattered around the city boundaries. It is said that his family secretly collected his remains for burial except for his head, and his decapitated ghost is still searching for this missing piece.

The location for their new trench was not difficult to choose. Laurel only had to screw her eyes shut tight and remember her dream; the spot where her brother had morphed into Napier was by a large oak — the only oak on the Meadow — and as Laurel instructed the team to set up fresh cordons, she felt a grim optimism about the day ahead.

They began work with a renewed surge of hope, chivvied along by a much more enthusiastic Robert. Paula had brought a small marquee from home, which she set up nearby to offer respite from the sun when needed.

But as the day grew to a close, an all-too familiar disappointment began to settle over the group, and Laurel's insides were writhing in panic yet again. Around mid-afternoon Tom had yelled in delight; he was uncovering what appeared to be a foundation trench for a large beam. It had turned out to be a Victorian drain. There was no sign of the skull, either.

Everybody sloped home apart from Laurel; she was not quite ready to return to her empty flat, which was now as cluttered as an animal's den. She lingered inside the marquee, her head in her hands. Dusk was beginning to fall and for the first time in days, the air was turning cooler. *In fact*, she thought, slowly looking up, *that's a pretty harsh breeze*. As the marquee's entrance flap trembled ever harder, a shadow appeared on the other side of the canvas.

Laurel's heart dropped in terror. She had no time to turn away before the figure was ducking into the tent; she instead clapped her hands to her eyes and waited for the deathly chill to pierce her core, yet some part of her was infuriated at his impatience –

"Jesus Christ, Laurel, what are you *doing*?"

She peeked through her fingers. Her husband, who she had not seen in four months, was standing in front of her, hands stuffed in his pockets.

"Jack. I thought you were someone else, I –"

"I rang the College, they told me where to find you. How's the search going?" When she did not answer, he moved towards her.

"You know why I'm here, Laurel," he said gently.

She stared at him blankly, her mind still whirling with thoughts of Napier, and stayed silent. He gave her an imploring look and took both his hands in hers. "Just sign them. Please. Stop second guessing it and let's move on with our lives."

Laurel let herself slide back into the present and she looked away from him, blinking hard. Deep down, she had known for months that signing them was the right thing to do. But those doubts... that fear of closure... it had all hindered her. She also suspected that Jack wanted to propose to his new partner, but could not bring herself to ask.

"Laurel, we had a good marriage for the most part. And what happened… happened. But, my God, all those hang-ups you had, all those beliefs in some curse after what happened when you were a kid…" His voice had become even softer. "I know you blame yourself for things. That blame and doubt needs to stop."

She exhaled hard and met his eyes, feigning the most composed expression she could muster. "Of course I'll sign them. Things have just been manic here." The image of Napier's decapitated body slid to the forefront of her mind again, and Jack frowned.

"Alright… but you still look spooked. What's the matter?" He looked so genuinely concerned that Laurel briefly considered telling him the truth.

I've made a deal with the ghost of a headless highwayman. He says he can help me find a medieval friary, and he needs help unearthing his own cranium. Yes, I know where to search for it. Well, because he sent me the location in a dream.

She smiled faintly. "Nothing, Jack. Everything's fine."

Thursday

Not half an hour after Laurel had dropped the signed papers into a post box on Walton Street, her trowel scraped against something hard, something off-white, something fragile and human. She glanced around to make sure no one was watching, then began to carefully, almost reverentially, push aside the soil. Such was her haste to uncover the skull that she broke her protective gloves; the mud caked beneath her nails and into the crevices of her palms as her discovery came into full view: eye and nose sockets, a broken cheekbone, a grinning mouth.

It would have to be sent away for testing, of course. She couldn't tell the age of the bone by simply looking. But Laurel knew that this belonged to Napier. She knew because she could feel his excitement. It was in her peripheral vision, in the sudden warm breeze that shook and swayed the trees around the Meadow. It was in the birdsong which heightened in volume as she wiped the soil from his forehead.

Nevertheless, as she gazed down at her find, sudden misgivings twisted her stomach and a whisper shot across her brain like a firecracker: *don't give it back to him.* She was kneeling, still blocking the skull from view. Perhaps she could get rid of it: shove it into her rucksack and hide it somewhere far away. None of the team would be any the wiser.

But it was too late. Yes, she could hurl it off the end of Brighton pier or down a well in the Outer Hebrides or into a plastic bin on a petrol forecourt. But he would never forgive her if she did not give him a proper burial, and the mere thought of any further night-time visits made her skin prickle with terror.

Besides, they had made a deal — albeit an unconventional one. Now that she had unearthed this, he could tell her where to find the friary. And what was it that Jack had said yesterday about *no more doubts*? A fresh resolve flooded her veins, and she turned to face the team. "Guess what, everyone?"

Evening was closing in and the site was empty apart from Laurel, who once again hung back in the marquee alone. She slumped in a chair and tried to ignore the alarm and guilt that was pressing in on her from all sides. The skull would give the College some press (despite Robert drawling, "not exactly Richard III, though, is he?"), but they now only had one day to find the friary, *and* she had dragged everybody to Port Meadow with no real evidence that the damn thing was here.

She picked up a soft brush and slowly began to sweep the

last few specks of mud from the top of the skull. Perhaps he saw this as a summons, for this time there was no mistaking the chill that crept across her bones, or the gloom that gradually settled around the marquee. Laurel knew that he had appeared a few feet away; her heartbeat increased rapidly, but she kept her eyes down and continued brushing.

My deepest thanks.

Laurel started; his voice was still that curious whisper-roar from the first night he had visited. She lifted her head and finally looked squarely at George Napier the highwayman.

He had not waited for the official burial to become whole again; a handsome head stood where there had previously been a bloody, maggot-infested stump. He could almost have passed for a present-day man, were it not for the faint shimmer about his being and his thoroughly eighteenth century waistcoat, britches and boots. With another jolt, Laurel noticed blood caked beneath his fingernails and the hilt of a knife tucked into his waistband. She snapped her eyes back to his; he looked wildly happy. And he was surprisingly clean-shaven, apart from a tiny nick where he'd cut himself... something twitched, stirred in Laurel's memory.

"The shaving mug," she said, "that was yours. Wasn't it?"

He smiled more widely, but didn't answer. "Tell me where the friary is," she continued.

She watched his mouth move as he answered; the words not quite in time with his lips, like a television's sound out of sync with its picture.

The place will be revealed in your slumber.

"That's no use," she said sharply. "It'll be too late, we need to get planning permiss-" But he was fading before her very eyes, the air was becoming thicker and warmer, and she was left alone once again.

As Laurel prepared for bed later, she was almost gibbering

with worry. How was she supposed to persuade the College, the council and the team that digging up a third location within a fortnight would be a good idea? She would have to beg the funders to extend their deadline, too. When she finally dozed off the dreams began, as shining and vivid as the first ones. A long dining table where a line of holy men were taking their evening meal. Rows upon rows of exquisite stained-glass windows. Then her brother, her dear little brother again, dancing and weaving in and out of the cloister arches...

Finally, her whole body seemed to swoop upwards and she was treated to a bird's-eye view of it all. She awoke as dawn was breaking, apoplectic with rage. Why, Napier was pointing her towards a field south of Oxford. Today it was known as Abingdon Road... the very site he had dragged her away from in the first place.

Friday

Despite yesterday's excitement about the skull discovery, there was a colossal amount of muttering and shaking of heads when Laurel announced that they would be returning to Abingdon Road. Robert was refusing to speak to her; he had folded his arms and stared at the sky while she desperately tried to explain her renewed trust in the original heat maps. But the project manager's wishes won out, and they were back at the first location by mid-morning.

"This your doing, love?" the JCB driver grunted at her, clearly unimpressed at being asked to dig up the very earth he'd scooped out ten days ago. Laurel just smiled stonily as he swung himself into his cab and began to re-dig the trench.

Their mattocks and spades made quick work of the soil, still soft from being disturbed the first time. They passed the point at which they had dug before and continued doggedly, their sweat soaking into the soil... surely they were now digging into the very bowels of Earth. And as dusk began to fall Paula gave a hoarse shout. Her spade had hit what appeared to be pebbled stone. The rest of the team closed in on her to help; within twenty minutes they had uncovered the top of a long wall which matched with Laurel's heat maps. When she announced that it was almost certainly the friary there was much cheering and hugging; Laurel was lost beneath a tidal wave of claps on the back, all irritation with her forgotten. Soon it became too dark to keep digging and someone shouted, "pub!"

As they set up more security cordons, Laurel spotted Robert trying to smile, but he couldn't hide his trademark grimace of envy which appeared whenever anyone outperformed him.

"Has anyone let the funders know? I'll phone them now," she said; Robert immediately looked panicked.

"No! No, Laurel I'm happy to -"

"Robert, I'm project manager," she said cheerfully, "I'll ring and you just go on ahead and get the drinks in." She left him standing stock-still by the cordons.

Amos answered the phone. He was their main funder, and one of her favourite people in the world. She was very relieved to be calling him with good news.

"Your team have done very well, Laurel, very well indeed," he said. "To find a skull and then the friary so quickly, and in two different locations — it beggars belief really."

"Well," she said, half-laughing, "your revised deadline certainly sped us along."

"Revised deadline?"

"You — you called Robert on Monday, said we had until Friday."

"Dear girl, we wouldn't do that! We wanted you to take your time, do it all properly."

"Never mind," said Laurel quickly. "My mistake. So, in terms of the final paperwork...?"

When Laurel hung up, she turned to see Robert in the same spot, his chin raised defiantly as though waiting for the argument. Stony-faced, she took a shaky breath, ready to unleash a tirade of vitriol at the second person who had double-crossed her in a week — but stopped herself. The skull was found and the friary was found. And she had no doubt that when she sat down this weekend and carefully constructed a full report of this blatant attempted sabotage, Robert would find his comeuppance too.

It was gone midnight by the time Laurel left the Turf Tavern; the team's jubilation had lasted all evening. The streets were quiet, but five minutes away from home she was met with the sight of two police cars and an ambulance standing outside a large detached house. Their blinking blue lights eerily lit the faces of a small cluster of onlookers, a couple of whom appeared to be filming on their smartphones. Laurel slowed down and stared; two paramedics were shuffling through the front door holding a stretcher, and the body was covered with a sheet.

"Never liked him anyway, flashy git," muttered a pyjama-clad man nearby. Laurel, already very uncomfortable at the sight of the blood-stained sheet, felt rattled at his words. She turned her steps towards home again, passing a policeman who was gabbling into his radio. "Violent homicide, boss. Young male lawyer. No signs of forced entry. Rolex and other valuables stolen." Laurel increased her pace, and it was only when she had shut her front door firmly behind her that she breathed out properly.

The warmth of the wine was still effervescing through her bloodstream, but she didn't feel like going to sleep yet. Surely Napier had finished with her now; she was no longer frightened of him — but her curiosity was piqued instead. Who exactly was this infamous figure who had helped her in the most inconvenient way possible?

She opened her laptop and began to quickly read through all the pieces she could find about the headless highwayman. There was one website she had missed the first time around.

The decapitated spectre of George Napier still stalks the streets of Oxford to this day, determined to find his missing head so he can continue to commit the despicable acts which made his death necessary in the first place. His main targets were those who were particularly boastful about their wealth.

Laurel snapped the laptop shut and stared into the middle distance, panic nudging at her insides again. She hadn't done anything wrong, surely? Because Napier had implied that he could genuinely help her. Because he'd have carried on terrorising *her* if she hadn't helped him. Because the mere *ghost* of a highway man (albeit newly-whole) couldn't harm anyone. Could it?

AUTHOR BIOGRAPHIES & STORY NOTES

Thomas Benson Thomas is 23 and works in Planning and Development in Summertown. A graduate of Lady Margaret Hall, Oxford in English Literature, this is his first attempt at writing fiction.

On 'Returning': *"Inspired by the Edward Thomas quotation included, my story considers how Oxford's past and present elide. Memory, regret, the past; the key themes of a traditional ghost story coalesce together in the mind of the narrator, who finds himself haunted by the past in more ways than one."*

C B Blakey Carl started writing in 2016. His first story 'The Way Through the Water' appeared in *Debut*, the first Oxford Writing Circle anthology. He is currently working on a series of interconnected short stories.

On 'Brass Lion': *"I've always been drawn to myths and folktales, they permeate everything I write. I've walked beside the canal through Jericho many times, but never at night. Such a peaceful place could be far more sinister after dark and might be home to all manner of creatures."*

'Doc' David 'Service of All the Dead', an early episode of *Inspector Morse*, had this author thinking that Oxford looked like a nice place to be. Years later he finds himself living there.

On 'A Piggyback on Puck Lane': *"The toll bridge in Cumnor is real but Tim-Tim didn't fall off it as described. That's possibly the only liberty I've taken in the telling of this story."*

Megan Davis Megan has been in and around Oxford for most of her life. As a place of many great fantastical worlds, she hopes to one day make her literary mark on the city too, even if it's just a small scratch.

On 'Three Weeks of Rain': *"The English drizzle isn't much to be proud of, but it is eerily atmospheric, and when one walks in cemeteries through that rain all sorts of ghostly imaginings begin to formulate..."*

Sam Derby Sam lives in South Oxford with his wife Caroline, daughter Hattie and two cats. He has never managed to leave Oxford for long after studying here almost 25 years ago.

On 'Annunciation': *"'Annunciation' is an attempt to capture the feeling of walking home alone through Oxford's medieval streets and feeling that one is slipping through time and space because so little has changed."*

Richard Edwards Richard — or Rich to the lazy and extremely busy alike — is from somewhere near Newcastle. After moving south he feels like he's trapped in Pygmalion.

On 'Ariadne's Afterdark Afterlife Amble in Oxford': *"I'll forever see Oxford as a town for tourists. It's how I was introduced to the place when I was a child. So here is a story about a man coming to Oxford and experiencing it as a tourist."*

Catherine Farfan Verse-dabbler, comma-tinker and killer-of-figurative-birds, Catherine's literary output started with the Oxford Writing Circle and she's not quite sure where (or if) it will end. So far she supposes it must be going ok, so you hopefully haven't seen the last of her.

On 'Ghost': *"Thank you to our own ghost for this poem. He*

may or may not have been a real person, but he really did usher us together in haunted Oxford pubs."

Jude Jones Jude writes SF and magic realism short stories. Her first novel was published on Bebo when she was 14 but requires translation out of textspeak before anyone else can read it.

On 'Lost': *"The libraries of Oxford were part of the inspiration for this ghost story, particularly the Gladstone Link, which is a little pocket of space-age buried under centuries of history. You can spend hours there, lost in books, in other people's worlds, or one you are building for yourself."*

Anna Lewis Anna Lewis is a biochemistry student in her fourth year at Oxford University and a writer of fiction, satire, and silly poems to entertain her friends. She is at any given moment most likely to be thinking about food. Find more of her writing at < www.aigroe.wordpress.com >.

On 'Urban Exhuming': *"Oxford's divided nature and rich history of the university are both made physical in the colleges, which form a significant part of many students' identities. This was originally a story about a failing relationship. It still is, but not the one I expected."*

Alice Little Alice enjoys writing of all kinds: it helps that she has beautiful handwriting and lots of nice stationery. She has had seven short stories published and is currently working on a piece of longer fiction.

On 'Concealed': *"'Concealed' was inspired by the house I live in which, thankfully, has fared better than the cottage in the story. I relish the idea that a sense of magic can persist even in a bleak suburb, and that ghostly happenings can take place against the backdrop of harmonious family life."*

Christine McDonough Christine is originally from Salt Lake City, Utah, and is an information designer. She is also an author, poet, archer, photographer, wheel-throwing potter, crochet master, painter, and former opera chorister, and would love an early retirement to try every other hobby on the planet. She travels, but never enough. The city of Oxford is her spirit animal.

On 'Buried in the Witch Raven's Book': *"I wrote this story in of one of the oldest and most secretive parts of Oxford's Bodleian library. I wondered at the ghosts who must haunt it... then pictured the characters there, reviewing stacks of old books. Secrets are for hiding things, and sometimes what you have to hide is truly horrifying."*

Peter Meinertzhagen Peter founded the Oxford Writing Circle in 2015 with the aim of creating a large and inclusive writing community welcoming of writers of all levels. It seems to have caught on. He works and lives in Oxford.

Sarah Milne Das Sarah loves writing, writers, wine and Oxford, so the Oxford Writing Circle is exactly her mug of Malbec.

On 'Sunday': *"The wonderful surname Iremonger, which I spotted on a gravestone in Oxford's Holywell cemetery, inspired this story of the living and the dead of the fictional Iremonger House."*

Jade Mitchell When Jade Mitchell was 10, she started writing gory stories to amuse her mates. Twenty-five years later, and at least her spelling has improved.

On 'Oubliette': *"I'd been in England two weeks when my friend took me on a whirlwind walking tour of Oxford. He told me about a secret network of butcher's tunnels under the Covered Market. And while I haven't been able to validate his story, I've never stopped thinking about it."*

David Olsen   David Olsen's *Unfolding Origami* won the Cinnamon Press Poetry Collection Award. His second Cinnamon collection and fourth US chapbook are forthcoming.

On 'Moonlight Sonata': *"Oxford's rich history of tortured saints, reclusive scholars, and embittered writers provides countless plausible examples of restless souls. 'Moonlight Sonata' evolved from my narrative poem exploring lunacy, in the original sense of the term: an intermittent madness arising from stresses associated with the full moon."*

Elaine Roberts   Elaine works as a marketer in academic publishing and has a BA in English Literature. She loves travel, good food and writing short stories. Often found staring out of the window.

On 'An Unconventional Deal': *"'An Unconventional Deal' was inspired by 'true' stories of the headless highwayman who still haunts Botley Road. What would happen if this disfigured spectre from the past struck a deal with a modern-day Oxford resident?"*

Ian Robertson   Ian is a biochemist with literary aspirations and dangerous ideas.

On 'The Ghost Hunter': *"This story is based on an idea I originally had for a TV series. It was inspired by watching* The Woman In Black *while writing my thesis, which led me to the question: what might become of an Oxford academic if they dedicated themselves to seeking out the supernatural?"*

Abigail Vint   Abigail is a professional writer and storytelling enthusiast and is consistently inspired by her new hometown, Oxford.

On 'When Invisibles Collide': *"Being invisible and feeling invisible can be the same thing on a busy Oxford street. I'm not afraid of the ghosts among us but more the connections we're missing with those who are still here but that we choose not to see."*

Alexander Walker Alex likes long walks on the beach, whiskey sours and penning short stories. He has a penchant for horror and heartbreak.

On 'Ruin': *"That house really does exist, in fact, I pass it all the time but there are far better memories stuck to it than the ones that inspired this story. Whatever ghosts still exist remain firmly locked away."*

Sophie Watson Sophie Watson lives and works in Oxfordshire and is currently writing her first novel.

On 'The Haunting of Hangman's Hill': *"For this story I wanted a ghost with unfinished business, so I settled on Mary Blandy, a Henley resident who was executed outside Oxford Castle in 1752 for poisoning her father with arsenic. Local ghost hunters claim her spirit still haunts the hill, professing her innocence and mourning her lost love."*

Tiffany Williams Tiffany is a writer whose perfect day begins and ends with reading. She grew up in Oxford and is now enjoying seeing new sides of it as an adult. OWC, being a circle, encompasses many of those sides.

ABOUT THE OXFORD WRITING CIRCLE

The Oxford Writing Circle is one of Oxford's largest and most vibrant writing communities. Its aim is simple: to encourage more people to write because through writing you can make anything. The group organises weekly events, including sessions to gain feedback on current projects, live writing workshops, guest speakers, and socials.

Find out more at < oxfordwritingcircle.org.uk > and on Meetup.